MW01697590

Murder in a Cornish Teashop

BOOKS BY FLISS CHESTER

THE CRESSIDA FAWCETT MYSTERIES SERIES

1. *Death Among the Diamonds*

2. *Death by a Cornish Cove*

3. *Death in the Highlands*

4. *Death on the Scotland Express*

5. *Death in the Crypt*

6. *Death in the Mayfair Hotel*

7. *Death in an English Village*

THE FEN CHURCHE MYSTERIES

1. *A Dangerous Goodbye*

2. *Night Train to Paris*

3. *The Moonlit Murders*

Murder in a Cornish Teashop

FLISS CHESTER

bookouture

Published by Bookouture in 2026

An imprint of Storyfire Ltd.
Carmelite House
50 Victoria Embankment
London EC4Y 0DZ

www.bookouture.com

The authorised representative in the EEA is Hachette Ireland
8 Castlecourt Centre
Dublin 15 D15 XTP3
Ireland
(email: info@hbgi.ie)

ISBN: 978-1-80550-443-6
eBook ISBN: 978-1-80550-444-3

1

'No, no, noooo...'

Maddie Penrose whipped the tea towel out of her apron pocket and frantically waved it in front of the oven door as it belched out another billowing cloud of smoke. This was not the afternoon of much-needed baking she had planned.

'Sorry, everyone!' She called over to the few unimpressed-looking customers who were hunched over the tables in the old, stone barn that was home to her grandmother's teashop. Though the term 'teashop' was stretching it slightly. 'Old barn filled with rickety tables, an odd collection of teapots and a very dodgy oven' was possibly a more accurate description, but putting that on the Cornish tourist board website certainly wouldn't bring in the customers.

Maddie felt sorry for the few anorak-wearing, slightly bedraggled tea drinkers who were sitting looking as if they really wished they'd walked the extra fifteen minutes it would have taken to get to the newer cafés and coffee shops in Pendragon Creek – the pretty coastal town just down the road.

Maddie opened the window, being careful to avoid knocking over an old stoneware pot and a faded display of postcards, which must have lived there since the mid-nineties. The sun had disappeared behind a dark, foreboding cloud and the sound of thunder rumbled across the fields. She could smell rain in the air, though it was holding off for now.

Maddie half-heartedly waved her tea towel around a bit more, then jumped as a gust of wind blew the A-board over outside and the light bulb above her head popped and blew out. She clutched the tea towel to her chest. She'd been in more stressful situations than this in kitchens, and she knew all she had to do was take a deep breath... which she did, and then immediately regretted, thanks to the acrid smoke that was still lingering from the oven's little tantrum.

No wonder her grandmother – Honor Penrose, though everyone knew her as Nor – hadn't been able to bake as much as usual. She must have been using the Aga in the farmhouse, the other side of the farmyard, and leaving this smoke-belching monster well alone.

Maddie had spent summers here at Folly Farm with her grandparents – and her parents and siblings, of course – and she often credited this *actual* teashop as her inspiration for her own career as a chef. She'd attended cookery school rather than university, excelled at it, and worked her way up through several restaurants and hotel kitchens. Maddie had done well, and a few years ago she'd beaten off much competition to become head chef at a cosy bistro called Chez Lucie, in the heart of one of south London's leafy suburbs. But the seven-day weeks and pressure to keep up the quality of the exceptional food had taken its toll on Maddie, and on a tearful phone call with her mother, she had agreed to hand in her notice.

It had also been her mother's idea, during that same conversation, that perhaps she should take some time out of London life and spend a few weeks with her grandmother. Now in her eighties, widowed, and in need of a new knee, Nor, according to Maddie's mum, wasn't coping so well with the teashop – and whole farm – as she once had. Maddie, though, remembered her running this place effortlessly. She had been the sort of woman who could crack eggs into a mixing bowl – for her famously delicious coffee and walnut cake with the secret-recipe nuts that Maddie and her siblings had fought over like jackals – while taking tea and coffee orders at the same time.

Maddie remembered the teashop filled with sunlight, delicious cakes, pretty vases of home-grown flowers and buzzing with chattering, happy customers... not this shabby place with a dodgy oven and five glum punters, some of whom had resorted to eating their own sandwiches. Maddie couldn't blame them. All the cake – singular – that had been available had been eaten hours ago when the first customers came in for elevenses and coffees.

She looked over to the ceramic display plate that used to be towered high with the freshest scones, but all she could see now was a very large crack running across the centre, half obscured by the one lonely scone sitting atop it. And next to it was the pot of the runniest jam known to mankind. She stirred the spoon around in it, musing that jam shouldn't be liquid. This was not jam, it seemed then, but maybe sweet strawberry soup? And she didn't even want to think about where the large catering-sized tub of clotted cream had gone, though she had narrowed her eyes accusingly at one of the farm cats earlier, suspecting that she might have found her culprit.

Maddie rested her hands on the counter and sagged her shoulders. She'd had better Saturday afternoons. A sudden crack of thunder startled her and reminded her that she really needed to find a new light bulb. Another crack caused her to jump again, but this time she stayed on edge... that wasn't thunder, or lightning. *Had that been a gunshot?*

Maddie forced a smile towards the customers, some of whom looked as startled as she did. She wished Nor was here with her. She'd sent her back to the farmhouse when the clouds had barrelled over, seeing that her knee had been hurting her. But Maddie would have liked her reassuring presence now.

'I'm sure everything's fine,' Maddie said to the room, really hoping that it was. A gunman on the loose was the last thing this place needed. Along with the unpaid bills – Maddie had seen the red lines running around the edges of the envelopes stacking up on the farmhouse's hall table – Nor had had a visit last week from the council. One of *those* visits. Nor hadn't told Maddie all the details, which was suspicious for a start, but the crux of it seemed to be that they needed to buck their ideas up, or risk being condemned – as that belching oven should be.

And to save Folly Farm, the teashop needed to be open for business. So here she was, with no cake, one scone, missing clotted cream, what sounded like a gunman on the loose and perhaps the sloppiest jam in Cornwall.

'Excuse me, could we have the bill?' the woman at the table under the window called over. She and her husband had kept their scarves on, no doubt because of the draught coming from the cracked windowpane.

Maddie looked at their table. They'd been good enough not to eat their own sandwiches, having nabbed a couple of scones before the pile had run out. Maddie had been able to find them a scraping of clotted cream while scratching her head over the whereabouts of the new tub, and she had felt bad about the jam, especially when she saw them both literally pour it onto their scones. She also felt bad that they'd been besieged for most of their tea by the big ginger farm cat, who could stretch his front paws right up to the top of the table, his inquisitive nose not far behind. He'd been a fixture at their side from the moment she'd brought the cream over. His name was Crumpet, and Maddie hadn't begrudged the couple as they'd politely shooed him away from their tea. It had been at that point that she'd narrowed her eyes at him and silently accused him of the larger cream theft.

'On the house,' she called back, much to the disdain of the

shop-bought-sandwich eaters at the table under the clock. She'd charged *them* full price for their refill of tea.

A sudden clatter at the door took her, and the remaining customers, by surprise. She looked up and saw it open, its hinges complaining as it was pushed with some force. A figure, silhouetted for a moment in the door frame, staggered in. He was a large man, and to Maddie's horror, he was holding a shotgun. Her heart skipped several beats, before she realised it was safely broken over his arm. But, as she focused on him, she noticed something else too. He'd been at her gran's jam, it seemed.

Oh dear, she thought. *Was he in earlier? Did it drip and run all over him?*

But he wasn't there to complain about jam. In fact, the red on his shirt cuffs and staining the sleeves of his wax jacket wasn't jam at all.

It was blood.

2

The teashop seemed eerily quiet for a moment or two, then suddenly there was a cacophonous noise of chairs being scraped back against the stone floor and gasps from the customers. What slim chance they'd had of enjoying their tea was now gone entirely.

'What the...?' Maddie slipped around the counter. She tried to cordially say goodbye to the nice couple who had braved Crumpet as well as the runny jam as they quickly left. She watched, agog, as they edged their way behind the man covered in blood as he walked down the middle of the teashop, between the tables, towards her.

The couple who had eaten their own sandwiches sat with their mouths open, the woman's hand clutching the anorak sleeve of her husband. The only other customer, a young man in a long black trench coat, seemed oblivious to the whole event, with his headphones on and his nose about four inches from the screen of his smartphone, the one can of Coca-Cola he'd ordered open on the table.

'Phone the ambulance, or the police,' the blood-covered man demanded and Maddie, her mind in a twirl, nodded before realising she'd need to know what to tell the police before she called them, or indeed if it should be the ambulance service instead.

She gestured for the man to sit down at one of the tables. Hoping she'd done the right thing (and that the shotgun would stay very much broken and not pointed at anyone any time soon), she grabbed the first thing that came to hand – one of her gran's old handwritten recipe books – and sat down opposite him.

'She's dead,' he panted as Maddie fished around in the pocket of her apron for a pencil, then quickly opened the recipe book. It was one of those old exercise books, with a school crest on the front and lined pages within, each one full of her grandmother's rounded, flowing writing. She pushed down on the spine, opening it up at a page with one of the shorter recipes on it, leaving her more room to scribble alongside it. Her brain, though decent enough, worked in its own way, and she'd learned over the years that she needed to write her thoughts down – important or not – to remember them. It was why she loved cooking. There was a simple set of instructions, a recipe that one could follow, and one action had to be done before another could. For example, you couldn't fry an onion if you hadn't already peeled and chopped it. If only this methodical approach could be applied to all walks of life...

Enough, she told herself, knowing her mind was getting distracted even as she sat in front of this distressed man. *Concentrate, Maddie!*

'Who's dead? What's happened?' Maddie asked.

'I don't know,' the man said, wringing his hands and then stopping as he saw, as if for the first time, the blood on them. Maddie tried not to look and instead she took a deep breath and gripped the pencil hard.

'OK then, well let's start at the beginning. I'm Maddie Penrose. And you are?'

'Clive Pendergast,' the man said. 'Nor's neighbour over at Hill Top Farm.'

'Clive, I think we might have met before. Nor's my grandmother,' as Maddie said this, he seemed to relax very slightly, his shoulders lowering a few centimetres.

'Good, good,' he said, though his mind was obviously elsewhere. He looked up at her. 'You have to call the police. I've just found a poor young...' He couldn't get the words out to finish his sentence.

Maddie gave him some room to come to terms with whatever horror he had just stumbled upon. She looked at him. She did recognise him now. He was large, though not overweight, and sturdy and fit for his age, which she placed at around fifty-five, or maybe a bit older. His gingery-red hair had receded over a freckled brow and his ice-blue eyes looked watery – whether from the shock of whatever it was he had seen or windburn from the fields, she wasn't sure.

'Of course I will,' Maddie reassured him, hoping the moment or two had helped him get himself together. 'But you need to tell me a little bit more about what's happened so I can tell them. Where is this poor young...'

'Woman,' Clive answered her as another roll of thunder rattled the windowpanes. 'She's by the old cow shed up by the sycamore tree. The wall... the stones... they must have fallen...' His voice trailed off.

'Where is it?' she asked, though the mention of the sycamore tree stirred something in her memory. 'Anything the police can use to navigate there?'

He looked up at her. 'Yes, there's a lane off Creek Road, it's single track and barely anyone uses it, but...' He looked at his hands as they lay flat on the table, like stabilisers.

'But what?' Maddie pressed him.

'It goes to the back gate of my farm.' He looked as if by saying this he was admitting to something, but he carried on, raising his eyes back up to meet Maddie's. 'But they can bring a four-by-four up the hill beyond the gate and reach the cow shed that way.'

'Right, OK.' Maddie had jotted those words down next to the opening ingredients of the recipe. She looked up to see the couple who had eaten their own sandwiches only now get up to leave and she shrugged an apology to them. The young man in the trench coat had left too and she couldn't remember if he'd paid for his can of Coke or not, but was too distracted now to worry about it.

She left Clive sitting at the table and walked behind the counter. She'd left her mobile in her bedroom – there were messages on it she had no inclination to deal with now – but knew there was an old landline phone nestled somewhere between the fire blanket and the toasted sandwich maker. Picking it up, she pressed the three numbers that no one ever wanted to have to dial into the handset and waited for the call to connect.

Moments later, Maddie had informed the dispatch of the situation and given them Clive's directions and her own mobile phone number, but was disheartened to hear that it might be half an hour or so before anyone could get to them. A dead body in London would have had the police there in moments, but she'd forgotten that Cornwall was such a large county that the police could easily be stationed an hour away.

She put the receiver down and fetched one of the novelty teapots from the shelf behind the counter, assuming a hot sweet tea was probably what they both needed. As she filled it with water from the boiling urn, she wondered about pouring some jam on the last scone for Clive, but decided against it. He needed sugar for shock, but strawberry soup was possibly pushing it. And being a true Cornish girl at heart, she couldn't serve a scone without a dollop of local clotted cream on top. Once again the missing tub of it nagged at her. Finding anything in this teashop had now been made harder by the light bulb blowing, but she was fairly sure a catering-sized tub of clotted cream would have been pretty hard to miss, even in the dimness of the cloudy afternoon light. But the thunder was, thank heavens, rolling eastward, it seemed, and the sun had reappeared now the clouds had skidded along the coastline. Maddie poured the brewed tea into two mugs and topped them up with a splash of milk and a heaped teaspoon of sugar each.

She returned to the table where Clive was sitting, with the recipe book clenched under her armpit, her pencil behind her ear and the two steaming mugs of hot sweet tea in her hands.

'I thought you could do with this,' she said, handing him one of them. Clive took it gratefully, nodding his thanks, and Maddie opened the recipe book up again ready to take more notes. 'The police would appreciate us going back to the scene to guide them in, and well, to keep it safe before they can get there, but I think you need a couple of gulps of that before you show me where it is. I added some cold milk so it shouldn't scald you.'

'You'll come too?' Clive asked, then continued before she could answer. 'It's not a pretty sight, I don't think you'd want to see it.'

'I don't want to see it,' agreed Maddie, 'but the police said we should do what we can to preserve the scene and I'm not leaving you to go back there alone.' She pointed at the tremor in the man's hand as he lifted the mug to his lips. As he sipped, she carried on. 'But before we go, and while you get some of that sugar into you, tell me what happened. How did you find it... her?'

Clive lowered the mug. 'I was walking the estate, you know, checking on the cows and the fences—'

'With your shotgun?' Maddie asked, indicating the firearm

now lying across his lap and remembering the gunshot she'd heard before.

Clive merely shrugged. 'Rabbits,' he said, before carrying on. 'Hiking season's upon us and you know how these walkers get when footpaths aren't maintained for them.' Maddie nodded, though despite spending holidays here in Cornwall, she'd grown up in suburban Surrey so really had no idea about rural footpaths and the politics surrounding them. He carried on. 'Got to the old cow shed and saw the tumble—'

'The tumble?' Maddie asked, pencil poised.

'Yes, the tumble. The stones all pulled down as if a wrecking ball had hit them. Turned the air blue I did when I saw it from afar, as that's a job and a half to put right. Local lads get bored and cause mischief, you see, and I thought they'd been up there and made a right mess, drinking their cider and hanging off the walls. But as I got closer, I could see something wasn't right with it all.'

'Why, what do you mean?' Maddie creased her brow.

'I could see something bright pink under the stones. I thought it was odd, so put a bit of speed on. Thought if it was those lads from town, I might catch them in the act!'

'Scare them off like the rabbits?' Maddie pointed the end of her pencil towards the shotgun again, but Clive shook his head.

'No, nothing like that. Shooting code never to point a gun, loaded or not, towards a person.'

Maddie flushed and took a sip of her tea, letting Clive carry on with his story.

'But when I got closer, I could see it was fabric, the arm of a coat, and there was no one, no lads, around. It didn't feel right. And bright pink isn't a colour the local lads wear, you see. Didn't feel right at all... and then I realised why.'

'What was it?' Maddie had her pencil poised, but the point of the lead almost stabbed through the paper when she heard what Clive said next.

'There was an arm in the sleeve.'

Maddie shuddered at the image. But what Clive Pendergast said next chilled her further.

'And when I got closer, I didn't just see the arm, but the hand too. And it moved.'

3

'She wasn't dead?' Maddie's pencil lead almost snapped off as she shot a look up at Clive.

'No. But she soon was, God rest her soul.' Clive shook his head, then blew on his tea to cool it. 'I tried to help.' He showed Maddie his hands, which still had a tremor to them. She could see now where most, if not all, of the blood had come from – his own fingertips, which were scraped raw from the effort of hauling rough stones off the injured woman.

'Then what happened?' Maddie pressed him. 'Did you manage to free her?'

Clive got up, ignoring her question. 'We should get going.'

'Yes, yes. Take the mug with you, keep drinking,' Maddie urged, taking her own mug and her gran's old recipe book back to the counter.

Clive took a sip and cocked his gun over his arm. Then he stopped and looked back at Maddie, as if remembering he hadn't answered her. 'Poor lass was crushed as bad as I've ever seen. No fight in her. She could barely get her words out.'

'She spoke to you?' Maddie asked, as she flipped open her gran's old recipe book on the counter.

'Yes.' Clive's voice lowered to a whisper. 'I could barely make it out. But it sounded like "Aren't you", then I didn't catch it, then "rock would tree help", but there were pauses and unintelligible sounds too.' He swigged from his mug, then put it down on one of the tables by the door and wiped a hand across his forehead, which only made him look worse, with blood now smeared there as well.

'Rock... Tree...' Maddie noted it down, then took a hurried sip from her mug. 'What did that mean?'

Clive shrugged and Maddie could see that his face was pale, drained of blood. She was worried that he hadn't drunk enough of his tea, but he seemed in a hurry to get back to the body. And he was probably right. But he did reply to her. 'I suppose she meant the rocks and was asking if the tree would help, maybe using it as a lever? I don't know.' He shook his head, and then in a whisper added, 'she died before I could ask.'

'The poor, poor thing,' Maddie said, putting down the pencil. She caught sight of her watch and remembered the police were on their way. 'Sorry, you're right, we should go. But you need to have a few more sips first.' Clive nodded and raised the mug to his lips again as Maddie asked one more question. 'She didn't tell you her name, did she?'

'No,' he replied as he put the mug down one last time. Maddie noticed the understandable tremble again. His voice was quieter and more reflective when he continued. 'And I didn't think to ask. It was all... It all happened so fast.'

'The poor girl,' Maddie said as she untied her apron and found her beat-up old denim jacket where she'd flung it earlier that day behind the counter. Her gran would need to know all about this, she'd *want* to know all about this, especially why she was closing up the teashop an hour or two early. But with no more customers in, no more cake or scones or clotted cream to serve *and* a dead woman out in the fields, Maddie made the only decision she could.

Moments later, she was escorting Clive out of the door as she locked up behind them, bracing herself for seeing her first ever dead body.

Clive led her out of Folly Farm and along the muddy footpath that she imagined most of the walkers who came to the teashop used, judging by the state of the teashop's floor, which she'd noticed earlier was covered in the same limestone grit and gravel as this path. The path itself was edged by a tall hedgerow on one side, sparse now due to spring only just getting going, and open fields to the other. It gently rose uphill and, after a few minutes, if she'd turned around, Maddie would have had the view of Nor's farm, with its stone outbuildings and beautiful Georgian farmhouse below. But Maddie pressed on, following Clive along the rutted pathway, careful of her own steps in case she twisted an ankle in their haste.

They crossed a stile, and from then on, Maddie wasn't sure which fields belonged to Nor and which ones were Hill Top Farm's, but judging by the name of Clive's farm, she reckoned the large sycamore tree standing right on top of the hill just ahead of them was his... and the site of the poor woman's death.

As she walked up behind him, she glanced back again at her grandmother's farm and the glittering sea of Pendragon Bay below it. Sunlight sparkled like diamonds on the water and she could see why so many hikers used this path and would seek a restorative cup of tea at the bottom of it. No wonder her gran's teashop had once been the bustling and cosy place she remembered. In a moment snatched from reality, she imagined how once again it could flourish, especially with summer coming, and how much she wanted to help make that happen.

Clive cleared his throat and Maddie's mind was drawn back to the terrible fate of the hiker who had been crushed by the falling 'tumble'; the stones that had once been laid carefully to make the drystone wall of a former cow shed, but had now tumbled to the ground. Made properly, as a centuries-old wall would have been, it should have been as solid as one made with bricks and mortar, so how had it fallen onto some unlucky walker? Perhaps she'd leant against it? Or pushed it? Pulled herself up on it? Maddie hated even thinking about it and wished for a moment that the only thing on her mind was what was vexing her about twenty minutes ago – dry scones and tumbling customer numbers, not dry stones tumbling onto unsuspecting hikers.

Clive, who seemed to have found an inner strength, and was forging ahead of her, came to an abrupt stop and turned around. 'Miss Penrose, I don't think you should come much further. She's... well, are you sure you can handle seeing this?'

Maddie looked past him, but all she could see was the ruin of the cow shed, its triangular ends showing where roof beams and tiles would have formed the shelter. The roof was long gone, along with its thatch and beams, and now one wall was too, and behind the farmer all she could see was the tumble that he had described. She took a deep breath, then girded herself.

'Clive, I think it's too late for that. You need to head off down towards the lane out to the main road and guide in the police. I don't know that route, but I'm here now so can warn anyone else off coming too close.'

Clive nodded and moved to one side before giving her a quick salute-style wave and heading off at an angle down a wide path that Maddie could tell was only ever used by tractors or four-by-four vehicles, rutted as it was, and with a hedgerow on either side merging into trees that formed an impenetrable arch over the lane. She watched as he disappeared down it, shotgun still broken over his arm. It made her think for one moment of the women in trendy London suburbs who carried their designer handbags in exactly the same way. She looked a while longer at where his back had been, unable to turn around to see what was behind her.

She knew what was there, after all. A dead young woman under a mound of stones.

A caw from a crow in the trees above her reminded her of her duty – preserving the scene from contamination, whether that be from other walkers or indeed animals – and how so very different today had suddenly become from her London life. She took a deep breath and turned to face the fallen stones.

Sure enough, Clive had been right and she could see the pink cloth of an anorak with a limp hand extended from it. The sight stopped her short, and she did everything she could to not look at the pink sleeve, and what it contained. Once seen, it was a sight she could never 'unsee'. She let her eyes rest on the stones instead, squinting one eye shut so that she really couldn't see the anorak sleeve.

Giving herself something else to think about, she analysed what else she could see. Clive had obviously been trying to move the stones from the woman's head and chest and she noticed a pile off to the side that he'd thrown clear.

At least she hadn't been alone when she died, Maddie thought to herself. Clive might not have been her first choice, but there had been a hand to hold hers as she passed away.

It was all suddenly a bit much. Maddie's nose fizzed and she could feel a tear forming as she thought about how scared and in what pain this poor woman must have been. She turned to wipe her eyes and stumbled away from the ruins, overcome suddenly by the emotion of it. She managed a few steps before finding a larger stone to sit on. It wasn't one from the tumble, or from Clive's exertions, but most likely a broken bit of stone trough from the days when this had been a resting spot for cattle.

Maddie sat and cradled her head in her hands, taking deep breaths. She didn't want to fail the police; be accused of getting distracted and ignoring her main mission of defending the scene, but she hoped that just being this nearby to the body was enough.

She wiped her eyes. After a moment or two, she looked up and was surprised to see the familiar bushy orange tail of Crumpet the cat. With no tables to beg at now the teashop was shut, the big old ginger tom must have followed them up the hill, either out of curiosity or in hope of teashop-style treats from a pocket.

'You're out of luck, Crumps,' Maddie said, awkwardly aware she was talking to a cat in the presence of a dead body.

Crumpet came up and bumped his head against her hand, then sniffed her outstretched fingers.

Tears, she thought. *Cats love salt*. But Crumpet's attention wasn't held for long by the saltiness of her tears that she'd brushed away with her fingertips. His sensitive nose had moved on and she watched as he raised his tail and sniffed with purpose. Her eyes followed him until he stopped at another stone, tail and whiskers aquiver. It was just like the ones from the cow shed, the ones that Clive had tried desperately to pull off the dying woman.

But this one was different.

Dark against the grey of the stone, red against the white of old lichen, was a smear of glossy red blood.

4

Maddie got up, wiping another stray tear from her eye as she tried to refocus on the bloodied stone in front of her.

It is blood, isn't it? she questioned herself, running through her mind all the things she thought – *hoped* – it might be instead. Perhaps a damp patch of moss, or was it reddish from the local ironstone leaching into the groundwater?

She reached down and stroked Crumpet, who was looking just a bit too interested in the red smear on the moss-covered stone, before picking him up and moving him to one side. He looked disgruntled and gave her a silent miaow to tell her off, but was soon nosing into the hedgerow, much to the alarm of several small birds nesting just out of reach.

Maddie looked at the stone. It was definitely blood. And fresh too. She looked back to the tumble, where the pink anorak sleeve was just about visible, and saw the pile of stones that Clive Pendergast had hurriedly removed in his futile attempt to save the woman.

This stone was yards away from that pile.

This stone had never been one of the ones that fell on the woman.

Maddie looked again at the blood on the stone. The sun passed behind a grey cloud and the world darkened around her. The fresh blood no longer glistened; its colour deepened and Maddie suddenly realised what it meant.

'Oh no,' Maddie whispered to herself, putting two and two, or at least stone and blood, together and making... murder.

Theories were now cascading through her mind. What if this poor woman had been hit over the head by someone, and this stone was the weapon? And then, thinking she was dead, they had pulled the stone wall down on top of her to disguise it and make it look like an accident?

Maddie's blood ran cold. The scene was made to look like an accident, but it wasn't.

And while accidents could happen when you were on your own, murder meant there was someone else involved – a murderer. And judging by the freshness of the blood, that murderer could easily still be around.

Noises from the hedge made Maddie whip her head around, her heart thumping. But it was only a harried starling beating its wings in order to scare away Crumpet, who had been joined by his partner in crime, a fluffy grey cat with a dark grey nose and large green eyes. This was Burned Toast, shortened to Toast by Nor, and, by all reports, an excellent mouser.

Maddie released her breath, watching as the two cats stalked the hedgerow, Crumpet, his eyes on the starling, Toast more concerned with catching whatever was hiding behind a discarded soft drink can. But she couldn't shake the thought that a murderer was possibly nearby. Maddie looked down the rough single-track lane that Clive had taken in order to wave down the police and guide them in.

Clive... He said he'd found this woman, but this was *his* land. He had even said that the single-track lane ran from the main road to his farm, and only his farm. Could he have killed the woman and created this whole scene in order to cover it up?

He'd literally had blood on his hands when he'd appeared at the teashop.

Not to mention, of course, he was nonchalantly carrying around a shotgun.

Maddie gulped. She wiped her sweating hands down the front of her jeans. *And I've just gone and walked up here with him...* She closed her eyes and berated herself.

Maddie now had no idea what to do. She'd promised the police she'd stay on the scene, but she may well have just walked into a murderer's trap.

She opened her eyes and lost another heartbeat as she saw Clive walking briskly towards her, the double-barrelled shotgun still broken over his arm. Could he have orchestrated this whole thing?

Maddie held her breath, aware that she had nothing on her, not even a pencil, or chopsticks, or even a wooden spoon that might have been in the pocket of her discarded apron. She had nothing she could protect herself with when faced with a tall, strong man, with a gun. Nothing that was except her gran's old recipe book that was rolled up tightly and shoved in her back pocket. Her hand reached for it, though she knew the only foe it could possibly take down was an errant fly.

She looked up, and Clive was closer, his cheeks flushed, his eyes gimlet-like in their intensity. Maddie froze. She wanted to flee. She knew she couldn't fight. Why was Clive back here without the police? Where were they?

Clive shifted the gun from his right arm to his left. If he cocked it, how long would she have before he could shoot? She looked around her, but apart from the hedgerow and the old cow shed, there was nowhere for her to hide. Clive's other hand was in the pocket of his wax jacket – a pocket deep enough to hold plenty of shotgun cartridges. Was this it? Was Maddie done for? Then, to her immense relief, Clive took his hand out of his pocket and waved at her. And, to her even greater relief, the front bonnet of the police Land Rover came into view behind him.

Maddie waved back, probably a little too enthusiastically, and then beckoned the police car over. It neatly overtook Clive, who was still red in the face and marching up the hill towards the ruins, before Maddie held up her hand to stop them before they got too close.

Two young constables jumped out and immediately took charge, asking Maddie so many questions that she felt quite ruffled. When had she arrived? What was she doing up here? When did Clive first come into the teashop? How did she know him?

Maddie 'ummed' and 'ahhed', though answered what she could, referring to her gran's recipe book at times, which seemed to only cause more confusion on the part of the young constables, especially when she misread her gran's old note about oats and crumble, instead of tumble. She pointed out the bloodied stone and that it was too far away from the ruins to have been part of that or the stones that Clive had removed. She noticed that Clive was interested in this fact too and wondered if she saw him blanch when she showed it to the police. She couldn't quite shake from her mind the image of him standing in the teashop doorway, blood on his hands and a panicked look in his eyes. Had he killed this poor woman, still lying under the tumble? Or had he truly been the Good Samaritan who tried to help her and listened to her dying words as she passed away? And, more importantly, how had that stone over there, the one that now had a neat little yellow triangle next to it, identifying it as evidence, become so covered in fresh, sticky blood?

5

Maddie let herself into Folly Farmhouse with a sigh of relief. The wide, sage-coloured door, with its brass knob and knocker, opened onto a rather grand hallway. A beautiful staircase swept down from the landing, its white spindles topped by a well-worn mahogany banister rail that curved to a neat scroll at the end. The walls were panelled and painted a soft pistachio colour, and, where space allowed, they were decorated with pastel-hued watercolours, painted by Nor Penrose herself. Framed in a mishmash of mahogany, gold or painted styles, these had the overall effect of making the hallway look like the peak of the summer exhibition at the Royal Academy. All of this was lit by a large glass and brass lantern that hung from the high ceiling on a chain and a half-moon-shaped fan light above the door, the dappled light from which played across the glass of the picture frames.

Two wide, panelled doors led off the hallway, one at the bottom of the stairs to the right and the other opposite it. To the right-hand side was what should be a formal sitting room, but it had become a dumping ground for most of Nor's arty bits and pieces she couldn't be bothered to lug upstairs to her attic studio anymore. Though, in Nor's defence, the light that poured in through the large sash windows was perfect for her painting and Maddie could see that the high-ceilinged, light-filled room made the ideal art studio. Even if the old sisal flooring was now liberally splattered with paint, and the sofas were 'reupholstered' with turpentine-smelling dust sheets.

The other side of the hallway was the dining room, with its dark-wood table and rather austerely uncomfortable chairs, definitely from a different era. Maddie remembered a few Easter and Christmas lunches around it, but it was no wonder Nor, and her guests and family, usually headed straight through to the large farmhouse kitchen at the back of the house. It had room enough in it for the four-oven Aga, a walk-in pantry, a large well-scrubbed pine kitchen table surrounded by an odd selection of mismatched chairs, covered in equally mismatching cushions, and off to one side two old sofas, which were arranged in an L-shape around an old boxy television set.

Before Maddie went through to the kitchen she stopped and looked in the gilt-framed mirror that hung above the hallway table. Her chestnut brown hair was a mess, curling at the edges of the headscarf she'd wrapped around it before doing battle with the oven in the teashop earlier in the day. Her eye make-up had run slightly, and she wiped at the base of her brown eyes in an attempt to make herself look slightly more presentable.

'What a day, and don't I look it,' she muttered to herself, as she straightened her shoulders and adjusted her headscarf. She took in the rest of her reflection too. Her cheeks were flushed, no doubt from the brisk walking, not to mention the shock of seeing what she'd seen today. There were still dark circles under her eyes from her late shifts at Chez Lucie, not helped by today's smudged mascara, and on top of that, apart from her flushed cheeks, her skin looked pale. Her denim jacket, an old favourite that had been with her since her culinary college days, hung loosely around her; she'd lost weight as she'd worked twelve-hour shifts and skipped meals to help the kitchen at the bistro keep up. Losing a few pounds should have made her happy – she was no stranger to licking the spoon, and on some occasions even the bowl, after all. But she could also see how it made her look drawn and tired. Today's traumas had not helped at all.

She forced a smile on her face and slicked a bit of lip balm on, then headed into the kitchen to tell her gran all about what had happened.

'Well, I never,' Nor said, holding a mug near her lips, gently blowing on the hot tea. One hand held the mug, the other stroked Crumpet as the large ginger cat lay fully across her lap. Maddie and Nor had taken up their cosy position on the comfy old sofas, and almost as soon as they'd sat down, steaming cups of tea in hand, Crumpet and Toast had decided to join them. Maddie idly rubbed the soft fur between Toast's ears as she recounted more of the story of the afternoon to Nor.

'It was horrible, Gran, it really was. But the police are up there now and I told them about that other stone I found and my suspicions about it.'

'I bet they didn't like some amateur sleuth jumping three steps ahead of them.' Nor raised an eyebrow over towards her granddaughter.

'They took it well if they didn't and said they'd let their chief know.' She paused as she sipped her Earl Grey, sweetened for the occasion to help with any lingering shock. 'I wonder what will happen next? I suppose an ambulance must have tried to get up that small track too.'

'It is naughty of Clive to let that lane get all rutted and overgrown,' Nor replied. She was a petite older woman, and dressed, as usual, sensibly but smartly. She had a knack of always looking perfectly put together and lived by the motto that it was 'nice to look nice'. It was true she had struggled recently with her arthritis and her knee, and obviously the teashop was getting too much for her to look after on her own, as well as the rest of the farm, but there was definitely plenty of life still left in Nor. In fact, Maddie found herself rather envying her sheepskin-lined, chocolate-brown suede ankle boots and natty fuchsia-coloured neckerchief that brought a pop of colour above her navy blue jumper. Not to mention her perfectly coiffed, if totally grey, bobbed hair.

'Was that lane not always like that then?' Maddie asked.

'No, it was once the main road up to the old cow shed – and by road, I mean single-track lane, of course. But it was used by the shepherd and cow-man, as well as those of us who wanted a shortcut up there for when Clive's parents used to host barn dances and summer parties. It was the perfect place for them, up there, with that lovely view of Pendragon Bay from the sycamore tree.'

'They had parties up there?' Maddie asked, pulling her leg out from under her before the pins and needles set in. A disgruntled Toast looked at her in disgust, before settling himself back down on her lap.

'Oh yes. In the seventies and eighties. We'd get a caller from Porthgowan, and he'd get us all do-si-do-ing with our partners and swinging ourselves silly until we were all far too dizzy to stand up straight. Your grandfather was a right one for swinging me far too fast – flew out of his grip and straight into that old cow shed once, but luckily it was full of fresh straw and cider drinkers, so there was someone to catch me.' She chuckled to herself at the memory, then frowned. 'Sad thought, though, that another young lady has met a sticky end there.'

Maddie narrowed her eyes at her grandmother. 'Sounds like your end wasn't too sticky. Just cidery maybe. Was there another young lady then?'

'Yes.' Nor concentrated on stroking Crumpet for a moment before she continued. 'We don't know how sticky her end was really, but back in the 1960s, that old cow shed was the last place that a local lass was seen alive, before she disappeared.'

'Really?' This was news indeed from her gran. Toast jumped off Maddie's lap as she moved her other leg. Despite loving the warmth of the cat's body on her, she was relieved to be free of the weight of him. He was obviously a remarkably good mouser, or perhaps Nor was softer to these two farm cats than she let on. 'So this was in the 1960s?' Maddie reached over for the recipe book and pencil that was sitting next to her on the sofa.

'Yes. 1965, I think... Oi, why are you writing in my recipe book?'

'Oh, sorry, Gran.' Maddie sheepishly put the pencil down. 'I had to grab something when Clive came into the teashop all covered in blood and you know what my brain's like – I have a tendency to forget things at the best of times – and I knew things he might be saying could be important.'

Maddie closed the recipe book, having noted down the date 1965 and its relevance to the old cow shed. And not meaning to be impertinent, but also not wanting to put this conversation off much longer despite the headline of the day being about the poor dead woman up at the old cow shed, and whatever had happened back in the sixties, she confronted her gran about the state of the teashop.

'... And by the way, no wonder your knee's playing up if you spent your youth being thrown around on the dancefloor by Grandpa,' Maddie finished off.

Nor looked at her with a glint in her eye, the first since Maddie had brought up the subject of the teashop a few minutes ago. 'Wasn't just the dance floor...'

'Gran!' Maddie made a face, but she laughed too. 'I don't need to know about that. But my point still stands. I'm worried about you running all of this on your own. Mum and Dad are too.'

'I know, I know. It's these hands.' She raised them in front of her face, one after the other, making sure not to spill her tea as she moved the mug between them. 'They're slowing me down. I can't make cakes as fast as I used to. But then I am eighty-two. Time to retire by anyone's book, but when I mentioned closing up, my friend Marge, who runs one of the shops down in the town, got all upset, saying I was a fixture of the community and owed it to the town to keep going... But I know really it's just because she likes her hot coffee after a sea swim and we're the closest spot to Pendragon Bay. I even had Jason asking if he could take it over.'

'Who's Jason and why would he want to run a teashop?' Maddie asked, shifting in her seat. The thought of anyone else manning that hot water urn made her uneasy. Defensive, even.

'Oh, he wouldn't want to run it as a teashop, but use the space to store more of his equipment. He's already renting the old barn the other side of the yard, you see. He's a young lad,' she paused and Maddie could see that Nor was trying to choose her words carefully so as not to offend. 'His manner is a little rough perhaps and I'm not sure he's... well, he pays me in cash—'

'Gran...' Maddie couldn't keep the warning tone out of her voice, even though she knew it could sound a bit patronising. 'You can't just accept cash these days.'

'I think it might have been cash or nothing though, ducky.' Nor fiddled with her neckerchief and Maddie suddenly felt very protective of her ageing grandmother as she continued explaining. 'But the cash is useful. I can use it to pay Clive for the hay for the horses, as he gets a better rate from the wholesaler when his doesn't come in off the fields, and young Pete from the town will do odd jobs for cash. So will Mandy and her daughter Bella, who come and do their horses and whatnot and sometimes do a bit of gardening for me. Needs must and all that.'

Maddie let it rest, but she wasn't happy with the situation at all. She got up before Toast could eye up her lap again and took her and Nor's empty mugs to the large ceramic sink. Seeing the plumpness of the cat, she thought it best to bring up the other mystery of the day.

'Where do you get your clotted cream from?'

'Farringford Dairy, just down the road, why?'

'We'll need some more. I was sure there was a full tub in the fridge in the teashop this morning, but it had gone this afternoon. I blamed Crumpet, but looking at Toast's undercarriage, he might have played a part.'

Nor tutted. 'Cats can't open a fridge and carry off a tub of cream. No opposable thumbs. Think what pickles they'd be if they could! What a nuisance though. Sounds like we might have a two-legged mouse, as well as the four-legged ones Toast likes to terrorise in the old hay barn.'

'Hmm,' Maddie agreed, realising that suspecting the cats had been a little childish. She would look into this Jason guy though. She didn't like the sound of someone who was a bit rough hanging around the farm, let alone eyeing up the teashop, especially if all he wanted to do with it was use the space as storage. Marge, whoever she was, was right. Folly Farm Teashop was a local institution – it couldn't just fizzle out and become some sort of shed. She needed to meet Jason and make sure he knew Nor wasn't a vulnerable old woman.

Glancing back at her bird-like grandmother, almost swamped by the large ginger cat on her lap, Maddie couldn't help but realise that, far from being the feisty, farmer's wife she'd always thought of her as, perhaps she was indeed a vulnerable old woman. And one with a teashop that desperately needed saving.

6

A sharp rat-a-tat-tat on the farmhouse's front door almost made Maddie drop her mug into the sink.

'It's all go here today,' Nor said, gently pushing Crumpet off her lap and brushing down the front of her jeans. Her fingers, though swollen at the joints through arthritis, fiddled with her neckerchief, arranging it just so.

'I'll get it, Gran, you stay there.' Maddie, still feeling protective of Nor having heard about Jason, gestured for her to stay in the kitchen. Wiping her hands on her sweater, which was just a plain jersey affair compared to Nor's rather lovely cashmere-mix, Maddie strode down the hall and was about to open the door when the harsh knocking sounded again. 'I'm here, I'm here...' she called out, unlocking the catch. 'Hold your' – she opened the door to see who was there – 'horses,' she said, letting the word hang in the air as she took in the sight of the police Land Rover. Not to mention the rather handsome man standing in front of her holding his police ID card up to her face.

'DI Trevelyan, Devon and Cornwall Police. Are you Miss Madeline Penrose?'

'Yes.'

She opened the door wider to let him in. He was tall, six foot two at least, and clean-shaven. His hair had a reddishness to it, making it auburn rather than brown, while his eyes were as blue grey as the sea on a February morning. He looked like an actor she'd seen playing a Tudor lord on TV; his face had that similar sort of intensity, of someone who had the weight of the world on his nicely broad shoulders.

Maddie spotted a colleague of DI Trevelyan's getting out of the Land Rover, but instead of joining them at the door, the woman – dressed in a grey suit and sensible shoes to match her sensible ponytail – headed over to the outbuildings. Maddie watched her for a moment then said to the detective in front of her, 'Would you like to come in?'

'If you don't mind.' Trevelyan said it as a statement, not a question, and Maddie wondered if someone could become less good-looking on further inspection, especially if that inspection included rudeness. Still, she found her eye darting to her reflection in the hallway mirror – just a quick check to see how she was looking – and wished that she was even half as well put together outfit-wise as her grandmother was today.

She followed DI Trevelyan along the hallway and noted, as he entered the kitchen, that he redeemed himself slightly by being courteous to her grandmother.

Maddie skirted around them and put the kettle back on the Aga, glad that it was still warm from the tea she and Nor had just had, so there wouldn't be a long awkward wait for it to boil. She then turned and, surprised, found DI Trevelyan just looking at her. Her hand went to her hair, still vaguely tied back under the headscarf, and she self-consciously flicked an errant curl out of her face.

'Miss Penrose—'

'Maddie, please,' she flustered, cutting him off.

'Maddie, I wanted to thank you for letting the constables

know about the stone with the, um...' he paused and looked at Nor.

'Don't be coy around me, Detective,' Nor said. 'Old age isn't for the faint-hearted; there's not much you can say that'll shock me.'

Maddie looked at DI Trevelyan and shrugged. He met her gaze, and for a moment Maddie wasn't sure where to put her hands or how to stand. She made do with leaning against the rail of the Aga, hoping she looked nonchalant. Nor, on the other hand, seemed far more poised and crossed her arms in anticipation of the detective carrying on. And he did, picking up where he left off.

'The blood-covered stone, then. It was useful to have it marked and noted in the first instance, before too many more of the team trampled over the scene.'

'Do you think it might have been used to murder her?' Maddie asked, finally finding something to do with her hands by taking the kettle off the boil and closing the lid on the Aga hotplate.

'We still can't comment on that, but we're pursuing all leads,' DI Trevelyan said.

'Of course. Tea?' Maddie asked.

Trevelyan nodded.

'And for your... partner?' she added, testing how he'd react to the word.

Trevelyan shook his head. 'DS Mitchell isn't a tea drinker.'

Maddie and Nor shared a look. 'Not a tea drinker. Right. So, is there anything else I can help you with?'

'Yes, as a matter of fact. I'm afraid I need a statement from you.' He pulled a notebook out of the messenger bag that had been over his shoulder and flipped it open. Maddie looked at him oddly, which made him continue, 'As long as that's convenient now?'

'Yes, of course,' Maddie said, squeezing the teabags out of

the mugs and dumping them in the sink. 'I just thought you'd have an iPad or something, not a good old-fashioned notebook.'

'Can't rely on all this modern technology,' Nor stated confidently. 'Batteries running out of puff and easily broken screens have nothing on the solid reliability of paper and pen.'

DI Trevelyan agreed. 'And they form a legal document too. Unhackable.'

Maddie passed him a steaming mug of tea. 'Go on then, when do you want me to start?'

'From as soon as Mr Pendergast entered your teashop, if you don't mind,' Trevelyan said, clicking the end of his ballpoint pen in readiness. 'And anything you might have seen or heard before that which you think might be of interest.'

Maddie took a seat at the kitchen table and gestured for him to sit too. Then she told him about the entrance that Clive had made at about three o'clock that afternoon, his version of what had happened and how she'd decided against giving him a cream-less scone, got some basic information from him, phoned the police, made him drink some sweet tea and then accompanied him back up the hill so that she could stay at the scene while he went down the lane to meet the constables.

A sharp knock at the front door neatly punctuated the natural end of her retelling, and Maddie got up to see who it was. When she opened the door, she found herself face to face with a woman about her age, the plain-clothes officer who had got out of the Land Rover with DI Trevelyan.

'DS Mitchell,' the woman said bluntly by way of a greeting. Now she was up close, Maddie clocked how glossy her brown hair was in its ponytail. Not a hint of frizz. And even though her grey suit was a bit shiny and ill-fitting, DS Mitchell did look annoyingly fit.

Not one for licking the cake bowl, Maddie thought to herself as she showed her in.

DS Mitchell walked straight past her and down the hall

towards the kitchen at the back, speaking as she went. 'Boss, can you come and see something out here,' she said, not even acknowledging Nor sitting at the table making light conversation with DI Trevelyan.

Nor, however, turned to her. 'Hello, Karen, how's your mum?'

DS Mitchell, who was still holding herself as upright as if a broom handle was stuck down the back of her jacket, crossed her arms. 'She's fine thanks, Mrs Penrose. Sends her best, I'm sure.'

'Good, good,' Nor said, catching Maddie's eye as the two police officers left the kitchen and headed back out to the farm.

Maddie looked quizzically at her grandmother.

'Very pleased with herself, isn't she, that one?' Nor mumbled, picking up her mug and taking it over to the sink. 'I know her mother, of course. She's a madam and all.'

'Gran,' Maddie hissed, though she couldn't help but laugh too. 'You can't say that.'

'I'm eighty-two; I can say anything I like,' Nor replied, though Maddie could see a smirk on her grandmother's lips.

'What do you think she wanted?' Maddie asked her gran, wandering back out to the hallway and then into the front room, Nor's makeshift art studio, in order to look out of the large sash window there and see if she could see what the officers were up to. She caught sight of them rattling one of the outbuilding's doors, and peering in through the old barn's dusty window, hands cupped over eyes to get a better look at the dim interior.

As she wondered what had caused their interest in the contents of her gran's old cow shed, she found herself looking at DI Trevelyan. 'Easy on the eye' is what Nor would no doubt call him, and Maddie would have to agree. His dark auburn hair was being ruffled by the spring breeze as she watched, and she thought back to those grey blue eyes that she'd found it all too easy to get distracted by as she was giving her statement. Well, he *was* easy on the eye... and also just her type. But what were they looking at? Or for? Surely, there was nothing to do with the murder in one of her gran's barns?

'Speaking of speaking my mind,' Nor called through from the kitchen, breaking Maddie's attention. 'I'm still not happy about you writing all over my best flapjack recipe.'

'Sorry, Gran,' Maddie called back as she let the lace curtain drop on the sash window, leaving the two police officers to whatever they wanted to look at. She walked back through the hallway to the kitchen. 'I told you, it was the first thing to hand when Clive burst in all covered in blood. I had to note down what I could before I forgot it. You know what I'm like.'

'Yes, but it says here, oats, three million, one thousand, nine hundred and sixty five grams...' Nor pointed to where Maddie had jotted down the date of that mysterious disappearance just after the amount of oats needed in the original recipe.

'No it doesn't, Gran. I was just putting that date after the amount of... Oh, never mind. And anyway, these recipe books should be typed up and printed out. Save them for posterity.'

'They wouldn't need computerising if people' – she prodded Maddie in the arm with one of her bony fingers – 'stopped writing all over them. There's more in there than you might think.'

'Sorry, Gran.' Maddie, remembering the few hours she'd spent apologising for draughts and the lack of any comfortable seating in the teashop earlier, changed tack. 'Your cakes are still amazing, that coffee and walnut was the only thing stopping a full-scale riot in the teashop earlier. Is it in here? You always said it was a secret recipe, especially that thing you do with the walnuts – it's delicious.'

'Pish,' Nor said, turning her back. Her hip caught the strap of DI Trevelyan's bag, pulling it off the table, its contents spilling out on the hard flagstone floor.

'I'll get it,' Maddie said, worried that Nor might really do her hip in if she had to bend over and pick up the bag's contents, which was mainly pens, a bunch of keys, a Swiss Army penknife and his notebook. Maddie scooped up the scattered objects and placed them on the table. Before she could stop herself, an urge had taken over and she found herself flicking through the pages of DI Trevelyan's notebook.

'Having a nosey?' Nor said, leaning over, while Crumpet skidded across the floor chasing a paperclip that Maddie must have missed.

'Can't help it, Gran,' Maddie replied. 'And I helped him out by telling him about the stone I found, so I just wondered...'

'Wondered what else might be in there.'

'And *who* that unfortunate girl is, more importantly. I just keep thinking of her as being "that poor woman under the rocks". I'd like to know her name.' Maddie riffled through the pages until she came to some bullet points that Trevelyan had made on the page just before his interview with her. Maddie held her breath.

7

'Trevelyan's notebook says she had no ID on her.' Maddie's voice was a whisper, more as a reaction to the fact she knew she was doing something very possibly illegal, rather than actually trying to stay quiet. 'Nor a bag or wallet.' Maddie looked at her gran, a new sadness crossing her face. 'Do you think she was mugged? Clive said that when he'd first seen the tumble, he thought it was local lads messing about. Maybe she was robbed?'

Nor shook her head. 'I shouldn't think so. You've been in London too long, my girl. That sort of thing wouldn't happen here in Pendragon Creek.'

Maddie, who maybe had less faith in her fellow man, tried to agree with her gran, but couldn't shake the 'mugging gone wrong' theory from her head.

'But if it wasn't a mugging, then there's a murderer out there who *meant* to kill her. I think that's worse.'

Maddie thought back to Clive and her suspicions around him. A random mugging that ended in a fatal tragedy was a horrible thought, but it would mean Clive wasn't involved, which was a good thing. The last thing anyone wanted was to spend their days wondering if their closest neighbour was a murderer.

Nor didn't help Clive's cause when she doubled down on her opinion. 'These hikers and walkers always have a backpack on them. And, more often than not, they're filled with nothing more valuable than a ham and cheese sandwich. Why would a mugger risk being arrested over nothing more than a sandwich?'

Maddie thought back to the couple who'd brought their own sandwiches to the teashop. 'We had some in earlier. Sandwich eaters, that is, not muggers. Or murderers, hopefully. They were blatant as anything, eating their sarnies like that.'

'They're the worst,' Nor grumbled, then continued. 'If people like them hadn't felt it was their right to do that, I might have tried a little harder over the last few years. Only so many coffee and walnut cakes and pots of tea you can make when all they want is mocha-frappe-latte-cinos and paninis. Or, worse than that, just a glass of tap water while they sit enjoying the warmth that I have to pay the bill for, while less-than-subtly munching on their own food. No wonder the council wants to shut me down.'

Maddie put the DI's notebook down and looked at her gran. 'Is it really that bad? I know you had one of *those* visits, but why?'

Nor shrugged, and Maddie thought she might be about to evade the subject again. But before Maddie could ask her, she answered. 'Some jobsworth at the council thinks there's no need for a teashop so far from the town centre and I'm ruining the countryside by encouraging litter. Well, there wouldn't be litter if they didn't bring their own supermarket sandwiches and cans of Coke.'

Maddie furrowed her brow and remembered the crushed and empty tin the cats had been playing with while she guarded the body. She should have picked it up and thrown it away, and she made a mental note to do just that when she next went up to that spot. In the meantime, though, she was fuming on Nor's behalf.

'They want to close Folly Farm Teashop just because some of the customers drop litter? That's ridiculous. Total jobsworthiness!' she agreed.

Nor stayed quiet, though her arms were crossed, and Maddie suspected that there was something more.

'Gran? Is that the only thing the council have against you?'

'Well...' Nor looked almost everywhere except at her granddaughter. 'I suppose there is something else I might have done...'

'You did what to the lady from the council?' Maddie was shocked, moments later when Nor had explained.

'In my defence,' Nor held her hands up, 'she had been a real prig about the eggs.'

Maddie opened and closed her mouth a couple of times. 'I still can't believe you put laxatives in her coffee. I'm not surprised she wants to shut you down.'

'She's overreacting.' Nor crossed her arms again.

'Hmm, having to break five times between here and St Ives for "emergency stops"—' Maddie made the quotation marks sign with her fingers as Nor interrupted her.

'Emergency plops more like.'

'Gran!' Maddie admonished her, but couldn't help twitch her mouth into a smile as she saw the glint in her grandmother's eye. Still, Nor's retelling of the story about the lady from the council and her understandable vendetta against the teashop did make Maddie worried. It seemed Nor had lost none of her spark, but they now stood in very real danger of losing the teashop. And having a murderer on the loose, in the very close vicinity, might be the final reason the lavatorially challenged lady from the council needed to shut it all down.

Maddie picked up the detective's notebook again. There

was nothing else in it of any use. He'd jotted down his note about the victim not having a bag on her, or any ID, and noted the bloodied rock. Alongside Maddie's own statement, he'd written 'seems trustworthy', which was nice, but, all in all, this fully trained policeman seemed as clueless as she currently was about who, what or why the murder had happened. Could she leave it up to him, and his probably equally clueless sergeant, who were both still nosing around the outside of the barns, to solve this murder before the council shut them down?

Maddie had never regarded herself as much of a sleuth, though she loved curling up on a Sunday evening with whichever Agatha Christie remake was on TV, pitching her own sleuthing skills against that of the fictional detective. She'd found, over the years, that if she wrote down the thoughts she was having as she watched, rather than just relying on her muddled memory at the end of the programme, she could deduce who the villain was long before Hercule Poirot or Miss Marple revealed all.

It was the same when it came to recipes, as she worked best when there was a nice clear step-by-step she could follow. It wasn't that she lacked flair in the kitchen, quite the opposite. In fact, Lucie Le Bon, who owned Chez Lucie, had remarked on more than one occasion that Maddie really should perhaps do all she could to use slightly *less* flair in the kitchen. Especially when it came to the carved fruit platters. There was only so much flair one needed with melon after all.

She glanced over to Nor's battered recipe book that just this afternoon she'd written a few notes in regarding the poor woman dead under the stones. Maybe if she could help solve this mystery, Maddie would prove that the way her brain worked was just as efficient as anybody else's. She'd then know that she wasn't that burned out or frazzled from the long days and nights working at Chez Lucie.

She pulled the book towards her, and ignoring the raised

eyebrow of her grandmother, she opened it up and looked at the words she'd written down.

Clive Pendergast – Hill Top Farm
Old cow shed – fallen stones
Last words – aren't you rock would tree help
Bloodied stone = murder
1965 – missing woman SAME PLACE

'I don't know what you think you'll find staring at those random words,' Nor tutted, as Maddie added *Clotted cream?* to the list. She wrote *litter* too, more to remind her to contact the council and find the representative she probably needed to apologise to with a very big, non-laxative-laced, cake. She looked up as the latch on the front door clicked. 'Quick,' Nor hissed and Maddie caught on straight away, finding DI Trevelyan's notebook and closing it up and hurriedly shoving it back into his bag.

'Detective Trevelyan,' Maddie greeted him as he and DS Mitchell appeared from the hallway into the kitchen. 'You forgot your bag.' Maddie pointed to the almost-too-perfectly closed bag on the kitchen table.

'Thank you, Miss Penrose... Maddie.' Trevelyan leant over next to her to grab his bag by its handle. Maddie caught a momentary trace of washing powder or fabric conditioner, along with something more woody and smoky. Not at all unpleasant.

'Was everything all right in my barn?' Nor asked, ignoring the triangle of looks that were passing between DS Mitchell, DI Trevelyan and her granddaughter. It was DS Mitchell who answered her with a frown across her brow.

'Rent it out, do you?' DS Mitchell flipped her own notebook open and held her pen ready to jot down Nor's reply.

'Yes. Mandy Leach has got the stables.'

'And the barn over there?' DS Mitchell asked, matter-of-factly.

'Jason Briggs has the east barn. For now,' Nor answered, coolly.

'Know him well, do you?' DS Mitchell asked.

'So-so,' replied Nor. 'Couldn't tell you his inside leg measurement, but I do know what he stores in there. Farm stuff. You know, trailers and tractors. Great big expensive ones, by the looks of it. For his business.'

'You've seen them then? Know what they are?' DS Mitchell's tone made the hackles on Maddie's back rise.

'I might be old, Karen Mitchell, but I'm not so blind yet that I can't see a tractor from fifty paces. Brought them in by night, mind you, though he said that was due to the insurance kicking in at midnight, I think.'

'And he pays you?' DS Mitchell asked, scribbling in her notebook furiously.

'Of course.'

'Been there long?'

'Few months.' Nor crossed her arms.

Maddie watched as DS Mitchell wrote what looked like more than what Nor had said in her notebook. Once she'd flipped it closed, she nodded to Trevelyan, and he turned to Maddie and Nor.

'Thanks again for your statement and help with the case, both of you. We'll be off.'

Maddie walked them both down the hallway and, once waved off, closed the front door behind them. A breeze swept through the courtyard of the farmhouse as the Land Rover's engine fired up and Maddie felt a shiver pass along her shoulders and down her arms. It had been a strange day, that was for sure. Strange and pretty horrific really, if she thought about it.

She turned around and leant against the closed front door as the reality of the day hit her. She had seen a dead body today.

Just the arm, to be fair, but still. Someone, some unknown woman in a pink anorak with no bag or ID had been killed – murdered – only a few hundred yards from this very house. It rather trumped the worries she'd had earlier today about the draughts from the cracked windows in the teashop, and the peeling paint on the walls. And that blasted oven. Not to mention the clearly wiped-clean windows of Nor's barn, where the police had done their best to peer into the darkness that contained whatever this Jason character was storing in there. She hoped they were just being nosey, interested in the farm and Nor's security levels, and turned her mind back to the teashop. Had one of the customers, or Clive Pendergast, been the murderer? Was whoever it was still here in the small town of Pendragon Creek? The thought she'd had earlier crossed her mind... maybe the reason why DS Mitchell had taken such an interest in the outbuildings was that they'd make the perfect hiding spot for a killer on the run.

Maddie turned around and quickly slid the deadlock in place across the sturdy wooden front door of the stone-built farmhouse. She wasn't prepared to take any chances tonight. Not when a murderer was out there.

8

Maddie awoke the next morning having slept badly. It wasn't that the bed she was in was uncomfortable, in fact it wasn't, it was sublime, especially compared to the one she'd had in London. It was one of the reasons she'd not argued too much with her mum and dad when they'd suggested she up sticks and go and have some R&R at her gran's – a small room in a shared flat in Clapham wasn't exactly the London life she'd planned for herself, especially now she was in her thirties. And the long evenings spent working at Chez Lucie had meant moving back in with her parents in leafy, suburban Surrey hadn't been an option – not to mention how boomeranging back to the their house would have been a hit to the ego at her age... But, somehow, leaving London altogether and getting stuck into Nor's teashop, well that hadn't seemed like quite such a step backwards in her career. In fact, she could probably put some of what she'd learned in London to use here. Loads of London chefs moved out to Cornwall to start up market gardens and 25-mile-menu restaurants. Some even got TV shows...

Maddie thought about her gran. *What had she said yesterday? Something about paninis... and how befuddled she was by it all*. Maddie felt sure she could bring a bit of cosmopolitan style to the menu of the Folly Farm Teashop, while not trampling all over her gran's legacy. As long as the council didn't shut the whole place down before she could get going.

She yawned, feeling groggy, despite the comfortable bed, with its soft mattress and vintage quilts. Yes, quilts plural, as Nor wasn't one to throw away something and Maddie was descended from a line of expert seamstresses, it seemed. The quilts in question were made by her great-great-grandmother and they were currently keeping her properly cosy, despite the early-morning chill in the high-ceilinged corner bedroom that she'd claimed as hers when she'd arrived a couple of days ago.

Maddie lay with her head cushioned by the duck-feather pillows, themselves in vintage linen pillowcases that smelled of lavender, and looked across to where a chink of light was coming through the thick chintz curtains. She had slept badly as she'd been thinking about the young woman crushed to death by the stones of the ruined cow shed. Crushed to death... but also hit over the head with a rock. The thought sickened her, and she wondered if the shock of it all had caused her to have such vivid dreams of giant cats roaming the grasslands above the cliffs and evil lurking in the beautiful Pendragon Bay. She was sure she'd dreamt about clotted cream and horses too, but it was all swirling back into the mists of sleep.

She pulled the quilts higher up to her chin, a task made harder by the weight of both Crumpet and Toast, who had decided her bed to be the comfiest one for their nap. Perhaps she should have taken her gran up on the offer of one of her sleeping pills, though that was another thing she needed to talk to her about. If Nor was in such bad pain she couldn't sleep, she really needed to get her knee op booked in.

Maddie sighed and raised her head off the pillow, straining her neck to see exactly where the cats were and which part of the quilt they weighted down.

'Farm cats, my a—' she mumbled, reaching out a hand for a stroke of the velvety soft fur on Toast's head. The cat gave a purr of satisfaction and Maddie relaxed back onto the pillow again.

Sunday morning or not, laying about like this wouldn't do, though, and as Maddie blinked away the crumbs of sleep from the corner of her eyes, she tuned in to the noises of the farm outside. Nor didn't just run the teashop from morning coffees through to afternoon tea; the Folly Farm stables were liveried and she had chickens who roamed about the courtyard and gardens, which needed an early-morning feed by the sounds of it. The clucking was getting quite animated, and Maddie was relieved that there wasn't a rooster to add to the din.

She gently nudged Toast and Crumpet out of the way and stuck one leg, then the other, out of the bed. She felt for her slippers and slid her feet into them, then shuffled towards the window before flinging open the curtains.

The view that greeted her, beyond the farmyard with its old stone buildings and flagstoned courtyard dotted with russet-red hens, and horses nodding their heads out of the stable doors, was that of the fields and pathway she'd taken with Clive Pendergast yesterday afternoon. Her eyes traced the line of the muddy path as it headed up towards the sycamore tree. She could just about make out the upper branches of the tree as it stood the other side of the hedgerow at the top of the hill. She couldn't see the old cow shed from here, but she knew it was there. And what – who – had been there yesterday. Maddie shivered as the memories returned; the tumble of rocks, the pink sleeve.

'This will get me nowhere,' she said to herself, or the cats, who had made nests in the disturbed quilts of her bed. She stretched her arms up high above her head, heard the familiar but slightly worrying clicking of her joints and then pulled her dressing gown off the wrought-iron bed post and threw it on.

Once she'd opened the pair of curtains at the other window, which overlooked the pretty cottage garden, she left the cats to their own morning baths and headed to the shower.

Nor was nowhere to be found when Maddie headed down for toast and marmalade, murmuring to herself that it was a better start to the day than almost being suffocated by the fluffy pairing of Toast and Crumpet. She loved her gran's home-made marmalade, which was traditionally made every January from the Seville oranges available in the local market. Nor always sent her grandchildren a jar through the post and Maddie had devoured hers by early March.

With a piece of thick toast, made from one of Nor's home-made loaves and slathered in the bittersweet orange conserve, in her hand, she stood at the back door of the farmhouse and slipped a pair of well-worn wellies on. She'd dressed today in denim dungarees, which she thought had looked quite fashionable and edgy in London – perfect for a Sunday morning at a Hackney farmer's market – but out here on a real farm... she tutted to herself. At least she'd left the headscarf off today or she'd look straight out of *The Good Life*. Still, if she was going to promote Folly Farm teashop to her as-yet-only-imaginary social media following, then this was the sort of look they'd expect. She glanced at her reflection in the glass pane of the back door and smiled at herself. Despite the tragedy and worry of the murder, not to mention the threat from the council, it was so good to be back in Cornwall. She felt like herself again.

Maddie closed the kitchen door behind her and wandered into the farmyard. She was sure her grandmother was feeding the chickens, judging by the happy clucking that was coming from the direction of the henhouse. She waved to a young girl who was mucking out one of the horses and walked over to say hello.

'Gosh, he's a handsome boy, isn't he?' Maddie said before introducing herself.

'He is, isn't he,' the girl beamed. Maddie put her at about eleven or twelve and smiled as she thought about how similar she probably looked at that age, with a face clean of any make-up, her long blonde hair in French braids and wearing sensible jodhpurs and a sweatshirt. And nothing more important to her in her life than her pony. Maddie had learned to ride here at Folly Farm when she'd been a kid, and she was glad that, despite the dilapidations in general, horses still called the yard home.

'What's his name?' Maddie asked, reaching out and gently rubbing the horse's muzzle.

'Cam – short for Camelot. Though I sometimes call him Canter-a-lot as that what he likes to do.'

Maddie laughed. 'That's a great name. Camelot, you are a handsome fellow,' she said as the horse whinnied in reply. 'And what's your name?'

'Bella Leach. My mum keeps the horses here and I come before school to help muck out. Except it's the holidays now, so I can stay longer and tack Cam up and ride him out. It was brilliant, I was here all day yesterday. It's nice because we don't have any other animals at home, so it's fun to come here to the yard. Are you here helping Mrs P with the teashop?' The non sequitur caught Maddie by surprise as she'd just been thinking about how nice it would be to ride out for a morning too.

'Yes. Sort of. I'm here for a few weeks at least, so I'll see what I can do.'

'Mum says it'll take a miracle.'

Maddie laughed. She always found the bluntness of youngsters amusing and Bella was no different. Maddie could imagine poor Mandy Leach blushing like anything if she'd heard her daughter parrot what she'd no doubt said. Maddie didn't mind though. Bella – and Mandy – weren't wrong. 'I'm not sure I'm a miracle worker, but I'll try my best,' Maddie said, before being nudged on the shoulder by Camelot.

'He wants a carrot,' sighed Bella, in the way children do, as if the very weight of the world was on her shoulders, rather than just a pony requesting a treat. 'And it's not like he doesn't get enough treats. I think Crumpet and Toast get jealous.'

'I think they might,' Maddie agreed as Bella fed her pony another carrot from the large bag by the stable door. Maddie said goodbye and left them to it.

With Nor still nowhere to be seen, Maddie found herself walking towards the large five-bar gate that separated the farmyard from the road out to Pendragon Creek – and the pathway to the old cow shed. She waved to Mandy Leach, who was mucking out another of the horse boxes, then a flash of white caught her eye and she went to look at it. Screwing up her nose at first, thinking it was bird droppings on top of the gate, Maddie almost ignored it, but then she looked a bit closer. It wasn't anything untoward from a bird. It was thick, pale clotted cream. And next to it was another splodge, but more in the shape of a cat's paw. Maddie nodded to herself. The mystery of the missing clotted cream was, just like the cream itself, thickening.

Still, the other more sombre mystery was still preying heavily on her mind, and something was drawing her up towards that cow shed, something that had made her brain swim in circles all night. Something about the tumble and the dead body which had lain underneath it.

Maddie strode out into the spring sunshine, yet with every step she took, she felt less confident. She couldn't shake the fact that barely twenty-four hours earlier a murderer had walked close to this same path.

A murderer who was still out there.

And who might return to the scene of the crime.

9

Maddie found herself out of breath as she retraced her steps from yesterday. Adrenaline must have powered her up the hill then, as she hadn't noticed how steep it was in parts. It always looked such a gentle climb from the house and teashop. No wonder walkers felt like they'd achieved something, even coming down the hill, after having walked these paths. She thought about the teashop's menu and pondered adding some more substantial dishes – a warming shepherd's pie using local lamb and properly fluffy mashed potatoes, or mac 'n' cheese using Farringford Dairy's own produce. Both of those would be easy to make in batches, but tempting enough to get the walkers staying and ordering more drinks... Oh and puddings, too.

It was with thoughts of steamed golden syrup pudding and hot apple crumble covered in custard – and that dratted oven which really would need replacing – that Maddie finally broached the peak of the hill and came upon the ruins of the old cow shed. She stopped short and rested her hands on her hips, letting herself get her breath back and swap thoughts of warm puddings for those of cold-blooded murder.

Maddie looked at the scene, now taped off with black-and-yellow police tape. The small yellow pyramid markers were still placed around and she noted the spot where Crumpet had found the bloodied stone. It was gone, but where it had been was marked and it was still noticeably further from the tumble and the stones Clive had been desperately removing – some of which seemed to have been taken as evidence too.

Her eyes swept back over to the tumble itself. It was now even more of a state since the paramedics, she assumed, had had to clear the stones away from the body properly. Maddie took a step or two towards the tumble, and noticed the number of footprints in the soft mud. If only she'd thought about it yesterday and looked to see if there had been a trail leading off in a different direction. But then those footprints could have been Clive's, or a walker earlier in the day, or the victim herself—

'Penny for them?' The man's voice, with its ever-so-subtle West Country burr beneath the middle-class accent, startled her.

Maddie looked up and saw the very person she'd just been thinking about, Clive Pendergast, standing the other side of the cow shed. Had he been there all along? Or just crept up the path while she'd been deep in thought?

The murderer often returns to the scene of the crime...

Maddie shivered at the unwanted thought, inspired no doubt by too much Sunday night Agatha Christie watching, and forced a smile at Clive.

'Good morning,' she managed. 'And I'm not sure my thoughts are worth much at all. I was just berating myself for not looking for any footprints yesterday—'

'Wouldn't have been much point,' Clive interrupted her. 'There's mud around the tumble, to be sure, but otherwise it's all grass and slicked down with rain after those storms yesterday; it'd never hold a footprint. And with so many walkers now spring's here, it'd be madness trying to pinpoint one tread from another, even down the lane to the main road.'

Maddie nodded. She didn't want to think of Clive as the murderer. He had, after all, done all he could to save the poor woman, or so he said. But she was still happy to keep the pile of tumbled stones between them, especially when he said, 'Felt I had to come back. Just to see.'

The murderer often returns to the scene of the crime...

Maddie shook the thought away and looked at him, realising the same could be said for herself. Perhaps, like her, Clive was still processing everything that had happened – coming back to the scene was a natural way of doing that.

She smiled at him and replied, 'Me too.' Then, after a pause, 'Did DI Trevelyan come and take your statement yesterday afternoon?'

'Yes, he did. Said they don't know her name or where she'd come from.'

'She didn't have any ID on her as she didn't have a back-pack or a bag. Which is odd, isn't it, as all the walkers do.' Maddie suddenly had a thought and she'd said it out loud before she could stop herself. 'Maybe she wasn't one of the usual walkers?'

'What do you mean?' Clive asked, his eyes narrowing.

Maddie tried to put her thoughts into words – or at least sensible, understandable words. 'Just that she might not have been your average hiker. Maybe she was up here for a reason? An assignation? But still... she'd have a bag...' Maddie tailed off as she lost herself in thought.

'Well, she wasn't just helicoptered in, was she?' Clive pointed out. 'She'd have had to come from Pendragon Creek at the nearest.'

Maddie nodded, accepting this logic and making a mental note of it. Then she asked, 'She didn't say anything else at all did she? When you, you know, were with her at the end?'

Clive shook his head. He reached up and took off his tweed flat cap, gripping it between his hands as he bowed his head. Maddie saw the breeze play with what was left of his pale ginger hair and he must have felt it too as he put his hat back on and answered her. 'Like I said yesterday, and like I told the police, she said those words about the rocks and the tree. I've thought about it and maybe she was telling me what had happened? Or suggesting how I could help get her out. Using a pulley from the tree to help remove the rocks, perhaps? She said "help", I remember that. I don't know. I... I've seen things as a farmer that most townies never do. I deal with life and death with the calving and all that, but I must admit, hearing that poor girl say her last words...' He paused and gathered himself, blowing out his cheeks as he exhaled. 'Well, it's not a scene I can easily forget, nor want to see or hear again.'

'It must have been horrible for you.' Maddie tried to find the words of comfort needed, but also couldn't quite get behind his theory. 'I'm sorry, but I can't believe she'd be lying there, dying, and working out ways of using a tree as a pulley system to remove the rocks from her. Especially not if she'd been hit on the head, too. Maybe she was more overcome by the beauty of it all round here, the more general rocks and trees by the coast. Maybe she actually had a lovely image in her mind and was talking about it...?'

Clive shrugged. 'I should imagine that's more likely. Pretty as anything round here and plenty of people come for their holidays and fall in love with it. Had one woman once chain herself to the gate as she thought my cows were trampling the bluebells.' He paused, and then shook his head at the private reminiscence. 'Still, better that than the folk who decide it would be nice to plonk a house or thirty right where we're standing. There's talk of adding these fields into the local plan. Saying the old cow shed gives precedence for building. Well, over my dead body! There's no way I would let anyone build on these fields.

And those local planners can remember that when they're hosting their meetings and putting flyers around the place. I won't have it, not at Hill Top.'

'There's planning permission to build up here?' Maddie asked, not quite keeping up.

'Not yet – and nor will there be, if I can help it. Local plans are how towns and counties work out where the new houses will go and there's people in the town would see this place built over rather than have it in their own back yards in the town.'

'But you don't have to have them here, if you don't want to?' Maddie asked, gazing down at Folly Farm and wondering how the view would change if thirty-odd houses were built just a few fields away.

'No, they can't compulsory purchase it, not while there's perfectly good brownfield sites around.' Clive crossed his arms, and when he next spoke, there was a note of suspicion in his voice. 'So, down from town yourself, are you?'

Town being London of course. DFL, or Down From London, was a slightly pejorative term used to describe the brigade of moneyed folks with very clean Range Rovers and brand-new Barbour jackets who bought up the old farmsteads and fishing village houses, slathered them in Farrow & Ball paints and shipped in John Lewis furniture. Maddie let the slur go. She was, recently at least, from London; but she was here to help Nor, not drive her four-by-four car, that she didn't have in any case, thoughtlessly through the lanes. And she had Cornish blood in her, she had to remember that.

'In a way, yes. You know my dad moved up to London? Aunty Rosie did too, though she's in Winchester now as Uncle Dave's job's out in Salisbury. Mum and Dad are in Surrey now too, where I grew up.' She noticed Clive raise an eyebrow at the mention of the county that was home to so many of Cornwall's tourists in high season. Maddie carried on regardless. 'I'm coming to help Gran for a bit. Get the teashop back on its feet.'

Finally a nod of approval from Clive. 'I can't judge, I suppose. My own two have fled the nest and gone to the bright lights of the city. Beatrice's in London too, heaven knows why, though she says there's more opportunity for someone in journalism. And Hugo is finding his feet in Truro.'

'Not so far then?'

'Might as well be Timbuck-Truro.' The grizzled farmer shrugged again, but then his face softened. 'He's back though for a bit. Helping me out with the farm and a bit of clay shooting. Nice to have him back.' He looked deep in thought for a moment, then said, 'Good that you've come to help Nor. Can't be easy for her now Aubry's gone.'

Maddie's grandfather, the magnificently named Aubry Peregrine Penrose, had sadly passed away after a brief but brutal battle with cancer a few years ago. Maddie conjured up an image of him, and it made her smile. He'd been eccentric to the extreme, with a vintage tractor in one of the barns and a penchant for wearing plus fours, those ridiculously baggy short trousers that golfers in the 1930s wore, along with bright yellow, knee-high socks. Sometimes baling twine would act as a belt, yet he'd almost always have a proper shirt and tie on, too.

Clive's voice cut through her thoughts again. 'Your grandmother is a marvellous woman and it's a fine farm. It would be terrible to see anything happen to it, or to her.'

Maddie thanked Clive, though she couldn't quite put her finger on why she suddenly felt out of sorts. Did he know about the visit from the council? Or Jason and his rent-in-cash ways?

When Clive nodded an abrupt goodbye, Maddie waved at him, then remembering one of her reasons for coming up here, she peered under the hedge. Sure enough, there was the can she'd seen the cats playing with yesterday. She stooped down and picked it up, holding it gingerly between thumb and forefinger in case some small creature should pop out of it. Once satisfied that it wasn't the home to the mouse version of a hermit crab, she carried it down the hill back to the familiar sights and sounds of Nor's farm. Clive's words of concern, however, were ringing in her ears. That's when she realised what was making her feel off.

Clive's words of *concern*... or was it a threat?

10

Maddie was greeted at the farm gate by Crumpet and Toast, who didn't budge from their spots on the top beam of the old wooden five-bar gate as she unhooked the catch and pushed it open. Any sign of creamy paw prints had gone.

'Eating the evidence does not stand up well in court,' she gently told them off, then shook her head in bewilderment at how the two cats could not only stay so balanced but also look completely unperturbed as they were swung back and forth as she closed the gate again behind her. 'You two should join the circus,' she said, then watched as Crumpet stretched himself with the grace of an Olympic gymnast and executed a perfect dismount. 'That's a 9.7, I'd say. Points deducted for looking far too smug as you did it.' She reached over and ran a hand over Burned Toast's velvety soft grey fur, and received a chirrup in return.

Maddie looked at her watch. It was coming up to ten and she knew Nor liked to have the teashop open and ready for punters by eleven on a Sunday, which meant getting in there and getting the tea urn fired up about fifteen minutes before. So, with a few minutes on her hands, she headed into the farmyard.

Peering into the kitchen window, she saw her gran with what looked like a freshly baked cake straight out of the Aga. At least she was still able to bake, though Maddie knew she'd have to take over that at some point if Nor's arthritis in her hands got worse, and her knee meant she couldn't stand for long. And she did really want to bring some new dishes onto the menu, too.

She walked across the yard and took in the buildings around her. The teashop wasn't the worst of the lot, and was really incredibly pretty, with its cottage-style windows and old stonework, but it certainly needed sprucing up. There were some tiles loose on the roof and the windows definitely needed a clean and repaint around the edges. The other old barn, the one rented by this Jason guy, looked worse, but, boy, did they have potential.

Maddie waved to Bella again, who was saddling up her pony ready for a hack, and then made a beeline for the rented-out barn. She remembered DS Mitchell had been interested in it while DI Trevelyan had introduced himself and started off the statements. Maddie was pretty sure DS Mitchell hadn't been daydreaming about whether this particular building could be converted into a bistro, or even a wedding venue, but the thought did cross Maddie's mind that DS Mitchell might have been daydreaming about something else. *Someone* else. DI Trevelyan really was easy on the eye...

Maddie shook the thought out of her head. A romance was not what she needed right now. She'd been seeing, sort of, one of the other chefs at Chez Lucie and it hadn't ended well when she'd handed in her notice and then told him she was moving about 300 miles away. And not just for a minibreak, but for the foreseeable future. Perhaps he'd liked her more than she'd liked him? And more than he'd let on. But romance wasn't on her bingo card at the moment. However, talking to her gran about the possibility of turning this old barn into a private dining space – complete with fairy lights strung across the beams, trestle tables decorated with wild flowers and flickering candles and a proper field kitchen at one end – was. Shame Nor had rented it out to Jason.

Maddie looked at her watch again. She still had a few minutes and Nor was no doubt at an essential and absorbing stage of the cake-making process at this very minute... perhaps creating the lip-smacking caramel-covered walnuts that decorated the top of her famous coffee and walnut cake. That pan full of melting butter and sugar (Maddie supposed – the recipe was, after all, secret) needed Nor's full attention...

Self justified, Maddie walked around the old barn, gently running her fingers over the rough-hewn stone, noting that it needed repointing in some areas. The windows were blacked out from the inside. *DS Mitchell wouldn't have seen a thing, despite her rubbing the dust off*, thought Maddie. She walked around the side of the building, where a wooden pedestrian door was positioned next to a larger set of wide roller doors. She remembered her grandfather used to ride his 'boneshaker', an old Massey Ferguson tractor, through those very doors. Even then, its red paint was peeling off and the seat was no comfier than sitting in a metal mixing bowl. Less comfy even. But there'd been so many times when Aubry had gunned up the engine, waved his tweed cap in the air and sung nonsense songs as he'd made all his children and grandchildren laugh at the sight of him. Maddie longed to see if the vintage tractor was still inside and instinctively turned the handle on the door. To her surprise, the door opened and she let herself into the dark, musty space.

The strip lighting flickered on. It made Maddie think of lightning bolts in an electrical storm, before the cool, white light stabilised and illuminated the decrepit barn. Maddie looked up to the rafters, half boarded with wide planks, but revealing the amazing proportions of the building.

This could so easily be converted into a fabulous bistro... Her heart quickened at the thought as her mind raced on. *Or opened up with more floor-to-ceiling windows and made into an events space, for weddings even...*

She stepped further into the barn and smiled as the sight of the red vintage tractor greeted her. She walked over to it and rested a hand on the wheel arch. Those vivid memories of her grandfather driving it, and giving all of them rides too, flashed back into her mind. It was hard to believe that this rickety old machine once tilled the fields, pulling harrows and ploughs, climbing the steep hillsides day after day. It barely looked more powerful than Nor's ancient Morris Minor, and was a darn sight smaller than the huge new version that was parked next to it.

Hang on a minute... Maddie thought to herself, as she turned and took in the brand-new tractor, with its wheels that stood taller than her and its gleaming cabin with an upholstered seat inside it, surrounded by all sorts of state-of-the-art equipment. *There's tractors and then there's... this!*

Maddie looked at the ginormous machine, which looked like it'd never seen a day's work in its life – she could serve a salad off the wheel rim it was so sparkling. Then she took a proper look. The whole barn, that she'd so far only been appreciating for its beams and proportions, and future ability to be strewn with flowers and fairy lights, was actually filled with brand-new farming equipment.

So this is what Jason's storing, Maddie deduced, walking around the various pieces of equipment, all as shiny and new as the massive tractor. Nor had said as much when DI Trevelyan had quizzed her. Maddie was running a hand over the as-yet-unused spikes of a bright orange chisel plough (which she only knew was a chisel plough because of the words emblazoned on the side, in jagged, shadowed capital letters: *CHISEL PLOUGH* 3000) when something caught her eye. Something pink. Careful not to damage said eye by accidentally bending down over one of the plough's spikes, she moved around the torturous-looking device and then crouched down to get a better look.

She had been right. Even with the occasional flicker from the strip light, she could make out the distinct pinkness of it. She reached an arm tentatively through the spines of the plough and caught a finger on a padded strap and pulled. The sight of it made her catch her breath.

It was a bright pink backpack.

Maddie fished it out from under the plough. She stood upright and held it out in front of her, both hands holding the edges of it. It was a backpack all right, and it matched the pink she remembered from the sleeve of the victim under the stones. Maddie shivered.

Had she just found the dead woman's missing bag?

She was about to look inside when a noise behind her made her heart quicken. Before she could look around, a strong hand grabbed her by the shoulder. Maddie froze.

11

Suddenly, all of Maddie's senses felt heightened. The smell of the barn became almost overwhelming: rubber, damp, oil, straw. The light, cold and pale from the strip lights, gave the drills and other machinery around her hard edges and dark shadows and the weight of the large hand on her shoulder felt as if it was forcing her, feet-first, into the concrete floor like a piledriver. She dropped the bag and closed her eyes, until the hand twisted and made her turn to face its owner.

'Who are you? Whatcha doing here?' The voice was rough, threatening. 'Come on?' it insisted, in its hard, demanding way. Maddie could feel the thick denim of her dungarees strap being pressed into her shoulder by this man's grip.

'S-so sorry, really sorry... I'm M-Maddie. I'm Nor's granddaughter.'

Maddie felt the hand gripping her relax, and then let her go. She sagged as she unclenched her back muscles. She turned to face him.

'Whatcha doing in 'ere?' The man, who was about five foot ten, shaven-headed and with a sparkling gem piercing in each ear, demanded an answer.

'I'm sorry... I... The door was open...' Maddie spluttered, but she did find herself subtly pushing the pink backpack behind her with her heel. Had he noticed it?

'Well, this is private property, innit?' the man said. 'But seeing as you're Mrs Penrose's daughter.'

'Granddaughter,' Maddie corrected him. 'And you are?'

He took a moment to answer, then crossed his arms and stuck his chin out. 'Jason,' he said.

Then, before he could speak again, Maddie blurted out her excuse. 'Hi, Jason. And look, I'm sorry. I'm staying with Gran for a few weeks or so, months maybe,' she thought out loud, 'and I was reminiscing about my grandad's old tractor, the Mass—'

'That old hunk of junk,' sneered Jason.

'Well, I wouldn't... I mean, yes, we call it the boneshaker. Used to, anyway. When he'd fire her up for us—' Maddie stopped, realising that Jason didn't need tales of her idyllic childhood here on the farm.

'She needs to get it out of here, tell her, yeah?' Jason said, his arms still crossed, which showed off his well-developed biceps and sleeve-like tattoos.

Maddie gulped. Arms that big just meant one thing. That he could throw a heavy punch. Or two things; throwing punches *and* that he'd be quite hard to get away from if he decided Maddie should stay put. And, the thought came to her again like a freakishly large wave down on Pendragon Bay; there was a murderer on the loose and this could be him. She had just found what might be the dead woman's backpack under his machinery, after all.

'I will,' Maddie whispered, suddenly very aware of how vulnerable she was. She stepped back to put some distance between her and Jason, but winced as she felt the sharp tip of a plough spike nudging against her shoulder blades.

Jason, however, stepped forward, his face closer to Maddie's than ever. 'Should've been vacant possession, yeah? The barn.

I'm paying cash.' He said the last bit as if it was an honour or a privilege given to Nor that she should take cash for the barn, not a bank transfer, say, or monthly cheques. Cash. Which can't be traced quite so easily.

'Of course, I'll tell her. I'm sure we can find someone to get it going.'

'Else I'll trash it, yeah?' Jason said this as carelessly as if he were talking about throwing away a used teabag. But something in that carelessness annoyed Maddie. Annoyed her so much that in that moment it trumped how scared she was of Jason, murderer or not.

'How dare you say you'll trash my grandad's old tractor. It's not yours.'

Her words obviously surprised Jason and his blond, barely-there eyebrows raised to almost meet his blond barely-there hair.

Maddie didn't let him interrupt her, though. 'Yes, you're paying my grandmother to rent this barn, but as far as I've seen, there's no contract, no written law that says she agreed to give you "vacant possession", as you call it, not when this building is hers, on her farm and it's quite frankly very kind of her to let it to you on such a casual basis. And I'm in here because I'm her granddaughter and, until I see a contract otherwise, I have every right to come into one of her barns – which was unlocked, I'll have you know – and visit an old family heirloom. And you shouldn't be so threatening to young women, after what's just happened. I've a good mind to tell the police about your behaviour.' Maddie had come close to jabbing her finger at his pumped-up chest, but instead she just vaguely waved her hand in the direction of Jason's torso. As she saw his face turn from looking shocked to something much angrier, she was glad she'd held back from the finger jabbing. And with the adrenaline rush gone, Maddie suddenly felt quite ill and a bit light-headed.

A trill rang through the air, which made Maddie jump, but

Jason merely reached into his back pocket and looked at the screen of his phone. With his eyes off her for a moment, Maddie reached down behind her, avoiding the sharp spikes of the plough, and caught one of the straps of the backpack with her finger.

'So, er, I'm going now,' Maddie said, not taking her eyes off Jason, who luckily had his eyes on his phone screen still.

'See you stay out of here, yeah?' Jason called after her as she quickly retreated out of the barn. 'And clear that old junk, yeah?'

'Can't do both,' Maddie muttered under her breath as she emerged into the daylight of the farmyard. The sunshine gave her a bit more confidence and she added, 'Idiot,' to her personal commentary.

She took a few steps, and felt better the closer she got to the back door of the farmhouse. Crumpet sauntered up to her, not a care in the world, and brushed up against her leg. Maddie exhaled, letting out what felt like about three hours' worth of breath.

'Where were you a moment ago when I needed you, eh? You could have jumped down on him from one of those mega tractors as easily as you jumped off the gate earlier.' She reached down to give him a scratch between the ears, which in turn meant the backpack slipped off her shoulder.

The backpack... Jason, despite his intimidation and threats hadn't called her out on it. Hadn't noticed it maybe? Or maybe he had seen her with it, but knew that if he tried to take it off her, he would have looked mightily guilty? He seemed the most likely person to have hidden it in the barn, after all.

Maddie kept walking towards the farmhouse, more than ever wanting to put space between her and Jason as another thought occurred to her; maybe he had seen her take the bag, didn't want to arouse suspicion by grabbing it back and would wait until he could retrieve it – by force if necessary – later? It was evidence, surely, from the murder up on the hill. She wanted rid of it, especially if there was the slightest chance that Jason would try to get it back from her. Best to call it in to DI Trevelyan and let him take it.

And she would.

But she might just have a little peek inside it first.

12

'There you are!' Nor exclaimed, wiping her hands with a tea towel, two sponge cakes and a dozen scones cooling on a rack behind her. The kitchen was temptingly full of the aromas of baking – nutmeg, cinnamon and coffee – and Maddie almost forgot all about her morning's adventures as she thought how delicious that cake would be once slathered in icing and decorated with half walnuts. 'I was wondering where you'd got to. And what have you got there?' Nor interrupted Maddie's brief daydream – well, cake dream – by pointing to the backpack.

'Oh, Gran, you'll never guess what,' Maddie said, taking a few steps towards the kitchen table and placing the backpack on it.

'That I've got to make another cake now all by myself as you've been scarce as rocking horse poo for the last hour or so?' Nor said, but she was smiling behind the ticking-off. She knew, as much as Maddie did, that although she was here to help her gran, the younger woman was also in much need of that good Cornish sea air and a bit of a change of scene from the whip-cracking of London kitchens.

'Sorry, Gran, but wait until you see this.' Maddie gestured

towards the backpack with both hands, her eyebrows raised in shock at her own doing, like a magician suddenly aware that they've *actually* managed to conjure a white rabbit from a hat.

'Is that the one I gave you for your ninth birthday? What was it, Hello Catty?'

'Kitty, and no.' Maddie shook her head. Although she'd loved that backpack, she concentrated on the bag in hand, which was, after all, worth two in the hedge and all that. 'I think this is the missing backpack from our murdered girl yesterday.'

'Oh blimey,' Nor said, staggering back a step. She was dressed this morning in her neat cigarette-style jeans and was wearing a jumper knitted into a pattern of sheep and cows in rows. A frilled collar of a starched-white blouse showed over the top and she'd even popped on a pair of cute, purple plimsolls. Maddie looked at her own feet, still in the wellies, and her denim dungarees that now looked more hackneyed than Hackney, and pondered where the stylish genes, if not jeans, had gone missing between her grandmother and herself. 'Well, where did you find it?' Nor asked, tucking the tea towel she was holding into the tied strings of her apron.

Maddie paused. Her excitement in showing her gran her find was tempered by the fact she knew – not that deep down really – that she shouldn't have been nosing around Jason's barn. Still, she had to own up to her grandmother, so with a voice tinged with less fervour and more candour, she admitted where she'd found it.

'Grandad's old barn, you know the one—'

'Rented by Jason. He was here just now.' Nor seemed to seize up a smidge, as if someone had walked over her grave. 'I hope he didn't catch you? Likes his privacy, it's why he's here and not using those modern storage places like the one the other side of St Ives.'

'He did actually. He's not a nice man, Gran, he was quite intimidating.' Maddie rocked her head from side to side, weighing up the situation she'd just been in in the barn. 'Though he probably thought I was trying to do something to that posh farm equipment he's got stored there. Said he wanted Grandad's boneshaker gone, too.'

'Oh, he's always asking for that. I told him if he can find me a mechanic who can get it going it'll be out of his hair in no time.'

'What hair he has got,' Maddie thought back to his shaved head. She was sure she'd caught sight of a tattoo on the nape of his neck too.

'So,' Nor pointed to the table, 'where was this then? In one of his big margarine tubs of a tractor?'

'No, tucked in under the Chisel Plough 3000.' Maddie fingered the strap of the backpack.

'Used to make do with the Chisel Plough 75 in my day,' muttered Nor. 'So, will you telephone that nice policeman then?'

'Yes, of course. Do you think he'd mind if we looked inside first?'

'Ha, yes. Of course he'd mind. But you're not going to tell him that, are you? What he doesn't know and all that.' Nor moved towards Maddie and the backpack on the table and raised an eyebrow.

'Gran, you're wicked!' Maddie laughed and then looked at the backpack. It was bright pink, with shoulder straps and an adjustable waist clip. The sort of thing that you could wear on a hike, as long as camouflage wasn't your main aim. 'She didn't mind standing out, did she?' Maddie thought for a moment. 'She wasn't hiding from anyone.'

'Not at first, at any rate,' Nor replied, her voice measured, but the implication of what she was saying sat heavy in the air. It was easy to get excited about solving a mystery, or even just knowing a little bit more about who the poor woman on the hillside was, but Nor's words were a timely reminder that they were dealing with a death. And more than that, a murder.

'There's blood, look.' Maddie pointed to the top of the bag. She recalled the rock on the ground with the blood on it, that deep red unmistakable.

'Here,' Nor turned away from the table and walked over to the sink. She opened the cupboard underneath and rummaged before producing a plastic packet that she tore open to reveal a large pair of bright yellow rubber washing-up gloves. 'Put these on.'

'Gran!' Maddie scoffed. 'No.'

'Go on. I know you've touched it already, but if you're going to go delving inside, it'll be best not to have your fingerprints all over it. DI Trevelyan had a soft spot for you, but you don't want to muddy the waters.'

Maddie opened and shut her mouth a couple of times, then, with a shake of her head, reached into her back pocket and pulled out her phone. Dialling the number that Trevelyan had left her with the day before, and was conveniently printed on a card that was lying on the kitchen table, she called in the find. A few moments later, she disconnected the call and updated her gran.

'He'll be here as soon as he can.'

'Time to get those Marigolds on then.' Nor held out the gloves again and gave them a little wiggle.

Maddie pulled a face, but reached out and took the bright yellow gloves from Nor and stretched them onto her hands.

'I feel like a prize idiot.' Maddie waved the ill-fitting gloves, with her hands in them, at her grandmother.

'Stop larking, ducky.' Nor nudged her and Maddie rolled her eyes.

With all the grace of a goose on ice, she managed to somehow undo the zip that held the backpack closed. And as gently as possible, and to Nor's wide-eyed expression of shock, she pulled out the first item.

13

'What on earth is that?' Nor stood back, and cocked her head, looking at the mysterious object from a different angle. Maddie, still in her rubber gloves, tried as carefully as possible to place the long, cylindrical piece of equipment down on the kitchen table. 'Is it a portable crutch? Some sort of grabber? Marge once got some fancy back scratchers with loofahs on them into her shop, they looked a bit like that, but scratchier.'

'It's a selfie stick, Gran,' Maddie told her. 'You use it for taking photos of yourself.'

'Oh.' Nor rolled her eyes. 'Jilly from the bakery has one of those. It's not as smart as that one though. She uses it to take photos of herself with the buns, you know those nice iced ones with the cherry on top – well, they hide her God-given blessings, if you know what I mean. She posts the photos to a website called Only Buns or something.'

'I'm not sure that's what that website's called, Gran.' Maddie didn't have the heart – or stomach – to correct her gran further or enlighten her about what Jilly from the bakery might be up to. She made a mental note to be cautious about ordering her loaves from her though.

'Oh well, she says she makes more money from doing things *with* baguettes than she ever did actually selling them—'

'Gran,' Maddie interrupted her by raising a yellow rubber hand. 'Please. And...' She indicated the bag and its current uber-importance and carefully delved in once again. This time, she pulled out a few wrapped protein bars, much to Nor's confusion as to what they were. 'Quick energy, lots of hikers have them,' Maddie said, counting out four of them.

'What's wrong with a flapjack?' Nor shrugged. 'Honestly, these new-fangled bars with added fibre this and protein shakes that... that's what puts teashops like ours out of business.'

Maddie nodded, though she liked the fact that Nor had said 'ours' and she felt the corners of her lips twitch as she tried not to smile in the middle of such an important task. She carried on, and pulled out a beauty counter's worth of make-up.

'Bronzer, foundation, primer, blush, highlighter, lip balm, lip plumper, lip gloss, extra-length five-times-volume mascara, eyebrow pencil, contouring brush...' She listed all the items as Nor's eyes widened in shock.

'That's more slap than the amateur dramatics society used in their last performance. And that was Jack and the Beanstalk and lots of the children wanted to be the beanstalk.' Nor looked shocked at the display on the table.

'Green then, I assume, not Hot To Trot Pink,' said Maddie, reading from one of the lipstick bases.

'Well, yes.'

Maddie kept fishing around in the bag. A side pocket with a very narrow opening was concealing something hard and bulky. 'Aha,' Maddie said as she pulled out an iPhone. The screen lit up as she held it, though denied her access with the wrong Face ID. What she did see, though, was a pretty, twenty-something-year-old woman, dressed in a pink floaty dress on the edge of a pier, looking back at her and laughing.

'Is that her?' Nor's voice was a whisper. 'Sweet little thing, wasn't she?'

'I don't know. Might be. Or could be a sister or a—'

'Girlfriend,' Nor proved her modern open-mindedness.

'Perhaps,' Maddie agreed, but she looked at the phone home screen and the pretty girl on it, smiling and carefree. She was wearing a lot of make-up and her right arm was held up in an unmistakable way. 'I think she's using her selfie stick though. I think it's her.'

Maddie took in the face of the woman for a little longer, then also noticed that she had hundreds of unread messages and notifications. Someone was missing her. Maybe lots of people. For the first time since she started looking through the bag, Maddie really hoped that the police would come quickly. She hoped that this *was* evidence and could help catch the poor girl's killer.

She reached in and found one last item in the backpack. It was a journal.

'Diary?' asked Nor, still inquisitive.

'No,' replied Maddie, who was struggling to flick through the pages while wearing the baggy-fingered gloves. 'It's one of those books that you can doodle in and write daily positive affirmations. "I deserve the universe's light" and "It'll all be all right in the end, and if it's not all right, it's not the end" that sort of thing.' Maddie noticed Nor nod sagely at the second phrase and carried on, actually reading pages within the journal. 'Here's a list, "Five Reasons I Always Knew I Was Special" and another one, "Positive Manifestations About My Future I Can Make Real".'

'Poor lamb, sounds like she was a bit confused,' Nor said, peering over Maddie's shoulder. 'Listen to this, "If I journey for the quest, does the quest become the journey?" That doesn't make sense. Neither does "Who are we, if we do not tread the same soil of our fore-mothers, listen to the wind in the same trees or build our home from the same rocks".'

'I think she was trying to find herself.' Maddie felt some affinity with the murdered girl. She liked to journal and doodle, positively manifest and all that. It was similar to how she liked writing things down. Calming her mind when it was at its most erratic, yet most creative. She sighed and quickly, but carefully, pushed all the girl's belongings back into the backpack. 'Perhaps her last words about the rocks and trees were in relation to that quote about the wind and building a home?'

'I don't think she's from round here, though,' Nor pointed out.

'We don't know that yet. We still don't know who she is at all.' Maddie shrugged and then she pulled off the yellow gloves, letting the rubber snap back and catch her. 'Ow,' she muttered as she threw them in the sink and walked over to the worktop, where she saw Nor's old recipe book sitting open on the side. She looked at the words she'd written the day before, the day Clive Pendergast had stumbled into the teashop. She added to them, thinking about her meeting with Clive up at the ruins first thing, as well as her scary moment with Jason just now. She also ignored the umbrage that was showing on Nor's face as she wrote so close to the original recipe.

Planning – houses at Hill Top
HER backpack – OUR barn – Jason?!

Was it starting to build a picture? *Like ingredients being added to the mixing bowl*, she thought, stirring them around in her mind. The only thing that was still missing was the girl's identity. But those items in the backpack, the high-tech phone, the selfie stick, all that make-up; it looked like the victim had been some sort of internet influencer, or at least a wannabe one.

Maddie had a thought and, grabbing a tea towel from the

rail of the Aga instead of the impossibly rubbery gloves, reached into the bag again and pulled out the iPhone. Placing it flat on the table, she then took her own phone out of her pocket and with the girl's iPhone activated took a quick snap of the home screen.

'What are you doing?' Nor asked, looking over her shoulder as Maddie cropped and re-sized the photo she'd just taken and then uploaded it to her phone's internet search engine.

'Reverse image searching. I think this girl would have been the type of person who'd have quite a large internet presence, so if we can give a search engine her picture it can then... Aha, look!' Maddie jabbed at her screen and enlarged the photo that had been called up by the browser.

'Oh yes, that's the same pretty girl,' Nor said, her head cocked on one side as if she were looking at one of her friend's holiday snaps. 'What's her name then? Who is she?'

'One sec...' Maddie clicked through another couple of links and then held her phone screen up so Nor could see it too. 'Chloe Hardy. She has the social media handle of @hardlyhardy.'

'Laurel or Thomas?'

'Sorry?' Maddie looked at her grandmother.

'Laurel and Hardy, or Thomas Hardy, which one is she hardly?' Nor replied.

It took a moment, but Maddie finally realised what her gran was on about.

'I'm going to say she's more Tess of the d'Urbervilles than bowler hats and silly walks,' Maddie said, scrolling through the pictures of a pouting girl.

'What's she like then?' Nor asked.

'Tess of the d'Urbervilles? I don't know, I haven't read that one,' Maddie replied, absent-mindedly.

'No, you numpty, this Chloe Hardy girl.' Nor pointed at the screen, leaning against Maddie's arm as the two of them flicked through some photos, predominately pink themed. 'Stop there,' Nor said as Maddie was scrolling. 'I recognise that view, I think.'

'And I recognise that pink anorak,' Maddie swallowed hard, then carried on. 'The post is from yesterday, about 2 p.m. It must be the last one she posted before she was...' Maddie clicked on the image and a reel started playing. Maddie turned the volume up on her phone in time to hear Chloe speaking to the camera.

"Hiya besties, Chloe from HardlyHardy here, just with a little update on my super-secret, super-exciting mission. Here I am in beautiful Cornwall, and as many of you know, I've been manifesting this for a while now. I can't tell you more, except that despite a little road hump in the way, it's all super-exciting and I will keep you posted. It just shows the power of believing that you deserve what the universe has in store for you and how important family is. Bye besties, stay real guys." The reel ended with Chloe making a victory sign with the hand not holding the selfie stick and sticking out her tongue through her Hot To Trot pink lips. Maddie felt weird. Hearing and seeing the dead girl she'd found yesterday. So alive, so vivacious. It all made it much more real.

A resounding *thud thud thud* made them both jump. Maddie quickly used the tea towel to push the iPhone back into the side pocket of the pink backpack and then nodded to Nor, who was already heading towards the hallway and the front door. Maddie's own investigating would have to wait, it was the police's turn now.

14

'Good morning, Mrs Penrose, Miss Penrose,' DI Trevelyan said as he walked into the kitchen. DS Karen Mitchell followed close behind and she nodded a hello this time too.

'Maddie, please,' Maddie said, beckoning the police over to the table where the backpack was lying.

'Of course, sorry,' DI Trevelyan said. 'Busy morning.'

'I can imagine. And I'm afraid we haven't helped by adding to your workload. But I thought you'd want to see this as soon as I found it.'

'Absolutely. Mitchell?' Trevelyan gestured for his sergeant to bag up the backpack into a large clear plastic evidence bag.

'Has anyone touched this, or its contents?' DS Mitchell asked, luckily not looking straight at Maddie or Nor as she was concentrating on handling the bag.

Maddie bit her lip. 'I touched it, of course. Had to pick it up.'

'Contents?'

'Um...' Maddie hated lying. And even though DS Mitchell was concentrating on bagging up the evidence, DI Trevelyan was looking right at her. Maddie made a quick decision.

'There'll be no fingerprints on anything. Not from us, anyway.'

'Not exactly what DS Mitchell asked, was it?' Trevelyan was looking at her.

Maddie could feel the blood rising in her cheeks. She turned away from the detective and said, as chirpily as possible, 'Coffee?'

Luckily for her, DI Trevelyan obviously decided not to question her further and said yes just as DS Mitchell said no. Maddie smiled to herself as she headed over to the Aga.

'Any updates on the case?' she called over to the police officers as she moved the old metal kettle onto the hotplate. She turned back to find DI Trevelyan looking at her again. To say it felt a little disconcerting would be an understatement, and she felt the blush rise in her cheeks again.

'Well, if anyone had delved inside the backpack,' Trevelyan said, glancing over to Nor, who was busying herself with Crumpet, 'and discovered some ID in there, they'd come to the same conclusion as we have. That our victim is a Ms Chloe Hardy from Lincolnshire, who checked into the Seaside View B&B last Thursday with her boyfriend, a Kieran Jones, also from Lincolnshire. He hasn't been seen back at the B&B since Chloe went missing, that's what prompted Mrs Laverstoke from the Seaside View to phone us. Says it looks like his stuff is gone but all of her cases are still there, and there's been no sign of either of them.'

'Tom,' DS Mitchell's voice had a note of warning to it, and Maddie noted the use of his first name.

There was a pause, which would have been even more horribly awkward than it already was if the kettle hadn't started boiling and Maddie splashed the hot water into a cafetière. Bringing it over to the table, being careful to not place it too close to the now-wrapped backpack, Maddie broke the silence.

'Thank you, DI Trevelyan.' Her formality was purposeful.

She could sense that Trevelyan – Tom – had overstepped the mark, and told her and Nor much more than he should have. That it was his junior officer who'd had to point it out made it worse. The last thing Maddie wanted was for him to get into trouble on her account. 'I can make another formal statement, perhaps to DS Mitchell' – she gestured to the sergeant as she walked over to the shelf and grabbed some mugs – 'about how and where I found it. But headlines are that it was lodged in some of the farm equipment stored here by a certain Jason Briggs.'

Placing the mugs down, Maddie noticed the looks that passed between Trevelyan and Mitchell. Maddie wanted them to do something about him, but she also didn't want to land her gran into any trouble, what with all the cash payments she'd received, and if Maddie's suspicions were correct, none of them would have troubled the taxman yet.

'If you could make a full statement, that would help.' DS Mitchell looked at Maddie for what felt like the first time. 'And you too, Mrs Penrose.'

'Me?' Nor was taken aback. 'I wasn't there when she found it. What do you need to speak to me for?' She'd reddened slightly across her cheeks and it was noticeable under the fine powder of her make-up.

'A statement on Jason Briggs, and how he's come to be in your barn would be a start,' DS Mitchell said.

'Why? Not illegal is it, to rent out a barn?'

Maddie could sense the tension rising. Not illegal to rent out a barn, but perhaps it might be illegal to not declare the earnings, or that they were in cash...

'We'd like to hear your side of the story all the same,' Mitchell added, no let-up in the iciness of her voice.

'Well, I don't have anything to say on the matter and that's all there is to it.' Nor crossed her arms over her chest. 'Man came looking for storage, I have space, he pays me money, 'nuff said.'

'We'll make some statements,' Maddie said, hovering a hand near her gran to placate her. She wasn't sure what had got her so worked up or why the police's request, though interesting in its own right, had got her knickers in such a twist. 'Coffee though first?'

'Afraid a few more questions first,' DI Trevelyan said, even as Maddie poured him a drink. 'Mrs Penrose, how well do you know Jason Briggs? I'm only asking, as if this is the backpack belonging to Chloe Hardy, which I'm sure it is, we have to know all we can about the man whose barn it was found in.'

'It's my barn,' Nor said, her arms still crossed. 'I just rent it to him.'

'And your relationship to him, is...?' DI Trevelyan continued. Nor opened and shut her mouth once or twice, so he helped her out. 'I mean, as in how long have you known him, have you been in business with him long, how did you come to terms on payments, how did you meet him?'

'Tom,' Maddie said hesitatingly, 'can this wait? Surely you have a backpack to analyse, it's obviously got blood on it, and Gran and I have a teashop to open. Maybe we can come in later and talk about this.'

'They're perfectly simple questions,' DS Mitchell added, unprompted, though she had taken Maddie's hint and had stood up from the table, and now held the bagged-up backpack. 'But she's right, guv, we need to get this blood sample tested.'

'Simple for you maybe,' muttered Nor as Maddie saw the two police officers out, with promises that they'd be in touch with full statements soon.

Pausing, once the front door was closed on the police, to catch how dramatically awful she looked in the mirror and push back a few stray chestnut curls into her ponytail, it was a minute before Maddie made it back into the kitchen. And when she did, she noticed that Nor, and her recipe book, had gone.

15

Maddie felt a certain unease as she opened up the teashop. DI Trevelyan had been asking questions that seemed to her wholly unrelated to the case and more related to her grandmother's farm, and possibly the income from it. This was definitely not the cherry on top of the visit from the council. Still, she didn't blame him for wanting to know more about Jason Briggs and how he came to be renting Nor's barn, but the questions on how he paid felt more accusatory towards Nor, not to mention their 'business relationship'. And her tax affairs were none of their business, although the jury was out on how much HMRC and Nor's accountant were troubled by the profits – or lack of – made on the farm.

'More hassle for them,' Nor explained as they arranged the cakes on the stands on the counter. She'd wandered into the teashop soon after Maddie had opened up, with no explanation for her sudden departure from the kitchen. The old recipe book had been tucked under her arm, though, and she'd placed it back on the shelf as she'd spoken, prompted by Maddie asking her about the farm. 'Think of the man hours, or woman hours, it takes to go through all my receipts for teabags, and where do I start when it comes to expensing the eggs.'

'Well, it depends how much they cost,' Maddie replied, not really thinking.

'How long's a piece of string!' Nor exclaimed. 'On one hand, they're free, on the other hand, I have to buy those hens, especially if Mr Fox comes to visit, and then feed them, and sometimes I feed them scraps and sometimes they forage around the farm, especially at harvest when tractors of grain trundle through, but winter months I have to buy more of those pellet things than I do in the summer.'

'OK, OK, I see. I think eggs are maybe something you don't need to trouble the taxman with.'

'Well, it starts with eggs and then all of a sudden I'm into oil for the tank that feeds the Aga, milk and cream from Farringford Dairy – but then I don't buy it as such, I swap it for chocolate cake sometimes, which Daisy Farringford likes for the kids, or so she says, and I get the cocoa from Julia at the deli, but I don't always buy that as sometimes she takes part exchange for my eggs... and, you see, we're back to eggs!'

'Which came first, the milkman or the eggs, eh Gran?'

'Well, they both come before the taxman in my book,' muttered Nor as she bustled around behind the counter and turned the hot water urn on. 'Check the level, would you, ducky.'

Maddie took the lid off the top and then poured in a couple of jugs of water from the tap so that the urn had plenty in it, ready for all the pots of tea it would soon – hopefully – be filling.

Nor finished icing the second coffee and walnut cake in situ, added her secret-ingredient nuts to the top, and cut it into generous slices. Maddie piled the fresh scones on a platter and placed the glass dome over them.

Whether it was just because the sun was out, or that word

had got out about Nor's 'cheffy' granddaughter being around, or worse, news of the murder so close to the teashop, but plenty of locals happened to stop by and linger over their morning tea and cake. Maddie found some old metal bistro-style tables and chairs in the store cupboard and, since the weather was looking better than yesterday, she set them up just outside the teashop so those who wanted could enjoy the fresh air and lovely views. She was also introduced to Marge and Julia, both of whom ran shops in Pendragon Creek. They had come in for a natter and a hot cuppa after their morning sea swim in Pendragon Bay.

Maddie was pleased that Nor looked jollier again, but she did wonder to herself if they should charge extra for people wearing those fleecy dryrobes as they seemed to take up double the amount of seats and drip seawater on the floor, too. And those drips were mixing with the gravel and dust from yesterday's walkers, which Maddie hadn't managed to sweep up since before Clive came blustering in... Anyway, Nor had enjoyed introducing Maddie to her friends and had promised them she'd be back out – or in – to the water as soon as summer was properly here.

'I don't think my knee could take the currents and it's too cold for me at the moment,' she'd said, exaggeratedly rubbing her hands up and down her upper arms.

'That's the point, Nor, it's good for you,' Julia had said and Marge had nodded enthusiastically.

'It does amazing things for your vim and vigour, Nor. Barry and I are finding we have so much more energy now I'm sea swimming and he's cycling. It's like we're twenty-seven again!'

'Isn't that how old you were when your eldest was born, Marge?' Julia had asked.

'Exactly,' winked back Marge, before collapsing into giggles.

Maddie had been called away by another customer, much to her relief, but the idea of a nice hot bath – as opposed to an ice-cold swim – was now lodged in her mind, especially as she poured boiling-hot water from the steaming urn into one of the novelty teapots. When had cold-water swimming been deemed better for you than a hot soak in a bath? Maddie shook her head as she laid up a tray of scones complete with clotted cream – the large tub of which had mysteriously reappeared – and with them the teapot shaped like an onion, and took them over to the table of similarly dryrobe-clad women, who waved over to Marge and Julia.

Despite not fancying joining them in the water, the gang of sea swimmers did create a lovely atmosphere in the teashop and it genuinely made Maddie so happy to see her gran moving among the tables and greeting the customers like the old friends they were. Maddie hadn't even minded giving up the last slice of coffee and walnut cake to a customer, even though she'd been eyeing it up for herself. It helped that it had gone to a man who had sung its – and its baker's – praises so much that Maddie thought she saw Nor blush.

But a literal and metaphorical shadow was cast over the teashop as the bulk of a man appeared at the door, blocking out the sunlight that had been streaming through it. Maddie's heart had sunk when she'd seen the bright white trainers and skinny jeans of Jason Briggs.

'Can I help you?' Maddie had asked, but Nor had bustled past her and ushered Jason to a table in the corner by the counter.

'Come on, Jason, sit yourself down. What would you like? On the house, of course.'

'*On the house?*' Maddie had hissed at her grandmother out of Jason's hearing when they were both behind the counter. 'Why on earth are you giving him freebies?'

'Never you mind, Mads.' Nor had brushed her off, but Maddie hadn't let it slide. When Nor was back from giving Jason a coffee and not one, but two chocolate bars, for free, Maddie nudged her again.

'Why the special treatment, Gran?'

'Think of it as a sort of tenancy discount,' Nor replied, busying herself around the counter.

Maddie frowned.

She watched as Jason unwrapped one of the chocolate bars and threw the wrapper on the floor. This incensed Maddie more than she could bear, and despite his threats this morning, she went straight up to his table, reached down, picked up the wrapper and then slapped it back on the table.

'Dropped this,' she said, seething.

Jason looked at her, swallowed his mouthful, then took a long sip of the coffee, never once taking his eyes off her.

Maddie faltered, though tried not to show how nervous she'd become, now her ire had subsided.

'What were the police doin' here?' he asked, his voice low, his fist now gripping the empty wrapper, crushing it.

Maddie gulped. 'J-just following up leads,' she stuttered, noticing the pulsing vein in Jason's forehead. He looked angry.

'Leads?'

'Yes.' Maddie edged herself back from the table, aware that the teashop was quite full and she didn't want a scene. She lowered her voice. 'Because of the murder.'

Jason said nothing, barely nodded, and let go of the chocolate bar wrapper. A flick of his finger and the litter skittered across the table and floated to the floor once again. Then he stood up, scraping his chair back across the stone floor. He looked Maddie straight in the eye before he pushed the half-full coffee mug off the table, making it smash and splinter on the floor.

'Oops,' he said, with a smirk, and walked out.

Maddie just looked at Nor, who shrugged and then, with a smile plastered on her face, handed Maddie the dustpan and brush and went over to greet another local customer who'd walked in just as Jason had left. Maddie did notice that Nor had lingered by the door though, once old Mr Enys, who was one of the local fishermen, had been greeted. It was as if she was watching every last second of someone leaving. The almost imperceptible nod that Nor gave herself as she turned back into the teashop confirmed one thing in Maddie's mind at least. Jason Briggs had left the farm.

16

Jason's visit had rattled Maddie. And what's more, it had reminded her, all too plainly, that there had been a murder, just yesterday, here by idyllic Pendragon Bay. It certainly wasn't what she'd expected when she'd come to stay with her gran for a few weeks, which, judging by the state of the teashop and the farm in general, might turn into a few months. And she had to admit, that murder aside, it was lovely being back in Cornwall, close to the sea. And perhaps, more than that, spending some time with her grandmother, who she'd packed off back to the farmhouse an hour ago, seeing how she was struggling with the heavier teapots and looking visibly tired.

Maddie locked up the teashop – having retrieved the now trusty recipe book from the shelf Nor had placed it on – and leant with her back to the pale green door, with its peeling paint and flaking off bits. But it had been warmed by the spring sunshine and it felt glorious against her back, like a hot stone massage from one of those fancy spas.

Ooh, there's an idea, she thought, mentally filing the genius plan she'd just come up with for turning the east barn into a spa, complete with hot tubs and a sauna. *From massage table to tea table – a treatment followed by afternoon tea with fresh scones and Cornish clotted cream...* The cream had reappeared this morning, or at least the tub it was in, had. She'd had enough to serve scones all day, but there had definitely been a big scoop out of it. She'd shown it to Nor before Jason had arrived, but she'd merely shrugged and said that little mice had big paws these days, which was as odd as it was cryptic and did nothing to stop Maddie from returning to her original theory that Crumpet was the criminal mastermind, the cat burglar, behind it all. If only he had opposable thumbs... or someone working on his behalf who did...

She let her mind wander for a moment more, closing her eyes as the sun sat heavy, but warm, low in the sky. She took in a deep breath. The sweet smell of fresh hay and the saltiness of the sea air filled her lungs and brought back so many happy memories of spending summers, and Easter holidays, and Christmas even, here at Folly Farm. It was so different from the suburban town she'd grown up in.

Maddie opened her eyes. She needed to forget about murder and think about more positive things, like ideas for different cakes, or whether the hikers and walkers of Pendragon Bay and Pendragon Creek would ever be tempted by a cruffin – the cross between a croissant and a muffin – and indeed if she'd have the time to make them as she wanted to do so much else to the farm...

She pushed herself away from the delicious warmth of the door and strode out across the yard, taking the same public footpath as the walkers would do to reach the town of Pendragon Creek. Making sure to close the gate behind her, she upped her pace, realising that the sun, though still in the sky, would be sinking below the glittering waters of the Celtic Sea soon enough. The exercise and fresh air in her lungs were both welcome after the hours she'd just spent in the teashop. *That*

Jason guy... What a creep. Maddie still wondered why Nor put up with him, more than that – pandered to him. *I know money's tight, but I'd have him out of there, and Grandad's boneshaker left well alone,* she grumbled to herself.

Maddie kept to the path, as she knew that the rough grassy verges and tufts, which were dotted with even tuftier sheep, could lead pretty quickly to rocky escarpments and deadly drops. But the view – oh the view – it really was stunning. She paused, just briefly, to take in the vast expanse of the sea, which she could see clear as anything now the pathway had found itself at the coast's edge. The bright spring green grass and the woolly sheep echoed the blue sky and fluffy clouds, with this sparkling blue champagne in between them.

Hmm, cocktails... Maddie's mind wandered again. *I could host a cocktail night. The first would be a blue fizzy one, topped with blackberries and...* The thought came and went and Maddie kept walking, downhill now as the hillside dipped down towards the estuary and the small town that was named after it: Pendragon Creek.

The town was picture-postcard perfect. It had a working harbour and a pretty little beach. Even the Co-Op was housed within an eighteenth-century fisherman's house. The footpath Maddie was on petered out next to some quaint cottages, but led directly onto the main road, which was called Fore Street. Along with the picturesque Co-Op, there were shops and galleries, their bow-fronted windows displaying everything from buckets and spades to bracelets and crystals.

As she paused to look into the window of an antiques shop, the tantalising aroma of proper fish and chips wafted past her. She looked along the road to where Oh My Cod had a queue stretching outside it. Maddie looked at her watch. Five-forty-ish, early for a fish supper, but then people seemed to eat earlier here than in London, where the only diners who'd come to the restaurant that early were the pre-theatre brigade who wanted instant service, lest they miss curtain-up. That brief memory of the stress of her London life sent an involuntary spasm through Maddie's shoulders. It had been the right thing to come to stay with her gran. She needed this slower pace of life, and if that involved chippy tea at five forty in the afternoon – or evening – then so be it.

She was tempted to join the queue, but remembered the left-over scone she'd snaffled just before she left the teashop. Maddie picked up her pace, determined now to get down to the Esplanade and walk to the end of the harbour pier before turning back, hoping that that would have been enough exercise to counteract the scone. And the cream. And the spoonful of jam. And the... Well, let's say it was first-week excitement. She'd stop eating all the produce tomorrow.

After a few more moments window shopping, Maddie finally reached the pier and took in a lungful of the sea air. It was bliss. The harbourmaster's office was closed for the night and the boats within the breakwaters bobbed gently on their moorings. Their bells and chandlery clanked away, adding their own notes to the cries of the gulls and kittiwakes that flew around, diving for minnows and, more usually, chips, sometimes out of the hands and newspaper cones of unsuspecting punters who'd taken their chippy tea to the beach. Maddie laughed, and held back her hair from the wind. The lighthouse on the headland had started exhibiting its light and the bells of St Mary's church, its spire just visible from the pier, announced evensong. Maddie turned around to look back at the town again. She saw the lights come on in the front rooms of the houses on the Esplanade and in the bedrooms and reception area of the bed and breakfast by the harbour's edge. She could see the name of it: Seaside View. It rang a bell.

'Of course,' Maddie said as the wind swept her words away. Then she thought to herself, *It's the B&B that Chloe and her boyfriend were staying in.*

Before she knew it, she was walking back along the length of the pier and heading towards the lit-up windows and welcoming porch of the bed and breakfast, her mind suddenly on murder again. And determined to find out more about the poor girl who died yesterday.

17

'Hello?' Maddie called as she pushed open the bright blue door of Seaside View. 'Anyone there?'

She looked around the reception area of the bed and breakfast, getting the measure of the place. The building itself was one of the old double-fronted Georgian harbour-front houses, white rendered with black-edged, deep-set windows. The reception was in what would have been the original hallway, with a staircase leading up one side, elegantly curved to a rounded end as it met the flagstoned floor of the hall. Maddie supposed it must have been built at about the same time as Folly Farmhouse, as it had similar proportions – high ceilings and panelled walls – though this hallway was much neater and tidier than the chaos of paintings that decorated her gran's.

A desk was set in between the end of the stairs and the front door, and behind it was a small wall-mounted run of pigeonholes, some of which held clunky key rings with simple Yale keys on them. On the desk, which was an old Regency-style mahogany thing, was a display of leaflets of fun and exciting days out in the local area and she made a mental note to visit the steam and traction engine collection one day, maybe with nephews in tow as an excuse. On the other side of the hallway was an upholstered bench, and next to it a standard lamp with a tasselled shade.

Old-fashioned but well-kept, Maddie thought, *a bit like our teashop, except we haven't got the well-kept bit...*

'Can I help you?' A lady appeared from down the hall and looked expectantly at Maddie. 'There was a bell if you'd needed me urgently.'

'Oh, it wasn't urgent,' Maddie replied. 'I...' At this point, she had to decide what to say. Should she come straight out with it and say she was looking into the murder of the woman who had been staying here? And then what? Be quite rightly asked to leave as being nothing more than a nosey parker. No, that wouldn't do, she had to be more subtle than that. Her mind blurred as she scanned the hallway for ideas, with her eyes luckily alighting on one of the leaflets on the desk that was advertising cream teas at a popular stately home. 'Thought I should come and say hello. I'm Maddie Penrose, granddaughter of Nor Penrose up at Folly Farm, and I'm helping her with the teashop.'

'Oh yes? Lovely to meet you Maddie, I'm Sheila.' She pointed to a sign on the desk that said: SHEILA LAVERSTOKE – PROPRIETOR.

'Lovely to meet you too, Sheila.' Maddie took her outstretched hand and smiled, meeting the genuinely warm one that crossed Sheila's face. She was a middle-aged woman, in her fifties perhaps, with a well-coiffed head of blonde hair, lightly salt and peppered with grey. She wore a floral blouse and a pair of comfy-stretch jeans; the sort of look that was smart enough to greet guests but meant she could turn down a bed and clean a room without worrying about what she was wearing.

'Folly Farm, you say? You'll know all about the murder up there then.'

Maddie nodded. She wanted to get into Sheila's confidence

– share a few secrets – but also didn't want to let on quite how much she knew in case Sheila told the whole town and DI Trevelyan got into trouble… and Maddie had the teashop door knocked down by nosey neighbours and irate councillors. 'It was horrible, I was there when Clive—'

'Pendergast? From Hill Top? Was he there, was he?' Sheila stepped behind her desk. It felt as if she was trying to put some sort of barrier between herself and talk of Clive Pendergast, or was that Maddie's over-imaginative mind getting the better of her again?

'Yes, Clive found the girl. And I followed him up the path and saw where she'd died—'

'Murdered, I hear,' Sheila interrupted.

'Yes, murdered,' Maddie agreed. News was obviously travelling fast through the small community. 'I called the police and all that.'

Sheila shook her head, a sign of pity and disbelief at the whole situation. 'Something like that happening just on that spot. And Clive of all people to find her. She was staying here, you know? Chloe, the victim.' Sheila fixed Maddie with a keen eye.

'Was she? Blimey. And that's her name is it?' Maddie said, putting those school drama lessons to the test. 'How horrid for you too. I hear she had a boyfriend with her, is he…' Maddie mouthed the word 'upstairs' and pointed towards the ceiling. Her conspiratorial tone obviously struck the right chord with Sheila, who leant across the reception desk.

'No,' she said in a whisper, even though Chloe was dead and this boyfriend of hers wasn't there. 'Left yesterday. Didn't pay the bill, though of course they'd booked for another two nights and as far as I knew she was still staying. Absolutely fuming he looked too.'

'Fuming? As in angry?' Maddie checked to see if she had the right end of the stick.

'Yes, angry as anything. Headed out, barrel bag over his shoulder and hasn't come back.'

Maddie, of course, knew that Kieran Jones had gone. DI Trevelyan had said the same thing. But it was interesting hearing it from Sheila. It was like when two different people gave you the recipe for something; muffins, for example. There would always be discrepancies between the versions. Blueberries, cocoa, fudge bits, baking powder... An ingredient or process that wasn't identical. Something that marked them as different. DI Trevelyan had never mentioned that Kieran had been angry. This was a new ingredient.

'That doesn't sound good. Being angry, I mean. And leaving you without the bill paid, of course. What time did he leave?'

'Before lunch,' Sheila replied. 'About 11.30-ish. I noticed as I was doing the bed in the Puffin Suite. I'm a stickler for getting rooms cleaned as soon as they're vacated for the day. You have to run a tight ship in a place like this. Keep on top of everything. Anyway, I heard the door slam and looked out of the window at the front, which I had open to air the room, and saw him with his bag over his shoulder, face like thunder.'

An argument with her boyfriend could well have been the 'hump in the road' that Chloe posted about, Maddie thought, remembering the reel she'd watched on Chloe's social media, filmed just before she'd been killed. 'Clive didn't find Chloe until much later, giving' – she stopped herself from using Kieran's name; Trevelyan had told her it, but Sheila hadn't yet – 'him quite a bit of time that he's possibly unaccounted for. I wonder where he went, when she went up to the old cow shed?'

Sheila shook her head. 'Maybe back to the Two Pelicans – the pub up the road. They spent the evening before there, shocked that I was just a B&B and wouldn't cater an evening meal. But, like I said, I saw him leave with his bag over his shoulder and didn't see him again.'

'Did he have a car?' Maddie asked. With the timing of his

departure being before Chloe was killed, she had to admit that the missing boyfriend, Kieran, was edging his way to the top of her suspects list. 'He could be anywhere by now if so, and I'm sure the police will want to speak to him.'

'Arrived by taxi from the station. No car between them.' Sheila shook her head. 'And yes, that nice DI did ask all about him and what time he left. I'm sure he'll be looking for him. Can't have got too far, as he'd be hitchhiking, unless they got a taxi to the station. I'm sure DS Mitchell will be all over that.'

'Do you know how far they'd come?'

Sheila ran her finger down the guest book. 'Lincolnshire, it says here.'

Ah, Maddie thought, here the recipes matched again. DI Trevelyan had said that too.

'Long way to hitchhike back to. And surely the police must be looking for—' she hesitated this time, waiting for Sheila to fill in the name for her.

'Kieran. Kieran Jones. DI Trevelyan knows all the details. I told him about the humdinger of a row the pair had had, too.'

'A fight?' This *wasn't* in Trevelyan's version of the recipe.

'Heard it through the walls. I had to knock on their door to ask them to quieten down as Mr Parry in the room next to them is a late sleeper. Cheek of it too, him shouting back to me in some phoney Cornish accent – honestly, people think everywhere west of Bristol we sound like yokels.'

'So rude, isn't it,' Maddie agreed, hoping her own voice never slipped into the local accent, lest it offended. She smiled at Sheila, and in her best London voice asked, 'So this was in the morning?'

'Yes, yesterday morning. Just before Kieran left. Hammer and tongs, they were. And him more than her, at least twice as much.' A scuffling sound at the door interrupted Sheila, who shook her head. 'Honestly, those seagulls are getting worse and worse. I can't leave the windows open any more in case they fly right in and steal the marzipan fruits I leave out for the guests.'

Maddie noticed a shadow pass the smoked glass of the panelled door, but her mind was on what Sheila had just said. Not just the thieving seagulls, though she could imagine a miniature marzipan apple sitting atop a perfectly plumped pillow, but the fight Chloe and Kieran had been having.

'Any idea what the fight was about?' Maddie asked, hoping Sheila didn't mind being probed about it.

She didn't seem to, and continued as if the clattering at the door had never happened. 'Oh the usuals, "you're so selfish", "why would you do this to me", "I'll make all of this worth your while" and then something about "you'll pay for this, you just see", which, I must say, in hindsight does sound a bit odd now that she's dead.'

'That really does sound like a big falling out.' Maddie wondered: *Big enough to kill over?* 'I hope they find him.'

'I presume they're looking for him,' Sheila continued. 'They said they'd take her luggage too, and I wish they would as I have another booking for that room. I call it the Sunset Suite as it looks due west over the harbour and gets lovely views as the sun goes down. One of our best too, newly refurbished.'

Maddie nodded as Sheila spoke. She couldn't help but feel that Kieran simply had to be the main suspect now in his girlfriend's murder. He'd been angry with her, stormed out, and then perhaps followed her up to the old cow shed and murdered her. Then, as Sheila chatted about the views from the Sunset Suite, aided now by the new sash windows, Maddie thought again about the walk up to the ruins and how hard she'd found it this morning. Carrying a big bag too, would someone do that on an impulse?

'Are you sure he took his bag with him?' Maddie asked again.

'Yes, two actually. One slung over his shoulder and another

gripped in his other hand now I think of it. Like I said, I was up in Mr Parry's room, the Puffin Suite, which looks right over the front there, too. Heard the door, leant out the window, saw the lad and saw his face as he looked right back up at me, or at least at their room's window, almost like he was giving her one last scowl. Proper cross he looked. I got back to turning down the room and heard the door go again, but I didn't check as I thought that must be her running after him. Lovers' tiff and all that. But then when he didn't come back, and then later when I realised she wasn't in the room, well, I'd heard the news in the town, so I called the police to say I think I knew who the dead girl was.'

'News travels fast, huh? Clive only found her at three-ish. When did you hear?'

'Filling up the car on my way back from the cash and carry, so must have been about six-ish. Daph who works there said a girl had been murdered up on the hills, poor love. When I got home, I checked their room and it was still empty. That's when I put two and two together, and phoned the police that evening.'

'Well done, without that info the police would have been scratching their heads for a while, I bet.'

Sheila looked pleased with the compliment. 'Just doing my bit. Now I wish they'd come and get her stuff. Her parents will want it, I'm sure.'

Maddie thought about Chloe's parents, and her heart sank. They probably knew Kieran too. What would be the point of him hitchhiking home, only to be recognised and arrested as soon as he got there? His word against the rumour mill and the police's suspicions... No, if he was the killer, he wouldn't be able to go home.

Maddie shuddered as a new thought entered her head; maybe he was still around here? Staying anonymous on the outskirts of town. There had been no sign of him since yesterday afternoon. Trevelyan would have mentioned if they'd known he'd called a taxi or been spotted at the station.

His girlfriend was dead. And the sun was setting now and soon it would be dark again, when the pretty rolling hills and dramatic cliffs became a dangerous and unforgiving landscape for those not used to them. For those from flat farmland like that of Lincolnshire.

Had he really climbed that hill, with two bags, and killed his girlfriend?

Or had he just left her after an argument and disappeared himself?

Or was he still here in Pendragon Creek? A desperate man who might do desperate things to get away with murder?

18

Maddie thanked Sheila for her time and left the B&B with promises to meet up again soon, perhaps at the teashop. She'd appreciated Sheila's openness with information, and hoped she'd trod the fine line between gossiping and giving too much away. Maddie hadn't thought she'd get so wrapped up in the whole murder 'thing', and her mind briefly flitted to the handsome policeman in charge.

Maddie Penrose, she scolded herself, as she walked down the cobbled street along the harbour. *This is not the time to be thinking of hunky men. You came here to get away from all of that.*

Still, DI Trevelyan did seem like a nice guy and, as her mother often told her, she wasn't so much on the shelf as propping it up until everyone else had a chance to get off – *No! Save yourselves! I'll just... stay... here...* Maddie was wrapped up in such thoughts as she dodged a discarded cone of chips being fought over by seagulls and headed almost subconsciously towards the sound of music and convivial chatter that was coming from a pub down the street. The pub was the bizarrely named Two Pelicans and it was the beating heart of Pendragon Creek.

Whitewashed with black-framed windows that bowed out into the narrow lane like the prow of an old warship, it was just up a steep, narrow lane from the Esplanade. Maddie remembered her dad telling her that it had been a fishermen's hangout in the 1800s and early 1900s. Then it had become more of a family-friendly restaurant when the tourists had arrived en masse in the 1950s. Since then, it had somewhat stayed in the red gingham tablecloth style, doing a roaring trade in high summer of fish and chips and scampi and chips and everything with chips. But in the evenings it was a bit livelier, with local musicians taking a turn on the small stage that was furthest from the bar.

Maddie pushed the door open and a blast of warm air greeted her, reminding her how chilly it had got now the sun had started to descend over the waters around Pendragon Creek. She wasn't surprised that a young couple like Chloe and Kieran had found this place when they'd come to stay in the small town, but the question was, why had they both come to this little coastal town in the first place?

Maddie stepped up to the bar and looked at what was on offer. A few local ales and not much in the way of wine. She'd become used to London's bars and nightspots, where you could order some abstract gin or small-cask rum, or a craft beer from Amsterdam or even a wine from Slovenia if you fancied, and the chances were the bar in question would have it. Or something even more out there and new-fangled – spicy margaritas and orange wine.

She furrowed her brow, deciding between brown ale, bitter or some gassy lager until a very familiar voice called over from the other side of the horseshoe-shaped bar.

'I'd have a G&T, ducky, safest option.'

'Gran!' Maddie said, shocked to see her octogenarian grandmother sitting on a bar stool across the way. She was even more shocked when she heard her say:

'Go on, Roger, give the girl a double. She's had quite the day.'

'Thanks, Gran,' Maddie said, sidling over to her and planting a kiss on her cheek before pulling up a stool next to her. 'What are you doing here, though?'

'Thought I should be tucked up in front of *Countdown* with my cocoa?' Nor winked at her.

'No, but...' Maddie shrugged. 'I just didn't have you down as a pub-goer.' Maddie looked around. A man with a long grey beard was setting up on the stage, an accordion on his knee. A TV, somewhat precariously hung from the ceiling by the bar, was silently showing the football and a man in a long overcoat was playing on the fruit machine.

'Not much else to do round here,' Nor answered her. 'And I'm eighty-two, not dead. Plus, I can't be doing with lugging those packs of mini tins of tonic in and out of the fridge. Easier to come here and pay Roger to do it.' She winked at the barman and passed over a ten-pound note to him as he placed a tumbler of fizzing gin and tonic, with a rudimentary slice of lemon in the top, in front of Maddie. 'Thanks, Roger m'lover,' Nor said, taking her change.

'Thanks, Gran.' Maddie chinked her glass against her gran's, smiling at the Cornish dialect. She'd forgotten how normal it was for friends to call each other 'm'lover'. It was a rather lovely way of greeting someone really. She looked at her gran and carried on. 'And sorry, I shouldn't be so presumptuous. Of course you should come to the pub. Good place to spend all that cash... And Roger looks... well, he's good for his age. Nice legs.' Maddie stuck her tongue out one side of her mouth as Nor nudged her in the ribs.

'That's enough of your cheek, young lady,' she said, a smile on her face.

'Tell you what though, I do need this. Thanks.' Maddie took a long sip and then put the glass down. She filled in Nor on her trip to see Sheila at Seaside View and Nor took it all in, gently twisting her glass around between her fingers as she did so. She stopped Maddie at one point in her story.

'What did she say exactly about Clive?'

'Just that it was horrible for him to find her. No, those weren't her words...' Maddie drummed her fingers on her forehead, wishing she'd written down what Sheila had said as soon as she'd left the B&B. What version of the recipe had Sheila given her...? 'That's it, she said, "Clive of all people" and then she seemed a bit odd, as if she wanted to distance herself from him.'

'Hmm, I don't doubt it.' Nor looked across the bar, but her eyes weren't focused on anything in particular.

'Gran, what is it? Why's that important? Has this anything to do with the missing woman in the 1960s?'

'Well, nothing's a coincidence, eh? You'll see a few eyebrows raised around here – and not just because some poor girl has lost her life up there. There's those around here who know more than they're letting on, I'm sure.'

'You're speaking in riddles, Gran. Who knows more than they're letting on? What's this got to do with Clive finding the body?'

Nor stopped gazing into the middle distance and fixed her ice-blue eyes onto her granddaughter. Then she said something that chilled Maddie right to the core.

'That Chloe Hardy, whoever she may be, might not be the first young woman to be killed in that spot. And more than that, Clive Pendergast might not be the first in his family to have something to do with it.'

19

Maddie almost spat out her gin and tonic.

'What do you mean, Gran?' She thought back to the sight of Clive Pendergast as he'd appeared bloodied and shocked at the teashop door yesterday.

Nor glanced at Roger, who gave her a knowing look as he wiped clean a tumbler fresh out of the glass washer behind the bar. Nor sighed. 'All right then, here's the tale, make of it what you will. Long before you were born, in fact your father was in nappies still—'

'1965,' chipped in Roger from the glass washer.

'It was indeed – well remembered, Rodge.'

'Not just a nice pair of legs.' He winked at Maddie, who blushed and mouthed 'sorry' at him.

Nor laughed, then continued with the story, her voice lowered to suit the sombre tone of the tale. 'So, 1965 as I said before. Your father was just a babe in arms and Rosie was a terrible two-er and I was knee-deep in the farm, as ever. Then word got out that Esther had disappeared.'

'Esther? So that was the name of the woman. You didn't mention her name yesterday. Did she have a surname?' Maddie rested her chin on her hand as she questioned her grandmother.

'She did indeed. Esther Pendergast.'

'Clive's wife?'

'No, his father's. This was back in 1965, remember.'

Maddie nodded, remembering meeting Clive and thinking that he looked to be in his mid-fifties, but he was healthy and strong, so could have easily been sixty and thriving off the fresh air and sunshine that a farming life allows.

'So what happened to her?' Maddie asked Nor.

'No one knows, ducky, just that she was last seen at the old cow shed, by Gerald Pendergast, Clive's father, or so he said, and then she was never seen again.'

Maddie frowned and then lowered her voice to ask, 'And no one found a body?'

'No, never. And she never made contact either. People say she had a sister up north, but when someone phoned her, she said she never heard from Esther. After seven years, she was declared dead.'

'Gosh. No wonder Sheila at Seaside View was so interested in it being Clive who found Chloe under the tumble. He must have grown up knowing all about that spot on his own farm. Oh dear, poor man, he'd been trying to free Chloe. Can you imagine the thoughts going through his head?'

'Doesn't bear thinking about, does it,' Nor said, downing her G&T and pushing the empty glass over towards Roger.

'Another one Nor?' he asked.

'No, better not. Early start as always,' Nor said, checking her handbag on the bar stool next to her and zipping it up. 'You stay, though, Mads, have another drink and get a taxi home. Mark King in the village will give you a ride, his number's on that pinboard over there.'

'Mark King, that's quite a name. Did his parents realise? Mark King. Marking. Weird.'

'Never thought of it like that,' Nor chuckled. 'Calls himself the Taxi King. Still, nice lad, he'll see you right.'

'I won't be late. And I won't go out tomorrow morning and abandon you to make all the cakes, like I did today. I'm sorry about that, Gran. And I'm sorry about being so bristly with Jason. I just don't like him.'

'Pays the bills, ducky, pays the bills. There's them round here that do a lot worse. And I can cope with the farm, you know.' Nor placed a gentle hand on Maddie's shoulder. 'I like Mandy who does the livery and her daughter is a sweetheart too, and I can potter with the cats and the hens, but that old barn was getting me down. Best have one rented out, even if the lad in question isn't someone we'd have a sherry with. Or a double G&T.'

Maddie nodded and kissed her gran goodbye. As she turned back towards the bar, and the fresh gin and tonic that had appeared before her, she realised that Nor hadn't mentioned the teashop or how she was coping with that.

Maddie sipped her drink and wiped a finger up the side, catching the condensation. She couldn't believe Nor's revelation. Clive's own mother had been killed, or at least went missing, last seen at the old cow shed. Nor hadn't said how this must have affected him, losing his mum at such a young age. He can't have been more than a baby. But did this coincidence make Clive look suspicious? Maddie thought about it as she sipped her drink. She didn't know. He had reason to be there, of course; he owned the land and had been out shooting rabbits. But what she had no idea about, and as far as she knew, neither did the police, nor Sheila Laverstoke, was what Chloe was doing there.

She thought about the reel she'd seen. Chloe was using her selfie stick, so she was alone when she'd recorded it. Maddie checked her phone and scrolled through to the account and found the timing of the post: 1.53 p.m. Over an hour before Clive had burst into the teashop. But if Chloe had been alone at 1.53, then she probably didn't run after Kieran, make up with him and take him to the hillside with her. And she certainly wasn't moping, as some people would after a humdinger of a fight with their beloved. She'd looked like a woman on a mission. Maddie put her phone down. Something didn't feel right about Kieran being the murderer, even though it made sense. Like knowing a tomato is a fruit, but also knowing it shouldn't go in a fruit salad.

'You look deep in thought,' Roger said, putting away the final tumbler from the steaming glass washer machine. Maddie had taken an instant liking to Roger. Despite the cringe-worthy moment earlier when he'd obviously heard her admire his legs – on Nor's behalf, of course. He was average height, wore a plaid shirt and, despite it only being spring, he was in baggy cargo shorts – hence the legs being on view. He was in his seventies, or so she thought, with grey hair that had all but disappeared from the top-most dome, and a dark grey, close-cut beard. All in all, he was friendly and looked like the sort of man who'd make a good scout master or outward bound instructor.

'I was thinking about the murdered girl at the ruins up on the hill,' Maddie replied, not feeling much of a need to hide her thoughts from him. No doubt the whole town was thrumming with the gossip; if any of the town were in the pub, that was. It was a quiet night, but Sunday often was; even in London, they'd struggled sometimes to fill Chez Lucie's tables on a 'school night'.

'Ah, a sad thing it is. I feel bad for those young people, if it's true he's missing too, and all.'

Maddie wondered why Roger didn't immediately assume Kieran was the murderer. He seemed to count him, if anything, as another victim of sorts.

'You don't think he did it? And is on the run?'

Roger thought about it. 'I suppose he could be. But he seemed to dote on her.'

'You were here at the bar when they came in?' Maddie shifted her weight on the bar stool and leant on the bar to listen.

'Oh yes, it's always me here. And yes, they were a lively pair. Couldn't take their hands off each other!' Roger chuckled. 'It's not quite high season, so we tend to get more couples without children here this time of year, but not like these two. We usually get the walkers, stately home visitors, you know the type. But she was dressed to the nines. Bright pink heels, shiny tops, plastic-looking trousers. Ready for a disco rather than a Sunday night in the pub.'

'Ha, not your usual types at all then.' Maddie glanced around at the few punters enjoying – if that was the word – the accordion-player's folk music. Plaid shirts and well-worn denim was about as à la mode as it got. Maddie turned back to Roger, thinking about what Sheila had said. 'No sign of any arguing then?'

'Not that I saw. On her phone quite a bit, which left the poor chap to play a few games of pool by himself as she yapped away making arrangements. But he bought the drinks and grinned at her like she was...' He stopped and thought for a moment.

'What?' Maddie pressed.

'Well, on a pedestal, you know? Can't say I blame him, nice-looking lass. But I think she knew it, and I don't mean that in a cruel way.' Roger wiped his tea towel along the bar. 'Not like the rich blokes that come off a yacht and bring their tenders into the harbour. Expect us to serve Dom blooming Pérignon or something.'

'Ha, I know the sort. We used to get them at the place I worked in London. Probably the same guys.'

Roger chuckled. 'Probably. They have that sense about them, you know...'

'Entitled?' Maddie said.

'Yes,' Roger agreed. 'And she were a little like that, bless her. Looked like she bloody owned the place – 'scuse my French.'

'Excused.' Maddie smiled and took a sip of her drink. Then, without realising she was musing out loud, she said, 'I wish I could see her phone records. See who she was talking to. That might help us work out why she was here.'

Roger nodded. 'Well, I can help you there.'

Maddie looked at him, cocking her head on one side. 'How?'

'Age-old way barmen have learned what's happening with the world since the first pub was opened; I listened.'

'Oooh.' Maddie leant forward and bit her lip in expectation. He had incredibly good hearing; she knew that from her blunder talking about his legs. 'What did she say?'

'Most of them calls started with the phrase, "Hiya Archer". And Archer isn't that common a name.'

Maddie shook her head. She didn't know anyone, here or in London, called Archer.

'So I reckon I know exactly who she was speaking to,' Roger carried on. 'That'll be Archer from up the road, lives with his mum in a little house just up from the petrol station. Been hard on them since his dad left them, so it was nice to see that some friends had come to visit. Uni friends, I thought.'

'Do you have a number for him?' Maddie asked, intrigued.

'No, and sadly you just missed him, he was over there earlier, on that fruit machine. You'll catch him tomorrow, though, if you want to.'

'Really?' Maddie asked, wondering even now if it was a good idea to do so.

'He comes in and plays darts on Mondays. About this time.'

Maddie thanked Roger, for the drink and the information about Archer. As she finished off her drink, she fished the old recipe book out of her bag and opened it up on the bar. She looked through the list of words she had written by the aged flapjack recipe:

Clive Pendergast – Hill Top Farm
Old cow shed – fallen stones
Last words – aren't you rock would tree help
Bloodied stone = murder
1965 – missing woman SAME PLACE
Clotted cream?
Litter
Planning – houses at Hill Top
HER backpack – OUR barn. Jason?!

And then she added:

Esther Pendergast (next to the bit about the missing woman)
'of all people' (next to Clive Pendergast's name)
C&K – lovers' tiff? Him more than her
Entitled
Archer

Maddie stared at the words as they merged with others, such as 'oats' and 'Lyon's Golden Syrup'. What was this recipe trying to tell her? Or was she working with all the wrong ingredients? When she wrote these lists while watching TV murder mysteries, she could almost always see the clues, or at least she knew what to look for. But now, with it really happening all around her, it felt a lot more confusing. Still, she'd persevere with her list making – if only to have something to talk to DI Trevelyan about when she next saw him.

She drained the glass and then, with a breezy 'see you tomorrow', she eased herself off the bar stool and popped the recipe book back in her bag. She found the noticeboard that Nor had pointed out by the door. Sure enough, the Taxi King was listed with a mobile number, which Maddie called. As she waited for him to answer, she scanned the notices. Zumba on a Friday with Kate at the Fisherman's Hall, bridge with Mrs Turner at the Atlantic Hotel ballroom on Tuesday mornings, meeting in the Fishermen's Hall regarding the local plan on Wednesday night, kids' highchair for sale, only twenty quid... Then her call was answered and Mark King, the Taxi King, said he'd be there in five minutes.

Rather than listen to the accordion version of 'Bohemian Rhapsody', Maddie stepped outside into the cool night air. The Taxi King had said he'd pick her up from the pub, but the road outside the Two Pelicans was narrow and one-way, so to save him going up it, she walked down the lane towards The Esplanade. Maddie wrapped her denim jacket as tightly as she could around her as she felt the chill come off the water. Yesterday's clouds and thunder had blown through, leaving a clear and moonlit night. But, as was so often the case, the clearer the night, the cooler it was.

As Maddie reached the harbour's edge, she could see the moonlight catch the ripples of the water. Leaning against the concrete wall of the harbour, not wanting to stray too far from the pub, Maddie turned around to look back towards the small town. She huffed out her breath onto her hands, regretting her choice to stay out so late in just her thin jacket. Looking up, she took in the buildings along the front, most of them old, like Folly Farm, but painted in pastel colours. And all of them gently glowing in the soft light of the moon.

All except the outside of the Seaside View B&B.

Maddie pushed herself away from the harbour wall and ran towards the B&B. It wasn't so much glowing, as flashing – its white-painted front alternating between blue and red, blue and red. Maddie could see police cars and an ambulance – how had she not noticed this as she'd turned the corner from the Two Pelicans? She ran the length of the harbour, ignoring a car signed Taxi King as it swept past her. She ran until the blue lights of the emergency vehicles made her want to shield her eyes.

A young policewoman stepped out in front of her as she neared the scene, and Maddie almost ran straight into her.

'Please, madam, don't come any closer,' the police officer said, holding out her hands.

'What's happened?' Maddie managed to ask, between gulping breaths. She craned her neck but couldn't see past the high-sided ambulance, with its back doors flung open.

The police officer, who looked pale and shocked herself, her face tinged blue by the lights, simply replied, 'There's been a terrible, terrible accident.'

20

Maddie took a few steps back from the police officer, then surprised even herself at what she heard coming out of her mouth.

'I... I'm staying here. Can I get into my room? The Puffin Suite.'

'I'm not sure.' the policewoman looked a bit confused. 'Hold on a sec,' she said, holding up a hand again as she spoke into the radio strapped to her shoulder. 'Resident out here, Sarge, says she needs to get in... OK, yeah, yeah, gotcha.' She looked back at Maddie, or at least where Maddie had been, but Maddie wasn't there.

With the adrenaline already abundant in her veins, Maddie had taken a split-second decision, and while the police officer had turned her head to her radio, she'd nipped around the side of the ambulance. The mention of the word 'sarge', which suggested to Maddie that DS Mitchell might be around, had been the clincher – the sergeant would have ruined her ruse. And now, leaning against the ambulance, catching her breath, she could see what had brought half of St Ives' emergency services all this way to Pendragon Creek.

Maddie felt weak as she saw what had happened and clasped a hand to her mouth. She closed her eyes but the image remained, flashing blue and red behind her eyelids.

Sheila Laverstoke was dead.

And more than that, she was hanging out of a window, her head limp over the sill. The large sash above her had been opened, but it was clear to see what had happened. Her neck must have been crushed by the weight of it. Maddie just hoped, for Sheila's sake, that it had been quick.

Maddie now wished that her curiosity hadn't got the better of her. She felt light-headed, and very, very cold. All she wanted was to go home, but she was sure she'd missed her taxi.

She stumbled away from the B&B, not caring now if anyone saw her. She just had to get back to the Two Pelicans, feel its warmth or see a friendly face.

As she rounded the corner into the lane, she saw the taxi idling outside the pub. Putting on speed and waving, Maddie rushed towards it. Opening one of the doors, she practically threw herself into the back seat, apologising to Mark, and garbling something about the tragedy at the B&B.

And on the journey home, Maddie shut her eyes, desperate still to erase the image of Sheila Laverstoke, dead, and dangling over the front of her own sash windowsill.

'There's been a terrible, terrible accident...' The police officer's words played like a soundtrack in her mind. Because Maddie could only think one thing.

A terrible accident... or was it?

The next morning, Maddie showered and dressed and hurried downstairs, where there was already the smell of baking in the cosy farmhouse kitchen.

Nor was listening to a local radio station, but turned it down when Maddie entered the kitchen.

'Sore head?' Nor chuckled as Maddie slipped into one of the kitchen chairs and cradled her head in her hands.

'No, I'm fine. Gran, have you heard the news?'

'News? Got it on now. Nothing more exciting than the DJ telling us about the Penbeagle Scarecrow Festival. We entered that once, you know. Used all of Aubry's clothes and dressed up this scarecrow in his old plus fours, one of his hats and those socks of his. The amount of people who said "Morning, Aubry" to the scarecrow was quite telling really...'

'No, Gran, not that news. It's Sheila at Seaside View. She died last night.'

'Sheila? Sheila Laverstoke? How?'

'Accident, apparently. Killed by one of those sash windows in the B&B. Fell on her neck.' Maddie shivered and raised a hand to her own neck as she did.

'Oh no, oh poor Sheila. And after she'd spent a small fortune on them too.' Nor shook her head. 'Oh dear me.'

Maddie got up and put the kettle on. As it started to boil, she could feel the thought that had edged itself into the side of her mind start to grow. She tried to clear room for it to spread, but her busy brain made it hard to give it space. Frustrated, she made herself and her gran a cup each of tea and went back to the table. She saw her handbag, which she'd dumped on the kitchen table when she'd got home last night, having fished around in her purse for a fiver for the Taxi King. Poking out of it was Nor's old recipe book.

'That poor old book won't last if you keep carting it about and writing things in it,' Nor tutted as Maddie pulled it out and opened it up.

'But it's exactly what exercise books like this are for, Gran.' Maddie hoped she wasn't pushing her luck. 'Writing in and taking places.'

Nor shook her head, but didn't stop Maddie from finding a pencil and adding some more words to the list she was building next to the flapjack recipe. She carefully wrote *Sheila at Seaside B&B – accident – new sash?* and then closed the book again. That thought would have to simmer and come together in its own time.

'You thinking Sheila's death is linked to Chloe up on the hill?' Nor asked, peering over Maddie's shoulder as she wrote.

'I don't know. But there's something I don't quite buy about Sheila's death being an accident. I can't put my finger on it yet though.' She put her pencil down. 'Oh Gran, it was horrible.'

Nor laid a hand on Maddie's shoulder. 'There, there, ducky. You've had a nasty shock and no doubt not a wink of sleep.' Maddie yawned on cue. 'But the police will look into it. And hopefully keep us posted. Poor Sheila, she was a lovely lady. Best keep ourselves busy though, only way to cope with this sort of thing.'

Maddie, who'd been brought up in a different era to her more stalwart grandmother wondered if maybe there were better, more therapeutic ways of coping with it; but couldn't deny that getting back into the kitchen would help her process her thoughts.

Maddie looked up at Nor. 'OK Gran, what can I do to help?'

'Well, come and measure this flour for me. I can't hold the sieve so well these days.'

Maddie leapt to her side and helped measure flour and sift it into a large ceramic mixing bowl while Nor cut up small chunks of fridge-cold butter.

'Now get your fingers in there and get breadcrumbing.'

'You know there are machines that can do this for you?' Maddie said, while she rolled up her sleeves and started working the mixture with the tips of her fingers.

'Oh, those Mixed Thermals? Can't see the point and it sounds like underwear.' Nor tutted again.

'Not sure that's their name,' Maddie chuckled to herself.

'And no, I didn't mean anything as fancy as a Thermomix. Just a food processor would do it. Couple of blitzes would save your fingers all this.' She held her sticky hands up.

'There you go, you see, I *have* got a processor. You. And look, you're almost there, just a few rubs more. And you'll have done it twice over in the time it would have taken you to get some contraption out of the cupboard. Let alone the washing-up.'

'You know what, Gran, there are machines for that too...' Maddie kept rubbing the butter between her fingertips, and dodged a piece of cheese that Nor flicked at her. It was all light-hearted enough, and a relief compared to the tragedy of the night before, but Maddie did think that Nor's reluctance to move into the modern day might be to do with how she felt about the teashop in general. She pondered this as she bread-crumbed the scone mix. But she was brought back to the here and now by Nor pouring in a cup of sugar to her breadcrumbs, then cracking two eggs into a well she'd made in the middle of the mixture and adding in a splash of milk. She passed her granddaughter an old ivory-handled stainless-steel knife and told her to mix it all, only using her hands again at the very end to bring the dough together.

It was obvious Nor was still on top of the cakes, they were as delicious as ever, and despite Nor's protestations about her ruining her old cook book, Maddie knew she barely needed a recipe to follow. But the building itself... Maddie looked out of the window and saw the peeling paint of the window frames and door. How much prettier would it look with them freshly painted? A new sign outside with specials of the day? She'd noticed a tattoo parlour in St Ives when she'd got off the train. Not that she wanted one, but tattoo artists were just that; artists. She reckoned she could ask one of the talented tattooers to come up with a pretty sign board, full of swirly writing advertising hot soup and a roll, paninis—

'Are you done with that yet? Don't overwork it, else they'll go tough.' Nor looked over Maddie's shoulder. 'And the sultanas are in the pantry. I'll get going on a cheese batch.'

'Righto, Gran,' Maddie said, focusing once again on the scone mixture, and trying not to trip over Toast, who was winding around their legs, in the vain hope of more cheese being dropped from heaven.

A few hours later and Maddie and Nor were busy serving pots of tea and spooning lashings of thick Cornish cream into ramekins – alongside the sloppy strawberry jam – and dishing out cream teas to the hungry walkers who stopped in. The sun had brought them all out – though Maddie was worried that it wasn't just the sunshine that had tempted them out to the footpaths. The headline on the local paper, which Maddie had just seen left on one of the tables by a customer, had splashed the news for all to read:

MYSTERY WOMAN DEAD NEAR PENDRAGON CREEK

Police investigate suspicious death of unnamed woman found under tumbled stones of disused cow shed – everything we know. Go to CornwallNow online for breaking news reports...

Maddie sighed as she read the lurid headline and call for people to go online – it was nothing better than clickbait. But it was interesting that DI Trevelyan hadn't released Chloe's name to the press. And last night's tragedy had been too late to catch the printers; no doubt it would be dominating the online headlines, though.

Maddie had picked up the paper, partly to read but also because she didn't like that headline and the whispered conversations people in the teashop were having because of it. Maddie felt terribly sorry for Chloe Hardy and what had happened to her, but she also didn't want the pretty town of Pendragon Creek, or the glistening Pendragon Bay, or worse, Folly Farm, being a pitstop on some dark tourist trail.

She took the newspaper back to the counter, along with a tray full of empty teacups and plates, and started gently washing them up. She tried to take her mind off the horrid headlines and think about what she could do to make the teashop the best thing about Pendragon Creek, despite what the woman from the council had said. Her mind's eye lit up with fairy lights, paper lanterns and al fresco supper clubs on long, warm summer's evenings. And then autumn and winter feasts in the barn next door and, an idea she was particularly excited by, a Christmas market in the farmyard, with local producers selling cheese, sourdough bread, honey, pies and pastries and, of course, steaming-hot cups of mulled wine.

Maddie's daydream was suddenly and violently shattered. She heard an almighty smash behind her – the shattering of the window; glass, wood and novelty teapots and all. Shards of glass and smashed pottery covered the floor of the teashop. Maddie turned around to see the teashop in chaos – customers pushing their chairs back, clutching their chests, checking on each other. Raised voices and angry words. Somewhere in the melee, she heard her grandmother's voice, but she couldn't make out what she was shouting. *A stick? Someone's sick? What the frick?*

'It was a brick.' Nor's hand, trembling, touched Maddie's shoulder and she looked up at her grandmother, who had turned pale with the shock of it all.

Maddie pulled herself together and stood up, wrapping an arm around Nor's shoulders as she surveyed the scene. The customers who were left looked equally as shocked and scared as Maddie felt. And Nor, though frowning, was also shaking as she pointed to the rough, terracotta house brick that was lying on the floor, only a few feet from where Maddie had been standing.

Maddie looked at it and a shiver raced down her spine.

It wasn't just a brick. Tied to it with rough baling twine was a piece of paper.

No, it wasn't just a brick – it was a message.

21

'Darn it,' Nor said, as her fingers struggled with the tightly knotted string. Maddie winced as she noticed how swollen Nor's knuckles were.

Fetching a pair of scissors from behind the counter, Maddie snipped the string. She let it fall away onto the table, which was already dirty with spilt tea and crumbs, not to mention shards of glass, splintered wood from the window and a cracked porcelain teapot that had once been in the shape of a cottage but had become collateral damage. Maddie ignored all of this for now and opened up the piece of paper.

'What does it say, Mads?' Nor asked, pulling her head back and forth trying to focus on the spidery writing.

Maddie sighed and passed it over to Nor. 'It says, "Stop talking to the police, or else".'

'Oh,' Nor said, taking it from her. 'Not very inventive, is it?'

'No, blunt and to the point.'

'Is it from the murderer, do you think?' Nor looked up at her granddaughter, the question echoed in her eyes. It was echoed around the room too, with the customers who had stayed now quieting their post-shock chatter and listening in at the mention of the M-word.

Maddie took the paper back from Nor and folded it again along the crease. She sharpened the fold with her fingers as she looked out of the window, in the direction that the brick must have come from. Directly in her eyeline was a pristine white BMW. Jason Briggs's car no doubt.

'Maybe, Gran, maybe,' she replied.

Nor followed her gaze and then gripped Maddie's arm with her fingers, her hands suddenly claw-like with their intensity. 'Don't you go interfering there, ducky. It's not worth it. Let's get this cleared up and I'll phone Derek down at the builders' yard and see if he can find us a new window.'

'Gran...' Maddie felt her grandmother's grip release as she turned and started apologising to the customers.

'Tea's on us, ladies and gents, and so sorry about that. Local youths is all. High spirits,' Nor's voice carried over the chatter.

One woman, dressed as if she was on her way to a rock concert rather than a walk in the hills, said, 'Do you think it's about the murder? The one up the hill there?'

'No, no,' reassured Nor. 'Not about that at all. Now I know you'll all want to hasten off and please do shake out your coats before you put them on. Glass gets everywhere, doesn't it?'

Her chattiness was in stark contrast to Maddie's silence. She just stood there, bemused at how Nor could act so cool and calm about it. Jason had just lobbed a brick with a threatening message through their window. And not just threatening in words; a stunt like that threatened livelihoods; lives even. If that brick had hit someone... it didn't bear thinking about. Maddie expected looks of horror and shock on the faces of their customers, and to the greater extent that was what she saw, though by the look of devilish interest in one tourist's face, this couldn't have been a more perfect interruption to her Cornish cream tea. It seemed some people liked a little a bit of drama with their Darjeeling, a crime scene with their clotted cream.

Maddie also wanted to know why Nor was insistent that she didn't go and find Jason in that barn of his and give him a piece of her mind. She was running through some of the tastier things she'd say when a broom handle was thrust into her hand by Nor and she was told to start brushing.

'You know Crumpet will be in here as soon as he gets a whiff of spilt cream, and I haven't got the time or money to be taking him to the vet with a cut paw.'

'Yes Gran, but...' Maddie began sweeping as she tried to phrase it. 'Why did you say that about Jason? Do you think it was him?'

'Never you mind, it's not something I want you involved in.'

That was it. Maddie had to know now why Nor was being cagey about it.

'Oh come on, Gran. I'm not a child. I've lived in London. I've seen a lot of things. I've *heard* a lot of things. Nothing you could say will shock me, or be something I need to be protected from. I'm here to protect you!'

Nor gave a pfft sound as she wiped glass off one of the tables with a thick cloth.

'Fine,' Maddie relented, sweeping glass into the dustpan that Nor had found under the counter. 'I'm not here to protect you, but you know what I mean. I want to help.' Maddie thought for a moment, remembering the questions from the police the other day; and Nor's reticence in answering them. 'And I want to know what's going on with Jason. You've been acting really oddly whenever he's mentioned or he's around.'

Nor finally stood still and let out a short, sharp huff. 'Firstly, no I don't need protecting. Not by my own granddaughter. And secondly, yes, I don't want you going and biting Jason's head off, as he might knock yours right off in reply.'

'Really?' Maddie recoiled, shocked.

'Really. I... I admit I didn't know what a piece of work he was when he first came and asked me about renting the barn, but Clive's son, Hugo, said it was all right—'

'Why run it past him? Why not Dad or Sam?' Maddie asked, assuming her father and brother might have been closer, as relatives, for Nor to bounce ideas off. 'Or even Mum, Daisy, Aunty Rosie, Uncle Dave, Jasper, Lily or me?' Maddie ticked her mother, sister, aunt, uncle and cousins off her fingers.

'Because he's the one that ran it past me. He's a farming equipment broker or something like that. Didn't Clive tell you? And a son of a farmer to boot. Deals in all these fancy machines and tractors and all that.'

'Like the ones Jason has stored in your barn?'

'Exactly. So I wasn't just a silly old woman and I did ask around about whether it was normal for businesses to find storage for their equipment, and Hugo and Clive said yes, and Hugo said Clive only said no because of the cows. But then...' Nor crossed her arms. 'Then Jason started talking money and told me how much he'd pay even though I'd asked for more, and then he insisted it was in cash, and my accountant – you know Mr Barrett down in Pendragon Reach – well, he wasn't pleased with that.'

'I should think not,' Maddie replied, though she was impressed that Nor had even told her accountant. 'How much is he paying you then?'

'Fifty pounds a month,' Nor replied and Maddie almost dropped the broom.

'Only fifty quid a month? That's got to be a two thousand square foot barn, Gran!'

'I know, I know,' Nor batted away her words. 'But at least it doesn't mean that I get in trouble paying too much cash into the bank, you see. Along with the cash I take in from this place, it all blends in.'

'Oh dear,' Maddie sighed, realising that Nor was being

used, not for laundering vast amounts of cash, but as an easy target with which to siphon off a bit. 'You know most London restaurants don't take cash any more for that very reason Gran. Got to keep receipts for everything.'

'I do, I do. Let's not start on that egg chat again though. You might find yourself summoning that woman from the council again, like some sort of evil pixie.' Nor shook her head and Maddie knew her gran was on the edge of having enough of this conversation. She'd turned her back on Maddie and was wiping down more tables and scooping up the broken glass in silence. The mention of the lady from the council, or more specifically what judgements she might make about the teashop if she heard that customers had just been in peril thanks to the farm's other businesses, made Maddie's blood run cold.

It didn't help that she also knew Jason Briggs was up to no good, she was sure of it. No one fleeced an innocent old lady, and no one threw a brick through the window if they weren't really trying to get their message across. And the message had been *don't talk to the police.*

You have to have a pretty good reason – or a pretty bad one – for people not to mention you to the police. Was it just his aggressive business attitude that he didn't want them alerted to, or was Jason Briggs also a murderer? Maddie had found Chloe's backpack in the barn *he* was renting, after all.

The sound of an obnoxiously loud engine caught her attention, the accelerator no doubt being purposefully revved to maximum effect. But by the time Maddie rested the broom against a table and looked out of the window, the white BMW had gone.

22

A few hours later and the teashop looked a bit less ruffled – though the same couldn't be said for Nor and Maddie. Maddie had insisted that Nor phone Derek at the builders' merchants, not so much to get the ball rolling on that, but so that her gran could take the old landline phone with a comedically long coiled cord, and sit down as she spoke to him. Her knee looked swollen and she'd been limping more since the brick came through the window. Meanwhile, Maddie had swept and wiped and done her best to use some brown tape to attach that dratted newspaper and its shock-tactic headline to the remaining glass and wood of the window. It would be no good at all if birds or bats decided the teashop would make a cosy nest for the night. And after that, while Nor waited on hold and then spoke to Derek, Maddie sat down at one of the newly cleaned tables and took out the battered old recipe book. It fell open at the flapjack page and Maddie quickly noted all the words that she'd already added in among the grams of oats and dried fruit quantities.

Clive Pendergast – Hill Top Farm – 'of all people'
Old cow shed – fallen stones

Last words – aren't you rock would tree help
Bloodied stone = murder
1965 – missing woman SAME PLACE *Esther Pendergast*
Clotted cream?
Litter
Planning – houses at Hill Top
HER backpack – OUR barn. Jason?!
C&K – lovers' tiff? Him more than her
Entitled
Archer
Sheila at Seaside B&B – accident – new sash?

She added: *Brick – warning* and almost stubbed out the pencil as she realised how intensely she was holding it.

The words barely made sense to her, yet eggs were nothing like flour, and neither of those was anything like butter, and yet they mixed together well to form the basis of so many recipes. There would be something that linked these words. Something that bound them together.

Don't get me started on the eggs again... Nor's words rattled around Maddie's brain and she almost snapped the recipe book closed. But her eye lingered on the name Archer and she remembered that Roger at the Two Pelicans had said he'd be in the pub that night, mentioning a darts match or similar. Could delving into why Chloe had been talking to him help eke out some more information for the police, hopefully speeding up closing this case and stopping these lurid headlines? Customers were all well and good, and any customer coming to the teashop for any reason was possibly a good customer. All the same, she didn't want Folly Farm, Hill Top Farm and Pendragon Bay to become a stop on a grisly murder tour; and these headlines and the mystery surrounding the case was making that happen.

Nor put the phone down and Maddie closed the book.

'He'll come himself with Tony from the glaziers in Portreath to fix it tomorrow,' Nor said, a note of triumph in her voice. 'And he'll take cash.'

Maddie had held back from lecturing her gran again on accounts, HMRC and the law, and had instead smiled and hugged her and suggested they go back to the farmhouse for their own tea. After fresh eggs had been boiled to soft, oozing perfection and slices of toast had been buttered and cut into 'soldiers', they both tucked in. Maddie wanted to ask more about Jason, but she also didn't want to upset Nor further on what was already a stressful day. Instead she broached the idea of going to the pub.

'Fancy a drink? I owe you from last night anyway, Gran,' Maddie asked. 'And Roger might sneak you an extra shot of gin if you're lucky.' She winked at her gran, who chuckled.

'That man might have good legs and be an incorrigible flirt, but the one thing he wouldn't do is give away a free drink. Tight as a duck's whatnot he is. Still, keeping an eye on the pennies is why the Two Pelicans is the only pub left. Did you know that when your grandad and I were young there were five pubs in Pendragon Creek?'

'Really?' Maddie was shocked. 'Where? And how could such a small town have enough business for five?'

'Not much else to do back then,' Nor said. 'No Netflix and thrills, or whatever it is you young people do. Lot of locals lost their shirts when some of the pubs folded though, as they'd had houses mortgaged on the wages they'd earned. The Fisherman's Friend went first back in the seventies, then the Smuggler's Arms and the Red Lion in the eighties. The Hope and Anchor, which was down by the harbour, that lasted until the nineties, and now it's just Roger and the Two Pelicans.'

'You'd have thought the amount of tourists here would have kept another pub afloat,' Maddie said, remembering how busy the town and harbour could get in high summer, especially around the midsummer festival, the regatta in August and the endless long summer days of school holidays.

'Needs more than a few weeks of sunshine in the summer to keep a pub going all year round. Different for teashops like us, we can just make cakes and buy teabags—'

'Yes, about that...' Maddie started, but stopped. Nor had a glazed look to her eyes and Maddie could see that she was tired. She started clearing up the empty egg shells and plates and dusted the table of crumbs. Nor took herself off to the comfy sofa and switched the TV on. Within moments, Crumpet and Toast had found their way onto her lap and across her shoulders and Maddie could see that she was set for the night. But with the sun still high enough in the sky for her to make the walk into town easy enough, she said goodbye and headed down to see if she could catch Archer in the Two Pelicans.

The familiar smell and sounds of a pub greeted Maddie when she pushed open the weighted swing door of the Two Pelicans. She could be in London, Liverpool or Llandudno; the patterned carpet, the trill of the fruit machine, the chatter of local voices, the smell of beer and chips and decor that wasn't so much dated as timeless. She'd heard that pub carpets were patterned so that spills didn't show up, but it always made her wonder why they had carpets at all? And indeed the Two Pelicans had some lovely original flagstones in the room just to the right of the bar where the ceiling lowered further and was made even more dangerous for anyone over five foot six by the deep beams that ran along it. Maddie looked and there was no dartboard in that side of the pub, so the one Roger must have meant that Archer would be playing at was the one in the furthest room, which also had a pool table. Maddie walked around to it, and sighed when she saw no one standing at the oche, no one even polishing a cue with the blue chalk and playing pool. She turned back to the bar and that's when she saw a familiar face. DI Trevelyan.

'Hi, Tom,' Maddie said, perching on the stool next to him.

He looked up and slopped his pint a bit when he saw who had addressed him. But it was only a moment before he said hello too.

'And what brings you down here?'

'I've left Gran on season two of *Bridgerton*, covered in cats. To be fair, I have thirty-year-old friends who would deem that, quite literally, the most perfect night in.' Maddie laughed and then said hello to Roger and ordered a gin and tonic.

'I'll get that,' Tom gestured to Roger.

'Thanks.' Maddie was going to protest, but actually she liked the fact that he'd just bought her a drink. She let that feeling sit there for a little while as they both sat in silence, not awkwardly exactly, but tentatively, until Roger placed her drink in front of her. 'How's it all going?' Maddie asked, hoping it would help herd the elephant out of the room.

'OK, OK.'

'So OK that you're in here nursing a pint?' Maddie said, pointing to the glass in front of him. He looked dejected. 'Sorry, I shouldn't make light of it. We had customers in today who I'm sure only came in thanks to CornwallNow and the newspaper headlines. And it can't help with Sheila's death adding to your workload too. I just want this cleared up so Gran's teashop can go back to normal, though, in some ways, normal was a bit depressing too.'

'Has she been struggling? Financially, I mean?' Tom asked and Maddie shrugged.

'She's in her eighties, Tom. I feel bad that all these years we've all just taken her for granted, and headed down here expecting her to host us for Christmases, summers and Easters. And thinking that the teashop would be preserved in aspic, you know, the same as it always was. But she's getting older. So yeah, I just wish this whole thing would be cleared up, justice done and all that, but also that Folly Farm could stop being the centre of all this macabre attention.'

Tom nodded thoughtfully. 'You and the whole community. I've had the chief on the phone. Truro's not pleased with our progress so far, even with the backpack you found.'

'I think that might have got me into trouble,' Maddie said then sipped her drink.

'Why? You handed it over to us. You're not in trouble with the law.'

'No, rather someone who's taking "the law" into his own hands. Jason Briggs sent us a rather brick-through-window-shaped message today and told me not to speak to you anymore.' Maddie thought for a second, then leant back on her bar stool to check there was no sign of Jason in the pub. Speaking to the police was one thing, being seen hobnobbing with the DI over a G&T was another, and she didn't want any more house bricks through any more windows.

'He what?'

Maddie turned back to look at Tom and was surprised to see how angry he looked.

'He hurled a brick through the teashop window. Pretty sure it was him. His car was parked right outside and he's a nasty piece of work. Got Gran to agree to some paltry rent for the barn and I'm sure he's up to no good. Pays cash too,' Maddie said, then regretted it. She didn't want to get Nor into trouble with the police.

But Tom's face was still clenched into a frown. 'Why didn't you say something? Call me? Us, I mean, the police?'

'It was just a brick,' Maddie said, though she analysed a

little in her mind why she hadn't thought to call Tom straight away. 'I was going to, but I needed to get Gran settled first, give her a bite to eat and make sure she was all right. Then I needed a drink. Long day.' She rolled her eyes. 'Gran phoned Derek at the builders' yard, they're going to fix the window tomorrow.'

'Have you got the note?' Tom asked and Maddie nodded. She reached into her bag and pulled out the recipe book.

'I slipped it in here.' She opened the book at the flapjack recipe and handed over the folded paper with the threatening note on it.

Tom took it and flipped it open and grunted. Then he looked at the open page. Maddie noticed his eye scanning her own list of 'ingredients' and quickly closed the book and rested her hand on it.

'Look, Tom, I know Kieran is probably chief suspect, but I was wondering if this doesn't hint that Jason might be the murderer. I found the backpack in his barn, he's obviously violent, I don't know where he's from, but maybe he knew Chloe, so maybe there's some background we – you – can look into.'

'Why didn't you phone me then, straight away, when you started suspecting him?' Tom's question was a good one and again Maddie shrugged.

'I don't know. Well, I do know, I suppose Gran said that I shouldn't make a fuss—'

'So your gran told you not to interfere?' Tom asked.

'Yes, for my own safety. Said Jason would knock my block off. Which just shows how dangerous he is, don't you agree?'

'Yes,' Tom said, then a moment later added, 'You had Sheila Laverstoke's name in your book too, why was that?'

Maddie stared into her G&T, the image of Sheila invading her mind's eye again. She pinched the top of her nose and closed her eyes, then, with a sigh, turned back to Tom. 'I saw what happened last night. Not the death itself,' she added hastily, 'but I was here in the pub and then when I left, I saw the lights and ambulance and all that, so I had to look. Tom, it was...'

Tom moved as if he was about to comfort her with a hand on her arm, but instead he gripped his pint tightly. 'I saw it too,' he said quietly. 'Poor woman.'

Maddie looked at him. Would he believe her when she said she thought it might be more than an accident? 'Tom, there's another thing. I don't know why, and heaven knows I have no proof of this, but it feels like it might not have been an accident.'

'Why do you say that?' Tom asked.

'The constable on the scene – who I should apologise to for lying to, but that's a different story...' Tom raised his eyebrows, but Maddie quickly carried on. 'She said it was a terrible accident, and it looked like it could be, but earlier that evening I'd met Sheila and she didn't seem the type to accidentally let a sash window fall on her.'

'That's accidents for you, you don't expect them,' Tom theorised.

Maddie shook her head. 'I know, but... then something Gran said later. Sheila had just spent money having those sashes renovated. A newly fixed sash shouldn't fall on you, not when the weights and ropes are all balanced.'

Tom was silent in thought. Maddie wondered if he was working out a way to extricate himself from this interfering busybody she realised she was turning into, but before he could answer her, the door to the pub swung open and, to Maddie's disappointment, DS Mitchell walked in.

'Evening, boss,' she said, then cast an eye over Maddie. 'Miss Penrose.'

Maddie nodded to her, though she could feel that elephant come charging back into the room as soon as the sergeant did.

'Ready?' said Tom to his sergeant.

'Ready, boss,' she replied. Then, in a low voice, she added, 'It's on.'

Tom nodded, knocked back the rest of his pint and gave Maddie a really strange look.

'Bye then,' Maddie said, filling the silence.

'Bye, Maddie,' Tom Trevelyan said. Then added, 'And sorry about this.'

23

Maddie twisted around on her bar stool and took another sip from her drink. From her position this side of the bar, she could see that someone was now in the back room near the dartboard. Archer perhaps. She took the old recipe book off the bar and put it in her bag, wondering how much Tom had seen of the 'ingredients' she'd been writing down. He'd noticed Sheila's name obviously, and they'd discussed Jason Briggs too. What might he have made of her notes about Clive and tumble though? And while her mind was on DI Trevelyan, she thought about what he meant by 'sorry about this'. Obviously it was slightly rude that he'd been called away, but not especially. They hadn't arranged to meet up after all, and she'd just come across him. He'd more than likely arranged to meet DS Mitchell; so why apologise to Maddie?

She shook the thoughts away, picked up her G&T and took a confidence-building swig as she walked into the back room.

A young man had taken up position by the dartboard, his feet lined up on the oche and his right hand held near his ear, a dart positioned ready to be thrown. If Roger was right, this was

Archer. Possibly one of the last people to speak to Chloe before she was killed.

'Hey,' Maddie said, trying to sound as cool and nonchalant as possible. 'Fancy a game?'

The young guy, who'd just hit a triple twenty, slowly turned to her, looked her up and down, and then said, 'Ten quid buy-in.'

'Oh,' Maddie's nonchalance was gone. 'Afraid Roger's taken my last note.'

There was a bit of tension in the air, then, luckily for Maddie, the young man relented and smirked. 'Don't worry. Thought you were a rich down-from-towner, but if you're on first-name terms with Roger the dodger over there' – he pointed to the bar – 'then I guess you're not.'

'Well, sort of. You might know my gran, Nor Penrose? From the teashop at Folly Farm. I've moved in for a bit to help her out.' Maddie took the opportunity to look this guy – Archer, she presumed – up and down, as he had her, as she spoke. He was wearing jeans and a heavy metal band T-shirt and his hair was slightly greasy and long. Maddie thought him to be a few years younger than her, but not much. What looked like a long black coat was slung over the chair closest to the dartboard and a smart phone was lying on the table next to a pint of Coke, its screen constantly lighting up as notifications flashed up on the home screen. A tatty ex-Army-style canvas bag was slung over the chair too, frayed and holey in places. Maddie furrowed her brow as she recognised the same red-edged style letter jutting out of it that she'd seen on her gran's hall table. An unpaid bill. Or two or three, by the looks of it.

She quickly drew her eyes back to his. He was the same guy at the fruit machine the night before, she was sure of it. Though he looked more familiar than that and she was annoyed that she couldn't place why.

'Oh yeah?' He reached over for his drink. 'So you are a down-from-towner then?'

'I suppose so, though I've got Cornish blood.' Maddie hoped this was enough to break down whatever barrier Archer had perceived there to be. Introducing herself properly might help. 'I'm Maddie, by the way.'

'Archer.'

'Cool name.' *Cripes, could I be any more awkward?*

'Yeah. So, darts?'

'Sure, I really haven't got any cash on me, though.'

Archer shrugged and handed over three darts to her.

'Do you coach people?'

'Nah, I just enter local leagues. Roger doesn't mind me practising here; there's not much room for a dartboard at home.'

'Do you live in Pendragon Creek?'

'Yeah, in one of the new-builds by the petrol station.'

Maddie threw her first dart, managing by some fluke to hit a double fifteen. They played a little and then Maddie brought up the subject of the murder.

'Did you hear about the girl up by the old cow shed? Happened a few days after I got here.'

Archer smirked again. 'Was it you then?'

'Ha,' Maddie was caught off guard, 'no. I was too busy trying not to burn the teashop down and find enough slices of cake for the punters.' She glanced over and could see Archer nodding. 'But it's really sad.'

'Have the police worked out who she was yet?'

'Yeah, they used facial recognition and reverse Google searching. From the phone they found,' Maddie hoped she disguised the self-satisfaction in her voice as she recounted how *she'd* worked out Chloe's ID.

'They found a phone?' He shot a dart straight at the board. 'That wasn't on the front page this morning.'

Maddie couldn't help herself. 'Actually I did.'

'You did?' Archer turned to her, obviously interested.

Maddie regretted letting him in so much. But he was looking at her quite intensely. 'I found the backpack, in one of Gran's sheds.'

'Wow, check you out, amateur sleuth.' Archer turned back from her and threw another dart.

'She was called Chloe Hardy.' Maddie hoped she'd done the right thing in telling him, even though he hadn't asked. 'Apparently what the police don't know is why she was here, or what's happened to her boyfriend.' She moved over to the oche and threw another dart, and frowned as it bounced off the rim of the board and fell to the floor.

Archer stayed quiet, but took his position and threw a neat dart bang in the middle of the board. Just before he threw his second dart, he replied to Maddie, never once taking his eye off the target.

'Funny thing is, I know exactly who she was and exactly why she was here.'

Bullseye, Maddie thought to herself, excusing her own pun.

'You do? So you know who she was? Why didn't you say?'

Archer shrugged. 'I didn't know that the girl I spoke to, and met here, was the one who had died, did I?'

'Oh, I see. I'm sorry,' Maddie said.

Archer shrugged again.

'Will you speak to the police then now?'

Archer threw another dart at the board.

'I think you should. This could be a big breakthrough for them.' She paused. 'What was it then? Why was she here?' Maddie asked, silently thanking Roger for his 100 per cent accurate intel on who Chloe had been speaking to on the phone.

Archer held his dart still and then aimed it perfectly into the triple twenty on the board. His smooth action, his deftness with the dart, suddenly made Maddie's spine shiver. She followed up her question with another one before he could answer her.

'Did you know her then? Look, Archer, I'm so sorry. I didn't realise she was a friend of yours, else I would never have started talking about her.' A little white lie, but she didn't want Archer thinking she was nosing around.

'Kind of,' Archer shrugged as he went up to the board to collect his darts. 'I'd met her online. She was interested in this part of the world and I said I could help her out.'

'How did you meet her? Social media?'

'Yeah, in a way. A forum. She was asking for help tracking down family members and I do a bit of online investigating and that. Know my way around an archive and how to access some data that others, well, you know... can't. Not sure I should tell the police that bit. Kinda why I've stayed quiet.'

Maddie nodded as it clicked. Archer hadn't gone to the police as whatever he did online probably wasn't exactly legal. Or ethical. But, boy, did that make Maddie even more interested in what he had to say.

'But you can tell me, what is it? What did she ask you to help with?'

'She wanted to find some long-lost family. It was a genealogy forum that we met on, you know one of those ones where you reach out for help with ancestry questions. Like I say, I'm in quite high demand 'cos of my skills in the area and when she asked if anyone knew how to research family in Pendragon Creek, it set an alert off – I have software that tracks things like that. So I answered her and before I knew it, she was here, which wasn't the plan.'

'What was the plan?' Maddie asked, wishing she could get her recipe book and jot all this down. She'd have to try really hard later to remember everything Archer was saying.

'Just that I would do some digging and send her what I found out. Then she could do what she wanted with the info, but then next thing I know, she's calling saying she's here with that boyfriend of hers and staying in Pendragon Creek and wanted to meet up to discuss the findings.'

'And did you?'

'Yeah.' Archer crossed his arms. 'You gonna throw or not?'

'Um, yeah, right, sorry.' Maddie quickly chucked a dart at the board, and grimaced as it pinged off the edge again. She looked at Archer instead. 'So, you did send her something? What had you found out? What were her plans?'

'I don't know why she wanted to meet. She was making a real song and dance about it all, and that bloke of hers looked massively unimpressed. Jealous, you know? I didn't like him. Anyway, she was excited about what I'd found and wanted to meet who I told her she was related to,' Archer said, matter-of-factly.

'Oh yes, and who was that?' Maddie tried to look and act nonchalantly, but as she threw a dart, Archer replied and her arrow not only missed the board, but almost took the eye out of the stuffed pelican that was decorating a shelf in the corner of the room. Maddie turned to Archer, not quite able to believe her ears the first time. 'Say that again? Who was she related to?'

'Clive Pendergast.'

24

'So, let me get this straight,' Maddie began. 'Clive Pendergast is the reason Chloe was here, in Pendragon Creek?'

'Yeah, I guess so. Chloe wanted help researching her aunt or something and Clive came up as basically next of kin.'

'Clive, who was the one who discovered her as she...' Maddie trailed off. She wasn't quite ready to share all the details with Archer. She glanced back towards the bar in the vain hope that DI Trevelyan might reappear there, but, of course, he and DS Mitchell had left a while ago with that cryptic sort of apology.

Archer was reaching for his coat when she turned back.

'Are you leaving?' Maddie asked the obvious, though she had umpteen more important questions she wanted to ask, such as how Chloe and Clive were related, how long Archer had been helping them, what he knew about Kieran the boyfriend, why he didn't like him and what he thought Chloe was talking about when it came to woods or trees.

'Yeah, there's a livestream I need to tune into,' was all he said as he downed the rest of his cola and grabbed his bag. A pen dropped out of a hole in the corner of it and he stooped to pick it up. Then, just before he left, he said, 'Any sign of her boyfriend?'

'No,' Maddie said, honestly. She wasn't sure how much she should let Archer know about how closely she was monitoring the investigation, but she couldn't see the harm in relaying what she'd learned from poor Sheila at the B&B. 'Apparently he left in an angry mood. Bag over shoulder, no taxi called, disappeared up the street. The police are looking for him.'

'Good. Didn't like him,' Archer said, that matter of fact tone to his voice again.

'Why not?' Maddie asked, genuinely intrigued.

Archer shrugged. 'Jock type. You know the sort. My money's on him.'

Maddie nodded, but she wanted more clarification than that. Why had Archer thought he was jealous? What of? Or who of? However, Archer looked at his watch and left. She picked up her own glass and took it back to the bar. With a nod to Roger, who gave her a friendly wave back, she left the Two Pelicans. She didn't have another fiver in her purse to give the Taxi King, and suspected she might not be his favourite customer after last night's dramas. In any case, the moon was now high and bright in the sky, and its refection off the water in the harbour and bay helped light her way.

She walked in the direction of Pendragon Bay from the town centre, noting Julia and Marge's shops on Fore Street, one selling interiors bits and bobs and ladies' clothing, the other a nice deli. She climbed the road as it went from being wide and pavemented to more of a pathway. The shops had given way to quaint cottages, some of them no doubt holiday lets. Finally, she was out of town and climbing the more rugged path that led up to the top of the cliffs.

Maddie took a deep breath. She knew this path so well, she reckoned she could walk it even if thick clouds covered the sky, but tonight it was stunningly beautiful, with the pale silvery light of the moon shimmering over the sea and long grasses. She looked out to Pendragon Bay, and with it being low tide, she could see the rocks that looked like a dragon with its tail; like those photos of the Loch Ness monster. One bump, two bumps and then smaller rocks in a line that resembled a dragon asleep in the shallow water. Maddie paused to take it all in. And she thought a little about what Archer had said.

Clive Pendergast hadn't said anything to her when he stumbled into the teashop two days ago, covered in Chloe's, and his own, blood, about knowing her; and more, being related to her. *Did he know? Could he have been hiding that knowledge as he'd bludgeoned her*— Maddie had to stop herself from thinking the worst about her gran's neighbour. Jason Briggs, though – she'd happily think the worst about him. He was a nasty piece of work, but was he a murderer? She'd found Chloe's backpack with her phone and journal in amongst his farming equipment. Had he stashed them there, thinking he could dispose of it all later once the police had gone? There'd been no wallet, no ID, but then Sheila had said neither of them had had a car, so perhaps she didn't have a driving licence, and who needs a wallet when your life can be on your phone? She didn't think he'd noticed her taking the backpack, but perhaps he had? Hence the brick and the warning...

Maddie shivered slightly as a breeze came up from the sea and reminded her that it was early in the year and, despite the warm spring weather, there was still a chill in the air. She wondered where Kieran was, having run off with his bag slung over his shoulder as soon as his girlfriend was murdered. DI Trevelyan must be on his tail. Perhaps that was the reason for DS Mitchell's interruption earlier – 'It's on,' she'd said. Maybe that was the hunt for Kieran. He and Chloe had had a fight, Sheila had heard it, and he'd stormed off. And not long after, Chloe was murdered. He had to be a suspect, too. Archer had said he looked jealous and was one of those jock types – pumped up on testosterone and primed for murder?

And Archer... he was an odd one, with his long black leather coat that was more ghoulish goth than coastal chic. Not that she minded that, there were already too many men around here who thought deck shoes and a gilet made you God's gift, but it marked Archer out as different. Non-conformist. And he did look familiar. But not in an old friend, I've-seen-you-around-since-forever familiar. Something nudged the sides of her brain. She'd seen him recently in some other context, she thought. London perhaps?

Maddie turned her face away from the ocean and its glistening waters and followed the chalk path, which practically glowed in the moonlight, across the top of the cliffs and along the fields towards Folly Farm. Her mind wandered away from the murder and more towards the teashop – the whole farm, in fact – and whether perhaps moonlit suppers or evening folk nights might be doable, with tiki torches lighting the way for the townsfolk to find their way to the farm. All you'd need was a few before the floodlights of the farm guided you down, their bright white and blue lights...

Hang on, thought Maddie, *blue lights?*

Maddie blinked in shock. Where the farm was, all she could see was flashing blue lights, and that could only mean one thing. The emergency services. The image of Sheila hanging out of the B&B window flashed across her mind. Had Nor had an accident? A stroke? A fall? Something worse... The possibilities ran through Maddie's head faster than she could run. Hours spent standing over stoves and working twelve-hour shifts on her feet had given her quite some stamina and she pushed through the shock and her racing heart, keeping her pace up until she reached the gate. She swung it open and left it that way, hoping that the chickens were all roosting and the horses were well stabled and wouldn't escape. If an ambulance needed to speed away quickly, she wanted no obstacles in its path to slow it down. Catching her breath as she rounded the corner of the barns, she prepared herself for what might have happened and what she might have to do to help Nor recover.

What she wasn't prepared for was what she saw next. The blue lights were still flashing, silently and without sirens, and they *were* the emergency services. But it wasn't an ambulance. The lights were atop a police car and Maddie gasped as she saw the familiar face of DS Mitchell putting handcuffs on someone.

Not just someone, though. Her own grandmother; Nor Penrose.

25

'Gran! GRAN!' Maddie yelled as she pelted across the yard. 'What's happening? What on earth are you doing?' She directed this last question to DS Mitchell, who had started to read Nor her rights. 'Gran...' Maddie's voice wavered, but DS Mitchell was relentless and Nor seemed speechless.

'... Do you understand?' DS Mitchell finished and Maddie watched as Nor just nodded.

'DS Mitchell, please, what's this all about?' Maddie reached over to touch the policewoman's arm, but was reprimanded immediately.

'Miss Penrose, don't—'

'Maddie,' another authoritative voice sounded and Maddie, who felt like she'd just been scorched, turned to face it. DI Trevelyan was coming out of the front door of the farmhouse, a plastic evidence bag in his hand.

'What's happening, Tom? We were just in the pub, and now this? What's Gran done? She can't have done anything, she's eighty-two, for heaven's sake! What's this all about?'

'It's OK, Maddie,' DI Trevelyan stepped closer, but Maddie

stepped back, and although she'd learned not to touch DS Mitchell, she stood protectively next to Nor, who had at least been allowed to put her Barbour wax jacket on before being handcuffed. She'd also managed to turn her collar up, and position her neckerchief in such a way that she looked like the most chic eighty-two-year-old farmer ever arrested, but the metal bracelets looked painfully heavy around Nor's slim wrists, and so utterly out of place and unnecessary.

'It's not OK. You've just arrested my grandmother. What's happening?' She hissed in fury at DI Trevelyan, asking the question for what seemed like the umpteenth time.

'We've arrested Mrs Penrose for handling stolen goods, failing to disclose knowledge or suspicion of money laundering and participating in fraudulent business carried on by a sole trader.'

'Gran? Gran hasn't done any of those things, let alone all of them. I don't think she'd even understand half of what you've said.' Maddie looked at her small, bird-like grandmother. She looked pale and Maddie hoped it was just the moonlight and the eerie glow of the blue lights. But Nor stayed silent, save for furrowing her brow at Maddie's insinuation that she wouldn't understand what was going on.

'We have links to Jason Briggs...' DI Trevelyan stopped, having received a pointed look from DS Mitchell.

'Is that your evidence there?' Maddie pointed to the plastic bag in DI Trevelyan's hand, which contained an eye-catchingly pink fifty-pound note. 'That looks more like you're nicking my gran's money.'

DI Trevelyan, receiving another cautionary glance from DS Mitchell, replied, 'Look, follow us down to the station and we can talk about it there.'

. . .

The farmyard had seemed impossibly quiet as Maddie had left it. She'd made sure the door to the house was locked, the gate was firmly closed behind her and that she could remember how to drive her gran's temperamental Morris Minor, which had more character in its clutch than some of the men she'd dated in London. One gin and tonic over an hour ago, though not ideal, didn't put her over the limit, so she'd driven to the central police station in St Ives about twenty minutes away. Luckily, she'd arrived just as they were processing Nor's arrest, so, in lieu of legal support, Maddie was able to sit in with her. During a quiet moment, when they were left alone, Nor explained what had happened.

'One moment I was watching that nice duke and that nice girl whose mum used to be in *Coronation Street*, cats on my lap, and then suddenly there was a hammering at the door and blue lights everywhere.'

'I'm so sorry I wasn't there with you, Gran.' Maddie reached over and held Nor's hand as it lay on the table. Nor squeezed her back.

'Not much you could have done, ducky. Next thing I know, that detective sergeant, whose mother'll hear about this, I can tell you, had started accusing me of aiding and abetting Jason, and saying all his equipment was stolen from farms down on the Lizard, and my barn was a holding spot before they went up north to auctions. Said the fact I'd taken cash and not turned Jason in when he'd been threatening to us made them suspect I know more about it that I was letting on.'

Maddie let out a long breath. 'I can't believe they'd think that of you, Gran!'

'Must say, there was a little part of me rather pleased they did,' Nor smiled.

'Gran!' Maddie took her hand off her grandmother's and turned in her chair to look at her.

'Oh, you know what I mean. Life in the old hen yet. And I didn't appreciate you telling them I was as thick as clotted cream and wouldn't understand anything. I know exactly what those charges mean. I've watched every series of *Law & Order*, you know.'

'Sorry, Gran, I... I just hated seeing you in cuffs and being treated like that.'

'I know you didn't mean it, ducky, but remember. I'm old, not stupid.'

Maddie felt awful. She hated being patronised – and she had been many, many times by ego-puffed chefs over the years – and was distraught she'd just done the same to her gran. Realising that the best way to get back on an even keel was to ask Nor about what she knew, Maddie was just going to quiz her more about Jason and ask if she'd seen him since brick-gate when the interview room door opened and DI Trevelyan and DS Mitchell walked in.

'Mrs Penrose, Miss Penrose,' DI Trevelyan said, formally. 'Are you ready for us to start our interview?'

Nor nodded and Maddie just sat there, staring daggers into DI Trevelyan's eyes. So this had been the thing he'd been 'sorry' about. The operation that DS Mitchell had called him away for. He'd literally bought her a drink and then left her in the pub while he went off to arrest her gran. Her thoughts were boiling up so much that she let all of that spew out in words about thirteen to the dozen, much to the shock of everyone else in the room.

'How dare you arrest my grandmother, and while she was alone in the house – well, with the cats, but you can't count the cats in this instance, even though they are important and not just farm cats... But, anyway, it's just ridiculous to pluck an elderly woman from her home late at night – what couldn't have waited until tomorrow morning, eh? And another thing, if you think Gran has anything to do with Jason other than innocently renting him a barn, at admittedly below market rate, but she's nice like that, then you've got another think coming and you should really be out there catching him, not ruining Gran's evening.'

'I haven't even turned the tape recorder on yet, Maddie,' DI Trevelyan said.

'It's *Miss Penrose*, if you don't mind,' Maddie told him, folding her arms across her chest. 'And as we're now on record,' she said as the detective pressed the button and they waited for the long beep, 'I'd like some answers from you.'

'That's not how this works,' DS Mitchell said, opening a folder of papers in front of her.

'I think you owe Gran here an explanation of why she's been arrested and hauled in here,' Maddie demanded.

'Well, that we can do,' DI Trevelyan said before DS Mitchell could open her mouth. 'We've been tailing Jason Briggs for a little while—'

'So you know he's a wrong'un?' Maddie said, exasperated.

'We call it "little fishing",' Trevelyan explained. 'Following the little fish until he follows us to the big fish.' He looked at Nor, which Maddie noticed.

'Oh, come on,' her exasperation increased. 'Do you really think my eighty-two-year-old grandmother is some kingpin to a crime organisation?'

Nor raised an eyebrow, but stayed silent.

'No, but we have to ask her a few questions,' DI Trevelyan continued. 'Why did Jason Briggs choose Folly Farm? How much did Mrs Penrose know about the contents of the sheds? Why did she accept cash payments—' He pushed the evidence bag with the fifty-pound note in it across the table.

'I was scared.' It was the first time Nor had spoken and DI Trevelyan and DS Mitchell both shifted in their seats, and looked at her. Maddie turned to face her gran too and listened.

'I've never come across a lad like him, all puffed up and very direct. He drove that big white car of his into the yard like he already owned the place—'

'When was this?' DS Mitchell interrupted.

Nor shrugged. 'Four, five months ago. But he didn't start renting the barns until I'd made some enquiries. References and that.'

Maddie nudged Nor. 'You said Hugo Pendergast had suggested it—'

'Let your grandmother answer for herself please, Miss Penrose,' DS Mitchell warned and Nor carried on.

'Maddie's right. It was the only reason I didn't send him off with a flea in his ear when he first arrived. And Jason gave me references too. Although one of the numbers I tried to contact rang out, the other was answered by a young lady. She said Jason was a nice man, good payer. And Hugo, who's my neighbour Clive's son, assured me it was all above board and storage spaces like my barns were something brokers needed. He said it was perfectly normal for businesses to need space in a hurry when equipment came in and the trade in used farming equipment was booming, what with the new ones being so expensive. And that makes sense. Have you seen the cost of a new tractor? Even Lamborghini make them these days! Bonkers.'

'Did you know that the equipment you had in your barns was mostly new? And all stolen?' DS Mitchell pressed further.

'No... no, I didn't. The stolen bit at least. They did look nice and shiny though.' Nor frowned and muttered, 'Should have guessed.'

'And you then set up a payment plan with Briggs? Cash? Nice and untraceable, isn't it?' DS Mitchell didn't let up.

'Well, it doesn't bounce like a cheque and you can't get to a bank these days anyway. And he didn't want the hassle of setting up a standing order, he said. So he offered cash and I said yes as by then I was worried I'd started wasting his time.'

'Why do you say that?' Trevelyan asked, more gently than his sergeant was prone to.

'Well, he told me,' Nor said, sitting back and crossing her arms. 'Said, "Look, are you wasting my time" and that sort of thing. All very menacing.'

Maddie's hands balled into fists in her lap, her fingernails digging deep into her palms. She hated hearing that.

'But you still let him move into your barn?' DI Trevelyan pressed.

'Yes,' Nor said, quieter now. 'What choice did I have? He was very persuasive.' She rubbed the tops of her arms, thin in their Liberty print blouse.

'Did he hurt you?' DS Mitchell asked.

'No, but... well, he wasn't a nice man. I see that now.'

'And he hurled a brick through the teashop window,' Maddie added. 'I'm sure we could get prints—' She stopped as DS Mitchell snorted.

'Bricks are notoriously hard to get prints from,' clarified DI Trevelyan. 'Too rough.'

'Like that Jason himself,' added Nor. She turned to Maddie. 'I'm sorry, ducky. When I said earlier that I was old but not stupid, well I have been a bit of a fool. I should have spoken to your dad, or had the nous to shoo him off before he got a toe in the door. I should have told him to bug—'

'For the benefit of the tape,' said DI Trevelyan, his finger hovering over the record button, 'the police in charge agree with Mrs Penrose. This sounds more like a case of cuckooing than little fishing. Interview terminated, ten forty-three p.m., Monday twentieth April.'

'Tom, are you sure?' DS Mitchell asked, after the recorder had bleeped. 'We had—'

'Nothing,' DI Trevelyan replied. Then he gestured his arm towards the door. DS Mitchell gathered the files up and with a shake of her head, left the interview room.

Maddie helped her grandmother with her coat and said, in a lowered voice, 'And what will you say if someone like Jason ever comes calling again?'

Nor slipped her arms into her wax jacket and then said emphatically, 'Bugger off.'

26

Despite his termination of the interview, Maddie was almost too cross with DI Trevelyan to speak to him. But the thought of the murder was still playing on her mind, not to mention the questions she held over Sheila's death. Plus, her recent chat with Archer had revealed a few more things that she knew the police should be told. So, despite her inner child wanting to just slam the doors shut on the old Morris Minor and drive off with a wheel spin – if that were possible in such a low-powered car with such a temperamental clutch – she turned on the steps of the police station and asked Nor to wait for her in the car.

'Only because I don't much fancy going back in there,' Nor said, taking the keys. 'Never thought I'd see the day that I was arrested. What will Marge and Julia say?'

'They never have to know if you don't want them to,' Maddie said reassuringly.

'Oh, they'll know, believe you me. It'll be round the town faster than a yacht on regatta day.'

Maddie shrugged at her gran, gave her another hug in solidarity and stepped back into the police station. Luckily, DI

Trevelyan was still at the front desk signing paperwork. She 'ahemmed' loudly in his direction.

'Miss Penrose,' he said once he'd turned around. 'Maddie.'

'Miss Penrose is fine. For now,' Maddie replied, though she caught herself adding the 'for now' bit and blushed. Recovering as quickly as she could, she beckoned DI Trevelyan over to where some plastic seats formed a waiting area in the reception space. No one else was there and she lowered her voice. 'I have some more information about Chloe Hardy.'

'About her death?' DI Trevelyan asked, his voice low too.

'Maybe, though more about her life. What she was doing in Pendragon Creek for a start.'

'And?'

'And I'll tell you, though you're not my favourite policeman any more.' Maddie blushed, surprised at her own flirtiness. *You're cross with him, remember*, she scolded herself. She readjusted her face to make her look as serious as possible and continued. 'Chloe was looking for family. Archer – oh, I don't know his surname, sorry – anyway, Archer from the pub was helping her. He told her she was related to Clive Pendergast.'

'Really?' Trevelyan looked interested. 'In what way?'

'Not directly, at least not in a long-lost-daughter-type way. Something about ancestry websites and all that. Following up some information on an aunt, I think. I should have written it down, but we were playing darts.'

'Darts?'

'Yes. Dart times call for dart measures.'

Trevelyan looked at Maddie, who instantly regretted her terrible joke. Then instantly made another.

'I'll stick to the point.'

Trevelyan shook his head, but flicked open his notebook and jotted a few words down. 'Terrible dart puns aside, this is good, thank you. Really interesting.'

Maddie was jealous of his note-taking. She needed to add

Archer's intel to her 'recipe' too. Plus, she'd just remembered something else.

'Archer said that he didn't much like Kieran though. A typical "jock" type, he said.'

Trevelyan noted this down.

'So, any sign of him?'

'Not yet, no. Though we've found CCTV footage of him leaving the town and heading out on the St Ives road. Looked like he was up for some hitchhiking. Timing is a bit off though, we don't see him until after 2 p.m., so he still might have gone up to the hill and killed her. We've got a message out to the truckers and bacon butty cafe owners on the lay-bys to keep an eye out, or ear to the ground. Nothing's pinged on his debit card and his phone's off.'

'That sounds suss. Archer didn't seem keen on him, but he might have known more than he told me. You, in a sort of formal capacity, should ask him.'

Trevelyan nodded. 'Yes, thank you. That's actually a really good lead.'

'Any news on Sheila's death? Has there been a post-mortem?' Maddie asked, hoping she wasn't overstepping the mark, but reckoning she'd been quite helpful, so tit for tat.

'PMs not in yet, but it's looking like an accidental death,' Trevelyan answered, lowering his voice. 'The sash window shouldn't have fallen on her, but they can lose their weights and fall. Sadly, she must have been leaning out at the time and right under it when it fell. It broke her neck and crushed her windpipe.'

'Oh.' Maddie felt nauseous and reeled back. 'Serves me right for asking.'

Trevelyan reached out and placed a hand on Maddie's shoulder. She wanted to shrug it off, as she was still furious after he arrested her grandmother. But she didn't. Before she could overanalyse the hand-on-shoulder thing, Trevelyan had taken it away and turned around to face the desk. He called out for DS Mitchell, and Maddie, remembering again that she was annoyed at him, and her, left them to it. She'd done her civic duty; now she just wanted to take her gran home and get them both tucked into their beds.

The old Morris Minor rolled into the quiet farmyard. Maddie cut the engine and got out, closing the gate behind her. Nor got out too and called over to her.

'Did you close that when you left to come and get me?'

Maddie paused and then stared at the gate, which she was now holding with both hands, having clicked it shut. She looked up at Nor, confused. 'Yes, I made sure I did. But it was—'

'Open when we drove through it just now.'

'Yes it was.' Maddie could see what Nor was getting at. 'I shut it behind me. I know I was in a rush, but I remember doing it.'

Simultaneously, they both looked towards the barn. The large roller door next to the pedestrian door that Maddie had snuck in through the day she'd found the backpack was up, and the barn was open to the world. And empty.

As they both walked towards it, the headlights on the car still on, and illuminating the cobbles of the farmyard, they noticed that absolutely every piece of farm machinery was gone. The smart new tractor, the Chisel Plough 3000, the trailers and ploughs. All gone.

All except Aubry Penrose's old boneshaker, which now stood alone in the cavernous barn.

'Good,' said Nor.

'Riddance,' added Maddie, and they closed the roller shutter down and headed into the farmhouse.

. . .

Maddie sat up in bed, at least one quilt pulled high up to her chin, and at least one cat purring somewhere beyond where her bent knees were obscuring the view. Resting on her legs, she had the old recipe book. She'd been desperate to write down a few notes in it since talking to Archer in the pub. She looked at the list she was creating.

Clive Pendergast – Hill Top Farm – 'of all people'
Old cow shed – fallen stones
Last words – aren't you rock would tree help
Bloodied stone = murder
1965 – missing woman SAME PLACE Esther Pendergast
Clotted cream?
Litter
Planning – houses at Hill Top
HER backpack – OUR barn. Jason?!
C&K – lovers' tiff? Him more than her
Entitled
Archer
Sheila at Seaside B&B – accident – new sash?
Brick – warning!

She tapped the end of her pen against her temple as she recalled the evening's information. After a moment, she wrote the word *related* next to Clive's name and *family tree* next to Archer's. Her eyes flitted over the two references to 'tree'.

'Of course, Toast,' she said to the purring grey lump at her feet, 'Chloe's last words included the word "tree". She wasn't trying to give Clive ideas about how to hoist the rocks off her. She was trying to explain in her last breath that she had looked into her family tree.'

Toast chirruped in reply and rolled onto his back, inviting a daring hand to tickle his tummy. Maddie knew better than to fall for that one, and instead looked back at her book.

What was the recipe creating? Had Chloe known it was Clive who held her hand as she died? Was she trying to tell him what she'd discovered?

Or had telling him what she'd discovered got her killed?

27

Maddie woke up early the next morning and shifted the pleasant weight of one of the cats off her leg. Why Toast had decided that her shin was more comfortable than the mattress, she wasn't sure, but then cats weren't known for their logic.

Maddie left the sleeping cat and pottered around, showering and dressing, before heading downstairs to where Nor was busy beating some eggs into sugar; the start of a sponge mixture. Maddie kissed her on the cheek and took over the beater, giving her gran's arm a rest.

'Thanks, ducky. There's one in the oven already, that's my second of the day.'

'Already? Have you been up since dawn?' Maddie asked, guiltily realising she hadn't actually set an alarm clock.

'Almost. It's going to be busy today. Thought I'd better bake extra.'

'Why busier than usual? Is the weather going to be good?'

Nor shrugged. 'Maybe. But it'll be busy as I'm pretty sure the news that not only was a murder committed on the hill just up there, but the lady that makes the cakes in the teashop was arrested last night.'

'Oh, Gran. I'm sure it won't have got out that quickly.'

Nor gestured to her mobile phone, which Maddie only really knew about in the context of the family WhatsApp group, where Nor would often send out-of-context photos with no caption, or cat memes. But now it was flickering alive, the home screen lighting up every now and again and Maddie could see that Nor had about fifty unread messages.

'It's got out all right. And I bet half those inquisitive minds will be round the teashop this morning in order to get the full story. I reckon it's what keeps Marge afloat in the sea – hot air and gossip.'

Maddie smiled. Nor might be rattled, but she was still herself. She continued making the cakes with her and eventually, once a batch of scones was in the oven too, she crossed the farmyard and opened up the teashop. Before she got to the door, she glanced over at the east barn. It didn't look any different from the outside than it had yesterday, but there seemed to be a sort of relief coming from it. And it set her mind off wondering what she could convince Nor to fill it with now... yoga and wine tastings perhaps?

Nor had been right, and the teashop was packed all morning. Marge had come in, with Julia in tow, and Nor had told them all about her arrest – slightly exaggerating some of it – and that Jason had upped and gone in the night.

'Didn't the police keep an eye on him?' Julia had asked, then bitten into her scone, which was light on the clotted cream, as Maddie had noticed once again that the tub had been mysteriously delved into. Maddie reached to the old recipe book that Nor had found on the kitchen table this morning and brought back into the teashop. She let it fall open onto the right page. She already had *clotted cream?* written on her list, but she added a *x2* to it before slipping the book back onto the shelf before Nor could see her scribbling in it once again. She could understand why her grandmother was a bit peeved at her writing in it, but there had seemed something else about her reaction to hiding it away. Protective of her old recipes, yes, but maybe hiding another secret too? Maddie would have used the recipe book to note down this thought, but Nor had come back to the counter.

'Julia makes a good point, you know,' she said, wiping her hands on the tea towel slipped over her apron tie string. 'Why did the police just let Jason go?'

'Little fishing they called it, didn't they? But why go to the bother of actively arresting you, making quite a show of it, and then not leave a patrol on the farm to monitor the man they accused you of aiding and abetting?'

'There's things that nice young DI of yours isn't telling us, I bet,' Nor said, raising an eyebrow at Maddie.

Maddie flushed. 'He's certainly not *my* young DI, Gran,' she retorted. 'And if that is the case, then that means he arrested you as some sort of show, which in a way now makes sense as they let you go pretty easily last night. And honestly, how dare he! How dare he use an old woman like that, for whatever plan he has brewing?'

Nor looked at Maddie with her ice-blue eyes. 'Less of the old, thank you.'

'Oh, you know what I mean, Gran.' Maddie reached out for her. 'It's just not done to use people like that. Good people.'

'I must say, I feel a little let down by Hugo Pendergast. He said it was legitimate, and if you can't trust your neighbours, who can you trust?'

Another group of guests bustled into the teashop and Nor turned from Maddie to welcome them in and find them a table, gesturing for Maddie to quickly clear away used teacups and wipe down one near a window for them.

The rest of the day carried on much the same, with locals

and tourists alike coming down off the cliffs and fields and ordering pots of tea and various sweet treats.

Something Nor had mentioned had played on Maddie's mind all afternoon, though. Hugo Pendergast. Could it be a coincidence that the son of the man who had found Chloe Hardy's body was somehow involved with Nor's current problem? In fact he had been the one to tell her that it was OK to let Jason Briggs rent the barns? Jason Briggs, who Clive Pendergast said was a wrong'un? It wasn't adding up for Maddie and she wanted to find out more.

Maddie had kissed Nor a quick goodbye at the door of the teashop as they'd locked up for the day. Nor was looking understandably tired and Maddie had made her promise that she'd do nothing more taxing than go and put the kettle on for her own mug of Earl Grey tea and put her feet up in front of *Pointless* or *Celebrity Bargain Hunt*.

'I'll be home to make us a tasty supper, Gran. I haven't properly cooked for you yet and I feel bad about it.'

'Ooh, one of your fancy French dishes from the bistro?' Nor had said, grinning at her granddaughter.

'Ha, maybe. Let's see what's in your pantry. It might be more freezer foraged than fine dining, but you definitely need the night off.'

'And where are you off to first?' Nor had asked and Maddie wasn't sure how to answer.

'There's something odd about Clive and Hugo. I mean, not *odd* odd. I haven't even met Hugo yet.'

'Clive thinks the sun shines out of his—'

'As I'm sure my mother does about me,' Maddie laughed as she interrupted Nor. 'Anyway, see you in a bit, Gran. I'll report back.'

. . .

It was easy enough to get to Hill Top Farm, though it did involve walking back past the ruined cow shed, and Maddie shuddered as she remembered what she'd seen there only a few days ago. She hurried past. There was no point looking around for further clues, not now the world and his wife had had the chance to walk past and mess it all up. Some bunches of flowers had been left on the tumble, just a couple, and there were no notes, but it touched Maddie that perfect strangers must have felt so moved by Chloe's death that they'd hiked up here to pay their respects. Perhaps not all the visitors to the site were there just to ghoulishly voyeur at recent events; some people had hearts.

Maddie carried on along the path and saw the rutted lane that linked to the main road – the one the police and ambulance had come up when she'd called them a few days ago. She remembered Clive saying that it had been the back route up to the farm, so bearing that in mind, she continued on the path she was on, which widened to take in the narrow lane that joined it, and walked another half-mile or so until she saw more robust buildings and what was obviously another farmhouse.

Hill Top Farm looked more industrial than Folly Farm. The barns were made of steel with corrugated iron roofs; big cattle sheds as opposed to her gran's old stone barn, outbuildings and stables. Maddie opened a metal five-bar gate and closed it behind her. The yard was laid to rough concrete, easy to hose down, and the barns opened onto it, with metal bars keeping the herd of gently lowing and mooing cows inside. Several old Land Rovers and some more modern Range Rovers were lined up in the yard, which seemed odd – so many cars for one man!

The farmhouse was similar to Nor's, stone-built and double-fronted with the sash windows symmetrical on each side. Maddie made a beeline for it and was about to knock on the front door when a sound made her jump.

Crack.

Crack. Crack.

The unmistakable sound of gunfire. And it was coming from just behind the house.

28

'Clive! Mr Pendergast!' Maddie shouted, her heart thumping as she looked about her. She banged her fists on the front door, but, as expected, there was no answer and no give to it.

Maddie stepped back from the front door, but in her haste, she didn't notice the heavy metal boot scraper on the doorstep and she tripped back, her arms cartwheeling in midair, until she landed with a thump in the flowerbed.

Crack. Crack.

Crack. Crack.

The shots sounded again, and Maddie panicked and floundered around in the flowerbed as she tried to get up, the sleeves of her old denim jacket getting snatched in the thorns of the early-flowering climbing rose.

'Oh bloody hell,' she said, looking at her muddy jeans. Her hands were just as dirty, and were useless when it came to trying to brush off all the soil from her knees and bum. Giving up, and not really caring how she looked at the moment, she skirted around the house, following the sound of the gunfire, careful to avoid trampling on any other flowers.

Crack. Crack.

'Clive!' Maddie called out again, though she was beginning to realise that the shots weren't as near as she thought they might have been. The noise was more of a ricochet. Still, gunshots so close to the house, and so close to the scene of a previous murder... Maddie was worried.

So worried that she jumped about six foot in the air when a firm hand clapped her on the shoulder.

'Maddie?' Clive said, as she turned around. 'What brings you here?'

'I... I was wanting to talk to Hugo,' Maddie stuttered as she took him in, alive and well, but carrying a shotgun broken over his arm, again. 'And then I heard the gunshots and I got worried, so I'm afraid I panicked a bit... and, er, I'll replace those tulips, sorry.'

'You look like you've been at the cow trough,' Clive said, and Maddie couldn't tell if he felt sorry for her, or was judging her appearance, just a tad. As for him, despite his smart tweeds, she could see that his fingers and hands were bandaged, obviously keeping dirt and gunpowder from getting into the wounds he sustained while trying to help Chloe, but they must have hampered his shooting somewhat.

'Sorry, again. Thing is, I saw all those posh cars and then heard the shots and thought maybe... I don't know, maybe Jason had left us and come to you, or gangsters, or...'

Clive laughed. 'Gangsters, oh dear. That's a good one. Those cars?' He pointed over towards the farmyard and Maddie nodded. He laughed again. 'That is a good one, I'll have to tell Brian that. And John. Ha. And Terry.'

'Who are they?' Maddie asked, not in on the joke.

'The owners of those smart Range Rovers. Or farm vehicles, as they'd call them.' Clive obviously found it all very amusing. Then he explained, 'And as for the gunshots, we're shooting clays.'

'Clay pigeon shooting? Here?' Maddie asked. 'I always

thought, oh I don't know, that you had to go to places that put on shoots. I didn't realise that you could do it in your own back garden.'

'Well, it's not exactly a back garden.' Clive led her around the house to where she could see that beyond what *could* be called a back garden, the valley dipped into fields, and in one of those several men were standing, pointing their guns in the air. She heard someone shout 'pull' and then there was another volley of gunshot. 'We have our own clay trap, so sometimes the other local farmers and I get some practice in before the pheasant season starts. My son Hugo's stopped by too, that's him down there in the red trousers.'

'Burgundy or tomato?' Maddie squinted down at the field.

'Tomato. So, no need to worry if you hear gunshots around the place.'

I think I will worry, thanks very much, thought Maddie to herself, though disguised her suburban ways with a smile.

'Anyway, said you wanted to talk to Hugo did you? What about?'

'Oh, it doesn't matter now.' Maddie, keen as she was to make Hugo explain himself over the whole 'introducing Jason to her gran' thing, didn't fancy heading down into a field full of guns. 'I'm sure I'll meet him soon. I just wanted to know how he knew Jason and why he'd said to Gran that he'd be OK to rent those barns to. You know she got arrested last night?'

'No?' Clive questioned, but Maddie wondered if he was lying. There was something a little bit off about his reaction.

'Yes. But let off quite quickly, luckily. One of the things she said to the police was that she hadn't felt like she was being preyed upon as Jason had been recommended to her by someone she thought would be in the know... your son, Hugo, who works in agricultural equipment sales.'

'Ah, well, I don't think you can go round accusing Hugo of setting Nor up with a wrong'un.'

'Can't I?' Maddie said, her eye flickering down just momentarily to the gun broken over Clive's arm as another volley of shots ricocheted around the valley.

'Now, look here, young lady,' Clive flustered, pulling his flat cap off and rubbing his free hand over his forehead. The wind swept up his gingery pale hair before he could put his cap back on. His blue eyes, unlike Nor's crystal clear ones, looked watery and pink around the lashes. 'Hugo is a good bloke, solid, good stock and all that. Whatever he said to your grandmother, it would be above board. I think wires might be crossed there.'

'What does he actually do?' Maddie stood her ground.

'Agricultural equipment sales, as you said,' Clive replied, a slight look of confusion on his face. 'In Truro.'

'Yes, but I mean, where does he source his equipment? Is it second-hand, spanking new, where is it made? You know, that sort of thing,' Maddie pressed.

'Well, I really don't know. I'm sure it's all legitimate, though, if that's what you're insinuating?'

Crack. Crack.

Maddie tried to work out the expression on Clive's face. It wasn't quite anger, but he was clearly getting defensive. Perhaps she'd pushed too far; she'd need to talk to Hugo himself, not his father, who might be overly protective, and not actually know anything either. And she didn't want to get on the wrong side of a man carrying a shotgun. Especially as she wanted to press *him* on something a little more sensitive.

'I'm sorry, I'm just angry on Gran's behalf. I hate that she's been used like this, and threatened too. Not to mention the trauma of last night.'

Clive nodded, and his expression changed again, this time to a frown of concern. 'That's natural. We all only ever want to do the best by our family. I can understand you're upset about Nor's predicament, but I can assure you, Hugo wouldn't have had anything to do with it. As I say, family comes first, and I can vouch for Hugo's character.'

Maddie still couldn't be 100 per cent certain that she was getting the truth from Clive; the assertion that family came above all else was a bit of a red flag. And made her think of the other thing she wanted to ask Clive about.

'Speaking of family, it must have been a shock to find out that you were related to Chloe, the woman who died.'

At this, Clive reddened. His eyes twitched and he could no longer hold her gaze. 'I... I don't think we were... we weren't you know, not really.'

'I realise that the word "tree" she said at the very end meant family tree. It wasn't to do with rocks and trees. Did you think that too when you heard it?'

'The matter is with the police,' Clive mumbled, then looked over his shoulder to where his friends were still shooting in the valley.

Crack. Crack.

He turned back to Maddie. 'If you'll excuse me, I have to get back down there. Terribly rude to leave them to it. Hosting, and all that.'

Maddie held eye contact with him, noting it was the first time since she'd brought up the connection between him and Chloe that she'd been able to. She nodded and then said, softly. 'I'm just trying to work out what happened. So that Gran's teashop isn't overrun by tourists wanting a piece of tragic history along with their scones. Not to mention the council getting it into their heads to shut us down. I don't want Gran's final years to be marred by that.'

Clive nodded. Maddie thought he looked like he was on the verge of saying something. *Confessing?* But at the sound of another volley of shots, he gave her a quick bow of the head and said, 'Excuse me, Maddie. But the police... they'll see it right, I'm sure. It's... it's complicated.'

He turned on his heel and Maddie could hear his name being called from down in the valley. She was tempted to follow him, ask what the complication was, but she knew that she was on thin ice. His reaction to her accusing Hugo of aiding and abetting Jason had been natural, but powerful, and although he'd softened at pleas to help her gran end her teashop days with a nicer clientele than just murder-tourists, she knew he was still hiding something.

Something about his connection to Chloe. Something she just hoped the police could unearth, if she couldn't.

29

Maddie walked back across the fields to Folly Farm. She felt herself quite on edge until she'd crossed the stile that separated the two farms' land, and even then, she felt uneasy. She could still hear the crack of shotguns reverberate around the valley and each time the shots were fired she tensed a little. Clive, though her gran's neighbour, was still a suspect. And the fact he'd said the relationship between him and Chloe was 'complicated' proved he did know of her claim to be related to him. Maddie wondered when he'd found out; before or after she was killed on his land? She was annoyed at herself that she'd chickened out of speaking to Hugo too. Despite Clive's insistence that he wasn't neck-high in whatever Jason was up to, she still wanted to give him a piece of her mind over it all. Maddie thought about all of this as she covered the last few minutes of her walk home.

A sight greeted her that she hadn't expected when she got to the farmhouse. Crumpet and Toast were noses down in a bowl of what looked suspiciously like clotted cream.

'Aha, caught in the act. Sort of,' Maddie said, picking one

cat up, then the other, in order to get to the bowl. 'And you know this isn't good for you, don't you?'

'Isn't it?' A small voice piped up from behind her.

Maddie turned around and saw Bella standing there, her horse's bridle in her hands, Cam looking on inquisitively, and even jealously, at the bowl of cream.

'No. Cats are naturally lactose intolerant,' Maddie said, and then cocked her head on one side. 'But you wouldn't know that if you didn't have them perhaps. You said you didn't have any pets at home, didn't you?'

Maddie stopped as she saw Bella's bottom lip start to tremble.

'Oh, Bella, I'm not cross.' Maddie stepped towards her, hoping to comfort her, but Camelot let out a whinny and Bella focused on keeping hold of his reins. Once the horse was steadied, Maddie apologised, 'I'm sorry. He's handsome but flighty, huh?'

'Yeah,' Bella mumbled. 'And I'm sorry about the cream. But I thought cats liked it and I always saw such a big tub of it at the teashop.'

'You're here early in the morning, aren't you, when the milkman delivers.'

'Mr Farringford from the dairy, yeah,' Bella said. 'We sometimes arrive at about the same time and your gran would always appreciate it when it was sunny and a bit warm if I put the milk and cream in the shade around the back of the teashop.'

Maddie nodded. It was all making sense. Almost.

'Bella, it doesn't matter if you did, but did you ever take the cream from the teashop fridge? As I'm sure, I—'

'Yeah…' Bella scuffed the toe of her riding boot on the ground. 'I might've done.'

'Saturday. The same day the young woman was… Well, on Saturday. That's when I noticed it.'

'You were busy with that guy, who wanted a Coke, but you

couldn't find the cans and had to go to the stock cupboard and then your gran's freezer to get ice as the Coke wasn't in the fridge—'

'Oh yeah.' Maddie rolled her eyes. Saturday had been a baptism of fire in the teashop and, looking back, maybe the smoke-belching oven hadn't been the only calamity. Nor's total lack of stock rotation had meant that there had been no tins of soft drinks in the fridge. So, she'd had to go to the stockroom, which was in another part of the teashop barn, but accessed from outside, and leave the teashop momentarily unguarded. The memory of it ran a little mental flag up a pole in her mind. The can of Coke was for... Archer! That's where she'd seen him before!

At least one little mystery was solved. Two, even, if you counted the Clotted Cream Grand Larceny.

Maddie smiled at Bella. 'OK, I get it. You snuck in.' Maddie chuckled. 'My fault for leaving the fridge unguarded. But perhaps no more cream for the cats? I'm starting to worry about Crumpet's waistline and Toast is, well, let's just say he might not be hitting the beach at Pendragon Bay in his Speedos this summer.'

Bella giggled. 'OK. I'll keep putting it in the shade, though, shall I?'

'Yes please. That's a real help. Though I'll try to get up earlier too.'

'Maybe you can ride out on Cam one morning. If you're up early enough.'

Maddie laughed. 'I'd love to.'

She waved Bella goodbye as the young girl went back towards the stables and Maddie carried the bowl of cream inside the farmhouse. She couldn't use it, and it couldn't go to the cats, or the chickens or horses, but there might be a local pig farmer who could make use of it. She smiled to herself. There had been an innocence in Bella's offer of letting her ride her pony. She was far too big for the thing, but Bella's suggestion had made her heart swell. Perhaps – murder aside – there was something rather lovely about being back on the farm.

Maddie found Nor, not with her feet up or watching the early-evening TV shows as she'd promised, but bent over the kitchen table, studying the tabletop intently. Maddie's warm and fuzzy feelings disappeared as she realised her gran was poring over the old recipe book she'd been writing in. Perhaps Nor really was quite cross that Maddie had effectively been defacing a recipe that Nor had been perfecting for sixty-odd years.

'Hi, Gran,' Maddie said, catching Nor's attention finally.

Nor looked up at her granddaughter and straightened her back while removing her reading glasses. 'Hello, ducky.'

Maddie braced herself for the telling-off. 'Gran, I'm sorry. About writing in that recipe book. I know I shouldn't have, it wasn't mine to take, and—'

'Oh pish-posh, I don't mind about that.' Nor looked at Maddie, then beckoned her over to the table with a bony finger. 'Come here and I'll show you why.'

Nor brought her finger down on the recipe book, but not at the flapjack recipe that Maddie had been writing next to. This page was for a recipe called 'Mrs WB's Cheese Biscuits'. Nor offered no insight into who Mrs WB was, but alongside the recipe ingredients (butter, flour and good, strong cheese in equal quantities), there were other words: *Esther, disappeared, sycamore tree, May 14, sister?*

'What's this, Gran?' Maddie asked, looking up from the list of scrawled words, so much like her own.

'Well, it could be the pot calling the kettle black,' said Nor, a firm grip on Maddie's arm as she pinned her with a gaze. 'Or an apple not falling too far from the tree.'

'Riddles again, Gran,' Maddie said, placing one hand over

the one her gran had gripping her arm. Then she realised what was going on. She looked at her grandmother. 'Did you write this list? Are you... Do you think like I do?'

'Always have, ducky, brain like a Chisel Plough 75, or at least the ground once it's been through it, full of holes... you know what I mean.'

Maddie just wanted to hug her. She'd wondered all her life why she hadn't been able to think 'straight' and why her thoughts were always so haphazard. Her dad, Nor's son, seemed to think in a totally ordinary way, as did her mum, who'd been a teacher, and her brother and sister who were doing well in their careers. And it wasn't like Maddie wasn't bright and achieving her dreams too. She'd done well to get to somewhere like Chez Lucie, but her mind had always been so busy. So hard to corral, as if trying to get her thoughts in a straight line was like herding cats. That's why she loved lists and recipes, as they ordered her mind – and it seemed Nor was the same.

But, despite this joy in realising that her gran was a kindred spirit in more ways than one, Maddie had questions.

'But what does this all refer to? You were making notes?'

'About Esther Pendergast's disappearance.' Nor nodded, running her finger over the list. 'It's like you said, it's too much of a coincidence that Chloe was killed just where Esther was last seen all those years ago. And with Chloe being related to the Pendergasts too.'

'But her surname was Hardy, not Pendergast,' Maddie mused. 'Of course, that could be a maternal line thing.'

'Exactly,' Nor said, pointing to the name *Esther* in the book, then running it down the list. 'Esther disappeared. And everyone thought she'd run off to her sister. And do you know where her sister lived?'

Maddie shrugged. 'No.'

'Well, I'd quite forgotten too. But then something jogged my memory the other day. When that policeman of yours—'

'He's not... Oh never mind, go on.'

'Well, when DI Trevelyan picked up the backpack you found, he was telling us that Chloe Hardy was from Lincolnshire. And that's what I remembered just now; that was where Esther's sister lived. In the fens. Or around there.'

'But Esther was never traced there, though? Was she?'

'No, but don't forget this was 1965. Lincolnshire was foreign lands! Police sent a search request and Clive's father apparently got in his Cortina and went to see Esther's sister, in an attempt to find his wife. But when he returned, he had no information, and of course the police had nothing on him, so we all took his word for it. She was gone and that was that. We called them bolters back then, women who just disappeared, though she didn't have much in the way of responsibilities.'

Maddie looked at the recipe book again. The ruined cow shed... the memories that must hold for Clive. 'She had a very young Clive, that's a responsibility. It must have been hard enough for him growing up without a mother, but then to have found Chloe in the same spot where your mother was last seen...'

Nor looked at Maddie, her expression incredulous. 'Oh ducky, no, no, no.'

'What?' Maddie was confused. She was sure she had it all correct.

'You've got your wires crossed there. The woman who went missing from under the sycamore tree, last seen there by Gerald Pendergast in 1965, was—'

'Esther Pendergast,' Maddie interrupted. 'His wife, and Clive's mother.'

Nor shook her head. 'No, Esther Pendergast was Gerald's wife all right, but she definitely wasn't Clive's mother.'

30

'I'm sorry, what?' Maddie took a step back from Nor.

'Whatever gave you that idea?' Nor said, closing the book and handing it over to Maddie, in a move that should have had a much more ceremonial or emotional feel, except that Maddie's mind was sparking all over the place wondering about Esther Pendergast.

'Well, just that everyone's been referring to Esther Pendergast and that she was married to Clive's father… oh.' Maddie realised her mistake. 'Married to Clive's father, but not his mother. His stepmother?'

'No, his father's first wife. Esther was a local girl, brought up at Hill Top Farm, in fact it was through her that Gerald held the estate, him being a younger son from another farm further south. She'd stayed to run the farm when her sister had married a farming chap in Lincolnshire, and Gerald took it on with her. Then when she went missing' – Nor pointed at the recipe book as if it held all the answers – 'Gerald pretty quickly remarried. And had Clive a year later.'

'Making him…' Maddie did the mental arithmetic. 'Oh, around fifty-nine. Yes, I guess he does look that old. I just assumed Esther was his mother, though. All this talk of how coincidental it was that Chloe went missing at the same spot. I definitely picked up on that.'

'Makes it more coincidental – or less, whichever – if you ask me,' Nor said, moving over to the Aga to rest herself against its warmth. 'The woman who originally owned the farm going missing there is more poignant than it being Clive's mother, especially if she's the one related to people in Lincolnshire, where that poor girl Chloe came from.'

'Something about a tree...' Maddie recited. 'That's what Clive said her last words were. And I'm pretty sure she was referring to a family tree, which means she knew she was related to Esther Pendergast. It's what all the ancestry searches were for.'

'And killed on the same spot as Esther, her ancestor, went missing. If that's not a "coincidence", I don't know what is.'

Maddie thought back to Clive's reaction when she asked him about his distant relation. 'Maybe it's not a coincidence at all. Chloe was up there, she confronted Clive, said she knew everything about her great-aunt, or whoever Esther may be to her, and he killed her, there and then. I've just spoken to him, Gran—'

'You what? In the middle of a clay shoot? He'll not have liked that.'

'You knew they were shooting?'

'I might be old, but I'm not deaf. You can hear it from here. Pointless sport.'

'Hugo's there. But I didn't much fancy facing off against a man with a twelve bore in his hands and trousers the colour of ketchup... Oh, and I owe Clive some new tulips. Anyway, he said it was complicated how he and Chloe were related. Which makes me think he obviously knew she wasn't related to *him*, but to his father's first wife. And I suppose that means she might have had a claim to the farm. It gives him huge motive to kill her.'

'Doesn't bear thinking about,' shivered Nor. 'I've had barn dances with that family. Gerald Pendergast was a fantastic dancer. Can't believe that of Clive either, what with the help he gives me come winter and the—'

'The fact his son was the one who introduced you to Jason blooming Briggs.' Maddie still hadn't forgotten that little plot twist.

'Hugo's never had much luck with his endeavours. Not an academic lad, so he struggled in school. Not sure he's held down much of a job since, so I felt I should support him when he asked if Jason could use my barn. Wish I hadn't now!'

'I'm still cross that he used you like that, especially taking advantage of your generous nature.' Maddie kicked the table leg, then winced as she remembered she was only in light plimsolls, not wellies.

'Well, what's done is done,' Nor said, then pointed at the recipe book that Maddie now held. 'I saw you'd jotted something down about Sheila on your list too. Do you think her death's connected?'

Maddie shrugged. 'It would be another strange coincidence if it wasn't. The lady who owned the B&B in which Chloe, who was definitely murdered, was staying has a very bizarre accident just a couple of days later... it raises red flags for me for sure. But...' Maddie sighed. 'If it wasn't an accident, the only other cause could be murder.'

The word hung in the air between them.

Maddie was the first to speak. 'I told DI Trevelyan that I suspected foul play. Sheila was too fastidious in her cleaning and you said she'd just spent a fortune on new windows, so I can't believe she'd have an accident like that. So, it's in the hands of the police now. But do you think I should tell him about Esther? Do you think he knows? If we think it's not a coincidence as well, then maybe we should tell him what we know?'

'I suppose so.' Nor crossed her arms. 'Though apart from my jottings in the book, I'm a little shady on the details. I can't remember what happened last Tuesday, let alone all those years ago.'

'I know how you feel,' Maddie said, gesturing with the recipe book. 'It can be hard to remember what's what. Hence the–'

'Writing it all down like a recipe,' Nor said at the same time as Maddie.

'Oh Gran,' Maddie said, wrapping an arm around her. 'We're like peas in a pod.'

'Well, this pea isn't sure if she owes that policeman of yours any favours.'

'He's not... No, quite right.' Maddie placed the recipe book down again, and twisted her lips around as she thought. She was cross with DI Trevelyan too. How dare he have treated her gran like that. And she'd already given him her best lead last night, telling him about Archer and the ancestry claim. 'He's probably worked it out already, what with Archer now part of the investigation.'

'Archer Lockwood?' Nor asked, pushing herself off and away from the Aga. 'He's back, is he?'

'Is that his surname? Beats "Archer Fromthepub", I guess. Anyway, Roger at the Two Pelicans said he'd heard Chloe saying the name Archer when she called someone on her mobile in the pub, and he put two and two together and worked out it was the same Archer who came in to play darts–'

'No doubt picked up from those Bristol guys he hung around with,' Nor said, shaking her head. 'Caused his mother no end of heartache when he ran off like that.'

'Ran off? Where from? Bristol? Which guys?'

'University of Bristol, no less. One of those fancy computer science degrees. But he didn't finish it as he got in with a set of hecklers. No, not hecklers—'

'Hackers?'

'That's the monkey.' Nor patted Maddie on the back. 'Ran off with them to some squat in Clifton and did who knows what. Something to do with bell ringing... it involved bongs at any rate.' Maddie stifled a smile at this as her grandmother carried on. 'His mother was livid. Wasted all that money on a degree course and spent the whole time on video games. But if he's back, maybe they've made up and he's on an even keel again. Never been easy for her since his father left them.'

Maddie nodded. She knew she was lucky to have come from a happy home with two loving parents, plus her brother and sister, Sam and Daisy. But what her gran said was making sense. Archer had boasted about his skills in getting information from digital files; the national and local archives and register officers and the like. And not always through official channels. It was how he'd found Chloe's connection for her.

'I wonder if he knew what Clive might do to Chloe if she confronted him? He didn't seem impressed that her boyfriend had just left her like that. He didn't like him at all actually.'

'Let's not go locking up Clive before we know what really happened. Innocent until proven guilty and all that,' Nor cautioned her and Maddie nodded again.

But there was something in that family link. Something that made Maddie think that Clive had to have some connection to Chloe's death. If the ancestry link was correct, then Chloe possibly had more of a claim to Clive's farm than he did. And surely that had to make him prime suspect in her murder?

31

Maddie had been true to her word and had cooked her gran supper that night. She'd found eggs – naturally – and made a quiche, whipping up her own pastry (of which she was justly proud, especially when Nor confidently said that it must be because she had naturally cold hands, and of course everyone knew the phrase 'cold hands, warm heart') and frying off some bacon lardons she'd found in the fridge, along with some strong local Cheddar-like cheese.

'Can't call it Cheddar unless it's from Cheddar itself,' Nor had said, handing over the sealed waxed paper packet with Farringford Dairy's logo on it.

'Like Champagne,' Maddie had laughed.

The evening had passed less dramatically than the one before, with the warm quiche served with salad leaves picked from the cold frame under the kitchen windowsill, and the two of them, plus Crumpet and Toast, curled up on the sofa. Maddie had told Nor about Bella and the clotted cream and Nor had laughed.

'No wonder these two were looking so pleased with themselves!'

'Cats that had genuinely got the cream,' Maddie had chuckled.

The next morning had broken and Maddie had woken far more refreshed than she had the previous one. The small factor of her grandmother not being arrested the night before had probably helped, as had the lack of feline accompaniment in bed. As much as she'd liked the novelty of having both Crumpet and Toast curl up with her as she'd first got into bed, she was rather relieved when she could uncurl herself from the torturous S-bend she'd manoeuvred herself into to accommodate them both on the mattress with her.

It was early still and she could hear the farm waking up. The smell of coffee was wafting up from the kitchen and Maddie got up and showered and was down by Nor's side as quickly as she could. It was barely eight o'clock and she had rather thought she'd be getting more of a lie-in during these recuperative weeks spent with her gran, but at least eight in the morning was more civilised than the dawn raids to the London markets she'd had to do most weeks while working at Chez Lucie. Smithfield for meat, Billingsgate for fish, New Covent Garden for fruit and veg and flowers for the tables... No, eight o'clock was a positive luxury compared to that! And to add to the luxury, Nor seemed to have it all under control, with scones baking, a sponge cake in the bowl (Maddie had to remind herself that uncooked cake mixture was not a balanced breakfast) and icing being beaten in the stand-up mixer.

'Go on with you, it's a lovely morning. Stretch your legs before the hordes arrive.' Nor shooed her out of the kitchen. Maddie wondered if it was a coincidence that she'd also had a message on her phone from her mum that morning asking how she was feeling and how life by the sea was treating her. Perhaps her mum had had a word with Nor and reminded her that Maddie was there to rest as well as work? She felt bad if so, as it was invigorating, and a totally different change of pace to her London life. And she smiled as she realised that neither she nor Nor had ventured to tell her parents about Nor's arrest the other night.

Some things that happen in Cornwall, can very much stay in Cornwall, she thought.

So, taking Nor up on her offer, she pushed her feet into the waiting wellies at the back door – a precaution against any latent mud that might still be around despite the dry weather; and on the other hand (or foot) a precaution against adders that might be sunbathing on the pathways recently emerged from hibernation. A nasty bite from Britain's only poisonous snake would be annoying – and just her luck.

Maddie closed the large gate of the farm and powered herself up the short but steep hill towards the old cow shed. But instead of going back, once again, to that grisly spot, she turned the other direction and headed along the coastal path. The tang of salt water was more potent up here and she breathed in great big gulps of it. Seagulls cawed and circled above, and once the path had levelled out and she'd caught her breath, Maddie ran, waving her arms in the air, letting out noises she wasn't sure were shouts or whoops or screams, but it felt like a release of sorts. Suddenly feeling self-conscious, she slowed her pace and shut up. She was, after all, on one of the more popular pathways now, and despite the early hour, she wouldn't be surprised if someone saw her.

She paused for a while to look out to the glittering waters of Pendragon Bay. She smiled, seeing the coloured swim caps of Julia and Marge, one bright yellow and one crimson red. At least she assumed it was them, though with summer around the corner, she knew the beach would become more and more popular with day-trippers and holidaymakers. More traffic for the roads and litter on the beaches, but also more money in the pot for businesses like her gran's teashop. She wondered if she could convince her gran to let her stay long enough to really make use of the summer trade? Get that toasted sandwich maker replaced with a panini press, fix that sodding oven and then... Her mind wandered as it so often did and she almost didn't spot the cobalt-blue piece of plastic on the ground in front of her. But she did, and she stooped to pick it up, thoughts of tourist litter still fairly high up in the jumble of her mind. Tutting to herself, she examined it and realised it wasn't just some waste plastic, but a USB stick.

'Old school,' she muttered to herself, putting it in her pocket, but not before noticing the initials marked on it in black Sharpie pen.

AL.

32

Maddie twizzled the USB stick around in her pocket. AL had to be Archer Lockwood, didn't it? Though she supposed it could be any one from Alan Lawrence to Alexandra Lee. This was a popular path after all.

Another thought occurred to her... Bella Leach, or as she might be... Arabella Leach? Would a twelve-year-old girl have a USB? If it was full of homework and exam notes, and rural broadband meant connecting to the school's cloud was impossible, then maybe. And if her name was Arabella, not Isabella. Or Clarabella. Maddie made a mental note to check, then remembered she'd rolled up her gran's recipe book and shoved it into her back pocket when she'd left the kitchen. So she did one better; she opened it up at the flapjack page and, fishing a pen out of her other back pocket, added *USB stick* to the list. And then next to it, *AL – Bella or Archer?*

Her eye cast over the list as she paused for a moment on the clifftop. The bit about clotted cream she thought she could ignore now, but the other words... *tree, tumble, shelter, missing woman...* they were all pointing towards Clive Pendergast.

Maddie looked around her. From the clifftop, she knew she

could take one of the pathways back inland and, missing the cow shed out altogether, drop back down towards Hill Top Farm's lower fields, and then climb back up towards the farm itself. It would take her no more than fifteen minutes and she was sure Nor wouldn't mind that she was taking her time. What she was going to ask Clive when she got there, she didn't know, but she at least knew now not to mind the sound of shotguns if she heard them and to take a wide berth of the field just behind the house. She was fairly sure that in her jeans and wellies, and in her faded old denim jacket with lots of old sewn-on badges on it, she didn't resemble a clay, or an out-of-season pheasant, but it paid never to be too careful.

Maddie thought about her options as she crossed the fields, climbed over stiles and edged her way through kissing gates. She saw the Hill Top cattle and kept her distance, veering way off the footpath in order to avoid the herd, which, of course, were standing right in the way.

'Cows are the worst,' she muttered to herself, betraying her suburban upbringing and hoping they didn't hear her and retaliate accordingly.

Finally, she found herself on the track towards the farm itself and she once again saw the metal five-bar gate that marked the edge of the concreted farmyard. This time, though, beyond it there weren't any fancy Range Rovers or rugged Land Rovers, except one.

The Land Rover that was emblazoned with the Devon & Cornwall police livery.

Its lights were flashing silently, which seemed odd this early in the morning and on a quiet farmyard.

Maddie carefully opened the gate, noticing how much lighter it was, being made of metal and not supporting the weight of two rather large cats, then carefully closed it again. Crossing the yard, her heart began to race and she went from curious to suddenly very, very worried. Beyond the familiar police Land Rover, she noticed another squad car and then also an ambulance.

Maddie broke into a trot as she saw a commotion come from the furthermost barn.

'Miss Penrose,' DI Trevelyan, who appeared from the barn, called to her. 'Wait! Don't come any nearer.' He sounded authoritative, stern. Serious.

She obeyed and stopped in her tracks.

'What's happened?' she called over to him, waiting until he was closer until she asked again. 'What is it? Is Clive OK?'

A brief shake of the head was all she had before the evidence was clear before her. Behind Trevelyan, she saw two paramedics push and pull a trolley from the barn, and on it was a black body bag.

'Oh no, oh no...' Maddie said, surging forward. She had no real love for Clive Pendergast, assuming it was him in the bag, but she felt winded knowing that someone else had died.

DI Trevelyan blocked her path and caught her up in his arms, holding her back. 'Miss Penrose... Maddie,' he said gently, pushing her away from him but still holding her by the tops of her arms. 'Please, let them do their job. It's a crime scene. You can't go in there.'

'Is it Clive? At least tell me who it is.'

Trevelyan nodded. 'It's Clive.'

'And a crime scene means you think it's murder? Not... well, not the other thing?'

Trevelyan took a deep breath. Maddie knew he had a habit of telling her perhaps a little too much of what was going on in an investigation and was usually only cut off by his more protocol-preferring sergeant. But DS Mitchell, if she was here at the farm, was busy elsewhere and Trevelyan broke his silence.

'Yes, we think it's murder. Shotgun wound to the chest. Two rounds, so one discharge from each barrel. Really nasty,' he added, rather unnecessarily at the end.

'I'm sure,' Maddie agreed, trying very, very hard not to imagine it. 'So it couldn't have been self-inflicted?'

'Not a chance. For a start, the angle would be impossible and the injury suggests the gun was fired from several feet away, not point blank. The entry wound is—'

'Oh horrid, enough, enough.' Maddie put her hand up. Trevelyan had dropped his hands from holding her now and she could feel the spots at the top of her arms where they'd been. She tried to ignore that, though, and concentrate on poor Clive. 'You said "for a start"... Is there anything else that suggests it wasn't an accident?'

Trevelyan nodded. 'Just a small clue, that being that there's no sign of the gun that shot him.'

'No sign? It's gone?'

'Yes, the shooter must have taken it with them. There was nothing by the scene at all when we got here.'

'Who found him? Was it Hugo? He's staying with his father...' Maddie paused, the realisation that someone else in this small community had just died. Someone's dad, someone's neighbour. And her heart went out to Hugo, despite never having met him, and being more than a bit cross with him. He had now just lost his father, and that was cruel. Unless... Could Hugo, who was undoubtably mixed up with some wrong'uns like Jason, have killed his own father?

The change in her facial expressions must have tipped Trevelyan off to her thought process. 'Yes, Hugo found him, but he's not a suspect so much as a person of interest. He said he saw his father first thing, then he got into the shower and when he got out, he heard raised voices in the yard. He took a few minutes to get dressed and dry and by the time he got outside, there was no one here, it was all quiet.'

'Too quiet,' Maddie said, adding to the report.

'Yes, that's what he said. "Too quiet". And he looked in the barns, couldn't see another car and then, well, then he found his father.'

'Dead? I mean, no last words like Chloe had?'

'Dead. Being shot in the chest will do that to you.'

Maddie grimaced. Still, she thought, it was only Hugo's word that he hadn't shot his father and she mentioned this to Trevelyan.

He nodded again. 'True, and I've seen some pretty good liars in my time, but he seems genuine. Obviously we'll take fingerprints and check them against any guns we find in the house. Clive and Hugo both have licences and the house has a gun safe.'

'He was shooting yesterday, I only saw him from afar, but Clive told me he was. There'd be witnesses too, the other farmers on the shoot. He might have easily handled one of his father's guns,' Maddie recollected, and Trevelyan noted it down in his notebook. 'How will you know if one is missing? And not just put back in the safe?'

'Every responsible gun owner in the country has their guns logged with the local police. Mr Pendergast was no different. Serial numbers and the make of gun are logged as part of the licence process. We've already checked and there's one missing from the safe. Current thinking is that Clive had it on him and somehow had it taken off him, used against him, and then the killer fled with it. We'll have dogs looking out for it around the local area, assuming it might have been dumped.'

Maddie nodded. 'When I saw him yesterday, he was just walking around with it broken over his arm.'

'Interesting, thanks.' Trevelyan noted that down.

Maddie looked back up at him. 'Hugo has to be a suspect. It was him that put Gran up to renting out space to Jason. He might be neck-deep in trouble. And there's no one else here.' Maddie looked around the yard. The only people apart from her and DI

Trevelyan were other police officers. She noticed DS Mitchell come out of the barn and glower at her. She tried a faint smile and then turned back to Trevelyan. 'Who else could have done it?'

Trevelyan inhaled deeply and slowly let it go. He closed his eyes for a moment and then looked at her. 'Look, if I tell you...'

'I won't say a word. And I might have something of interest for you too...'

He narrowed his eyes at her and rubbed his chin. Maddie noticed that he hadn't shaved this morning and this oddly intimate sight of him – not ready for the day – made strange things happen in her stomach. She tried to ignore them and looked at him expectantly.

'Whatever you have to tell me regarding a case, you should tell me.'

'I will, but first...?'

He nodded his head over to one side. 'Follow me.'

Maddie did and they walked away from the barn and the police cars, over towards the other farm gate, the one that led to the main road. Maddie noticed a little yellow pyramid thing on the ground by the gate with police tape round it. She recognised it as the same sort of marker they'd placed all around the tumble when Chloe's body was found.

'What's that pyramid thing marking?' she asked Trevelyan, unable to get close to whatever it was due to the tape. She could see that it was white, though muddied; like a piece of A4 paper that had fallen to the ground, perhaps.

'Evidence that someone else might have been here this morning. It's a print-at-home train ticket.'

'What does that show you? Just a QR code and a destination?' Maddie shrugged.

'This one was booked in advance and has the seat number and passenger's name on it.'

'Oh,' Maddie said, looking up at Trevelyan. 'And?'

'And it belongs to Kieran Jones.'

33

'Kieran? Chloe's boyfriend.'

'The very same,' DI Trevelyan said, guiding Maddie back away from the e-ticket.

'He was here?' she asked. 'Have you found him? I mean, he's been missing, hasn't he, since Chloe's death?'

'There's been no sign of him, yet.' Trevelyan exhaled, and Maddie realised the effort that must have been going on behind the scenes to find the missing boyfriend. 'But we've had a couple of leads, eyewitnesses who think they saw him in St Ives. We're checking CCTV, but scrolling through hours of footage takes manpower and we're understaffed as it is.'

'But this places him here, back in Pendragon Creek—'

'Yeah, but we don't know when. That train ticket is the one he and Chloe arrived in St Ives on.'

'And that was a few days ago, so he could be anywhere now,' Maddie said, crossing her arms, but Trevelyan corrected her.

'That same printed-out e-ticket was his return ticket too. So unless he had it saved on his phone, or printed out twice, that muddy bit of paper by the gate was his pre-paid way out of

Cornwall. And since he hasn't pinged on any surveillance systems, we think that might have been his only copy.'

'He might have paid in cash?' Maddie suggested, the thought of it sparking a possible connection in her mind between him, Jason and Hugo. 'That wouldn't set any alerts off, which might have happened had he paid by card.'

'True, but we asked the station master, as the ticket machines at St Ives don't accept cash. He'd have to have paid at the kiosk, and they have CCTV, which we're checking, but they didn't recognise his description.'

'I see,' Maddie shrugged. 'So what do you think it means? That it dropped out of his pocket and he was here?'

'Exactly. We think maybe he suspected Clive of killing his girlfriend, then laid low, moving out of town but staying here in the countryside, then took his revenge when Clive was alone, using the victim's own gun before running off again. We're going to start the manhunt. Anyway, what did you want to share with me?'

Maddie fingered the USB stick in her pocket. By rights, she should hand it in as possible evidence, but her fingerprints were quite literally all over it now, and anyway, she hadn't quite forgiven Trevelyan for how he'd treated her gran the other night. But she had said she'd trade...

'Gran told me an interesting bit of, well, local gossip. About Clive's dad's first wife.'

She recounted the story of Esther and how perhaps it wasn't a coincidence that both Chloe and Esther had links to Lincolnshire. Maddie liked that Trevelyan was taking notes as she spoke; it made her more confident in her own theories about the links.

'Thanks,' was all he said though at the end. 'That is interesting. But my main priority now is this manhunt for Kieran Jones. We haven't got the officers to concentrate on both and since

Chloe's leads are getting colder by the second, we've got to prioritise Clive's death now.'

Maddie nodded. But she and Trevelyan stayed rooted to the spot, as if each was waiting for the other to move first.

Finally, he said, 'Anything else?'

Maddie frowned. There was something else, but she was conflicted about bringing it up. She had to mention it, though.

'Jason's gone. Left the farm, emptied out the barn. All before we got back from the station the other night.'

Trevelyan held her gaze and she tried to work out what he was thinking. After a moment, he sighed and just said, 'I know.'

She watched Trevelyan walk away and, feeling more than a little confused, let herself out of the gate.

As she crossed the fields, the wind picked up and a shiver crossed her shoulder blades. The bright spring greens and perfect blossom whites and pinks of the hedgerow suddenly became muted as a thick grey cloud blotted out the sun. The world became darker and Maddie hurried home, this time with only one thought in her mind. A killer was on the loose, and possibly very, very nearby.

Maddie shivered again as the biting wind caught her at the top of the cliffs. She constantly turned around to see who might be at her back – but it was just the wind, pushing her, whipping up her hair and drying out her eyes so much so that she almost stumbled blind along the grassy path at the cliff edge. *No wonder people fall at times*, she thought, as she careered onward, grateful that she knew every inch of it so well from summers and holidays playing here with her brother and sister.

At last, she dropped down off the higher-most point and the wind gave way, but the sense that she was being watched, followed even, didn't leave her and she upped her pace, wary of stumbling but wanting very much to be back at Folly Farm as soon as possible. Back with her gran. Whether to protect her, or the other way around, she wasn't sure.

There was a murderer on the loose... The thought returned to her. And one that had just committed the act, probably less than an hour ago, very close to where she was now, and possibly still with the missing gun on them.

Maddie gripped her coat around her and couldn't describe the relief she felt when she saw Folly Farm emerge across the fields. She broke into a trot as soon as she could see the gate and almost cried out in joy when she spotted Crumpet and Toast jump up onto it, their tails held proudly high, and their ears twitching forward as she ran to them.

'Boy, am I glad to see you two,' Maddie said, sharing out head scratches and chin tickles to the awaiting cats, who, as elegantly as ever, were able to balance impeccably on the gate top as she swung it open and closed again. Only once it was clicked shut did they both jump off it and follow her, like bodyguards, to the kitchen door.

'Morning, ducky,' Nor called out, mixing a bowl of cake mixture. 'Just in time to help with this one.'

'Gran...' Maddie started and then burst into tears. She wasn't sure why, but the retelling of the morning's grim discovery took it out of her. Although she didn't know Clive that well, and even thought he might be Chloe's killer, she bawled her eyes out as she sat at the kitchen table and recounted everything she'd seen and heard at Hill Top Farm that morning.

'Well, there's a thing,' Nor said, shaking her head as Maddie finished her sorry tale. 'Poor Clive.' She had turned quite pale and Maddie realised that the shock of it wasn't just affecting her.

'Are you all right, Gran?' Maddie reached a hand over. Nor took it, placing her other one on top too.

'I will be. Dear Clive though. I've known him since he was a boy.' She moved her hand and pulled a hanky out from her cardigan's sleeve. She dabbed her eyes and shook her head. 'And they suspect the boyfriend of that poor girl? Well, if he did do it, then I suppose he probably killed her too. I feel bad about us suspecting Clive at all now.'

Maddie wiped away a tear with the heel of her hand. She hated seeing Nor upset and realised she'd never seen her grandmother cry before. She wasn't sure what to say, except, 'I don't think we were far off. He must have had *something* to do with it, else why would he be targeted now?'

'Where there's smoke there's fire, you mean?' Nor said, squeezing Maddie's hand.

'Yes, exactly. If it is Kieran, then he obviously suspected Clive of killing Chloe. He must have known they were related too.' As Maddie dug into her pocket for a tissue to blow her nose, she found the USB stick she'd picked up on the pathway on her way to Hill Top Farm. She pulled it out and placed it on the table with the initials facing up.

'Who's Al?' Nor asked.

'I assumed initials, A L, but you're right, it could be Al. Short for Alistair? Or Alex?'

'Alan, Alyn or Allen,' added Nor, reaching for it, but Maddie gently batted her hand away.

'Fingerprints, Gran. Bad enough that mine are on there. Do you think I should plug it into my laptop and see what's on it?'

'Could be full of those computer germs,' warned Nor. 'You know the illnesses computers pick up from each other. Nasty. Katie down at the Pendragon Centre for the Over Sixties said we should all be very careful about putting our dongles places, and clicking on pop tarts.'

Maddie smiled for the first time since she'd walked into Hill Top Farm.

'I think you mean pop-ups. But yup, you're right, Gran. Bugs and viruses are dangerous for computers, but I'd be really unlucky to get anything just by looking at what was on this. And don't you think AL could refer to Archer Lockwood?'

'Archer? And his computer thingies. Yes, maybe.' Nor agreed. 'I'd definitely give it a dose of Dettol though if it has come from him. He was always a grubby child. Not dirty, but you know, grubby.'

Maddie shook her head in mock dismay at her gran's judgements on the young man, and with a promise from Nor not to touch the USB stick while she was gone, she dashed up the stairs to her room and pulled out her laptop. She'd not had the need to use it yet since arriving, and it felt oddly incongruous opening it up on the kitchen table and waiting for the screen to wake up and ask for her password. Luckily, it was an older model with a USB port still on the side and once she'd noticed, but ignored, the emails that were stacking up in her inbox which had popped up automatically, she pulled the top off the stick and plugged the USB in.

A file instantly appeared, its blue folder icon had a name that Maddie knew meant that this should be handed over to DI Trevelyan straight away.

Almost straight away.

She had to have a look first.

Because the folder was labelled: Pendergast/Hardy family tree.

34

'I can't open it, it's password-protected,' grumbled Maddie, as she futilely clicked on the icon again and again, only to be met by an impolite 'bong' sound each time.

'Probably best get it to that DI of yours—'

'He's not mine,' Maddie said, automatically.

'We'll see,' said Nor, bending over the Aga and opening the oven door. A sudden gust of sweet baking aroma filled the air and Maddie took a deep breath. What was it about delicious smells that brought you right back to a time and a place? Her mind hopscotched back to the first day that she'd helped out at Nor's teashop. The day Clive had burst in, covered in blood and announced Chloe's murder. Maddie knew there was some connection between him finding Chloe's body and him now being killed – but what was it?

'They still haven't found Kieran,' she said to Nor, as she helped her release the cake from the springform tin and get it onto the cooling rack.

'I hope they do,' Nor said, meaningfully. 'I hope they do.'

. . .

Nor's words ran through Maddie's mind as she served customers in the teashop. She was also annoyed by an online review that she'd seen pop up describing the teashop as 'dirty'. It had been when she'd unplugged the USB and quickly logged in online to check her emails when the alert had come up saying the teashop had a new review. 'Floor covered in chalk dust and muck. Cake was nice though. Two stars.' Maddie had looked at the date. Saturday. Good thing the reviewer hadn't been there when Clive had burst in, else that two-star review would have dropped even further, no doubt. And yes, the floor had been dirty, she'd noticed that too, though had been too busy battling with the oven to do anything about it. And it was the floor after all, not the plates or cutlery. She just had to hope the lady from the council didn't read it and add it to the rap sheet. Maddie sighed. Still, it stuck in her mind and she'd added it to her recipe.

Julia came in and Maddie waved at her and gestured a nice quiet table under one of the windows. Once she'd taken a pot of Darjeeling and two slices of Nor's delicious coffee and walnut cake over to a pair of walkers, she stopped by Julia's table and said hello.

'Hello, Maddie, how are you?' Julia asked, before introducing herself properly. 'I know we met the other day, but Marge does rather like to chat. I'm Julia Miller-Bakewell—'

'Oh, from Miller & Bakewell, in town?'

'That's right. Though most people just call it the deli!' Julia laughed.

Maddie liked her. They made a bit of small talk about restaurants and where Maddie had been working – 'Ooh I've heard of Chez Lucie, very posh,' Julia had said at one point – before Maddie thought of asking her about the latest news from town. Miller & Bakewell was just a road away from the Seaside View B&B after all, and Julia seemed like someone who'd be in the know.

'Oh it was awful, Maddie. The police were there for hours the morning after poor Sheila was found. Seems a lot of work for an accident.'

'Maybe it wasn't?' Maddie raised her theory, and Julia frowned.

'You don't think it was?' Her voice was hushed. 'Me neither, and the word going around is that she'd had a little trouble in the B&B recently.'

'What sort of trouble?' Maddie wished her notepad was her recipe book.

'Raised voices heard along the street, which wasn't normal for Sheila. She kept a very tidy house and never had yobs staying. It's terrible, though, what's happened to her.' Julia shook her head. Then changed the subject. 'Will we see you both later?'

Maddie raised her eyebrows. 'Where? What's happening? Not sure Gran and I have been invited to anything,' Maddie said, though was unconfident. She was known to accept invitations and then immediately forget them, and fail to turn up altogether when the time came. A brief dalliance with a Filofax in the mid-2000s had helped, until that too became a physical representation of her brain and wouldn't close properly on all the jotted-down notes, mementos, receipts and flyers she'd stuffed in there.

'The town meeting to do with the local plan. Marge and I have bent Nor's ear about it something rotten, she'd definitely know it was on. You two have to come.'

'I've heard it's happening, but what's it all about? Planning permission is it?' Maddie replied as Nor joined them, having heard her name.

'Hello, Nor, love,' Julia greeted her. 'Just filling in your granddaughter here about the meeting tonight.'

'Oh yes,' Nor nodded. 'In the diary.'

Maddie still looked confused, so Julia continued. 'It's not to do planning permission so much as whether we should allow the local plan to include the fields over by Hill Top to be released for planning eventually. They border right onto Nor's fields, you see.' She nodded at her friend, who grimaced. 'Not right now, but if it goes in the twenty-year plan, it could happen any time. Of course, Clive will be there tonight and be all "over my dead body" about it, though it would be him who would profit if the land could be developed.'

Maddie felt the colour drain from her face. She looked at Nor, whose face was ashen too, and then turned back to Julia.

'What is it, love? Did I say something?' Julia looked perplexed.

Maddie nodded, then shook her head. 'It's not you, it's just... you haven't heard. Clive Pendergast was murdered this morning.'

'Murdered? Murdered!'

'Sorry, Julia, m'lover.' Nor put a hand on her shoulder. 'I should have phoned you straight away. Bit of a shock for all of us.'

'Murdered?' Julia asked again, looking from Nor to Maddie.

'Just this morning. And when I got there, the police were all over the farm, and news was that Clive had been shot dead with his own gun in one of the barns.'

'Well I never,' Julia said, visibly shocked. 'That's terrible. Do they know who did it?'

'No,' Maddie replied, honestly. 'Though, of course, they're thinking it's connected to Chloe's murder.'

'Are they now? Why's that?'

'I'll get your order over to you,' Maddie said, 'and let Gran explain.'

As she walked back towards the counter to fetch Julia's scone and tea, leaving Nor and her friend to discuss the latest tragedy in the neighbourhood, she thought about what Julia had said. She'd used a common turn of phrase... 'over my dead body'.

Clive had used it too when he'd mentioned the local plan. She was glad Nor had already pencilled the meeting into her diary as she thought it would definitely be a good idea to attend. Because an inkling told her that this discussion over the local plan had something to do with Clive's very recent, and very dead body.

35

The Fisherman's Hall was crammed with locals, the chatter and general noise of voices filling the space as much as the people themselves. Maddie and Nor entered through the main door of the old hall, so-called as back in the 1800s it had been the place where the fishermen could come and discuss industry matters and congregate when needed. It had merged with the needs of the general townsfolk and was now the town hall, complete with staging for the amateur dramatics society, soft-play mats for the mother and baby groups and a portrait of the king hanging above the clock on one wall. Tonight, there were chairs set out in rows, with an aisle created down the middle leading towards the staging. A-boards stood on the stage with plans and maps pinned on them, plus there was a cinema screen pulled down from the ceiling and a projector on a tripod, all ready for a PowerPoint presentation. A trestle table was placed between two of the A-boards with four chairs behind it, no doubt for the councillors and perhaps someone representing a local developer.

Maddie had asked Nor about the meeting earlier in the day, after Julia had left and in a quiet moment.

'Oh yes, some adjustment to the local plan now the old airfield has been deemed too polluted to build houses on. Turns out diesel and old ordnance from the war doesn't appeal to a nice housing developer and they've pulled out. I suppose you can't blame them. Who'd want to buy a house knowing an unexploded bomb from World War Two was possibly underneath your shed? Or let your kiddywinks play in the grass knowing it was soaked with diesel all those years ago. I don't go for these conspiracy theories about phone masts giving you the ague, but you can't argue with that sort of thing.'

'And they're suggesting Hill Top Farm instead,' Maddie had said, and Nor had pursed her lips and shaken her head.

'Clive would never have allowed it. Not on his family farm.'

'Over his dead body,' Maddie had whispered to herself. 'Over his dead body.'

Familiar faces sat on the chairs, while some mingled in the aisle. Nor was immediately swept up by Marge and Julia, who had bagged a row of chairs in the middle, and Maddie waved and mouthed something about joining them in two minutes. First though, she headed for the bar, which was set up in the old kitchen serving hatch. She loved that a town meeting couldn't possibly happen without liquid lubrication and smiled when she saw Roger from the Two Pelicans behind the makeshift counter.

'Two glasses of white please, Roger,' Maddie said and he nodded at her as he unscrewed the top off the cheap white wine.

Seeing her wince slightly, he said, 'At least it's cold. Want some ice in the glass too?'

'Why not, thanks,' Maddie agreed and took the glasses from him, passing over a tenner from her purse. 'What brings you here tonight?'

'I've got the licence to sell alcohol here too,' Roger replied. 'And it's quiet in the pub tonight, as all you lot are here, so I thought I might as well set up shop and listen in at the same time.'

'Anything I should be looking out for? As a relative newcomer?'

'Oh, just handbags at dawn between the red and blue councillors. That could be a fun spat. And I always like to see who's on which side. Helps me with the chat at the pub. Wouldn't do to go bemoaning the outcome to someone who supported it when they next come in for a cider.'

Maddie liked his pragmatism. And decided it would be a good idea too – to see who she recognised and which side they came down on. Especially if it involved Hill Top Farm and the fields near the old cow shed.

The meeting started with the usual preliminaries – and continued using such jargon that what was actually a very important issue for the whole community, and intrinsically interesting, became so mind-numbingly boring that Maddie wasn't the only one who had finished her glass of well-iced wine and was staring around the room as the councillors droned on. She caught the basics through the bureaucracy: as Nor had said, the airfield, which had been deemed a brownfield site and therefore good to build on, was in fact contaminated and the developer who had pushed for it to be included in the local town plan's housing target had pulled out. The town now needed to decide which other places could be used for housing and, of course, this was where the controversies started.

Maddie was surprised to see that there were a few locations put forward. The suggestion for halving the primary school's playing fields got a lot of jeers until it was pointed out that half the field was on a slope anyway, which also possibly explained why the school's fledgling football team rarely hosted home matches, not since they lost to St Ives Juniors twenty-seven nil, purely because of gravity. One of the old derelict pubs was proposed, along with its pub garden, to be turned into flats. Maddie noticed Julia and Marge, sitting on her row, were for the inclusion of the area of land just to the east of the town, beyond the petrol station, which would mean more home-owners could walk into Pendragon Creek and use the shops.

Reading from a sheet in front of her, one of the councillors listed Hill Top Farm and there was a mixed reaction – some boos, some cheers.

'The current landowner has said he's not willing to sell to developers, though,' the councillor said and Maddie realised that no one in the room, apart from her, Nor and Julia (and let's face it, by now Marge), knew about Clive's murder. Maddie nibbled on a fingernail. The meeting was continuing while she weighed up the pros and cons of announcing to the room that Clive was dead. Over his dead body... that's what Julia had said earlier, as had Clive himself before he'd died... Some hands were raised and Maddie realised that a vote was being had – in Clive's absence – and Maddie quickly looked to see who was in favour. Not her gran, nor Marge and Julia who liked the peace by the bay for their swimming, and Hill Top's far fields were too far for people to walk in everyday for gifts and cakes and what-not. Maddie saw Roger from the pub with his arms firmly crossed, but Archer, who must have snuck in just as the meeting was starting as he was standing near Roger's hatch, had raised his. That didn't surprise her; Archer wouldn't want the new-builds in the land next to where he and his mum lived, unless they brought better Wi-Fi connection with them perhaps. A man in the row next to her was voting in favour too, while several of the row in front also nodded and shrugged and put their hands up.

Clive wasn't here to vote or veto or whatever it was he should be doing to protect his farm because he was dead. Maddie was struck by indecision over what to do about telling the room. Would this vote be binding? Was the future of Pendragon Creek riding on this? Maddie was about to put her hand up, not to vote but to say something, when the lead councillor was interrupted mid-sentence. Everyone's head turned as the door to the hall opened and, much to the councillors' and crowd's surprise, DI Trevelyan and a few uniformed police constables walked in.

'We're keeping it all very civilised, officers,' one of the councillors said. 'No need to help keep the peace in here yet.' She gave a nervous laugh, which was mirrored by a few others in the hall.

'Nothing of the sort,' Trevelyan started, then raised his voice so that the whole hall could hear him. 'I'm afraid I have some news which may well have an effect on the outcome of this meeting. This morning, at around eight thirty, Clive Pendergast was found dead on his farm. It wasn't a natural death or misadventure. He was shot and killed by some as yet unknown assailant. He was murdered.'

The ripple of gasps and whispered confidences swept around the room. Maddie kept her ear out for anything anyone was saying – any 'I told you so's or similar. But there was nothing there but genuine shock, which turned to grief pretty quickly for those who knew Clive. Maddie looked across Julia and Marge to Nor, who had her head bowed, as if in silent contemplation or prayer. Unable to catch her eye, she looked around the room again. A room of friends, neighbours, townsfolk and councillors. Maddie's main suspects were still Jason and Kieran – connected both to Chloe and Clive – but was she right? Or was one of these shocked and grieving people the murderer?

Maddie felt a shiver across her shoulders as the thought occurred to her... Was the murderer here in the room with them now?

36

'Well, that was quite the entrance,' Maddie said to DI Trevelyan, as the crowd filed out of the hall, heads together gossiping about Clive. 'I didn't think that was in the policeman's handbook?'

DI Trevelyan looked over her head as she spoke, eyeing the room. Maddie noticed him cock an eyebrow at someone, but even though she turned her head to see, she couldn't work out who. There was no uniformed officer there at any rate. Then she realised, and Maddie looked up at Trevelyan. She tried not to concentrate on the particularly nice colour of his eyes and more of what those eyes were showing; concern? Stress? Cunning?

'You did that on purpose, didn't you?' Maddie asked, thinking about what Roger had said about keeping an eye on who supported which motion in the meeting. But rather than keeping tabs on who wanted houses and who didn't, Trevelyan had been interested to see who had reacted to the news of Clive's death.

Finally, Trevelyan looked down at Maddie, who felt very short all of a sudden. 'Plain-clothes officers were in place—'

'To see who reacted to the news of Clive's murder?' Maddie asked, though it was more of a statement.

'Exactly,' Trevelyan agreed. 'I'll get a debrief from my team. Karen's been here all night, did you see her?'

'No,' replied Maddie, simultaneously wondering why she felt odd at his use of his colleague's first name, while also annoyed at herself for not spotting DS Mitchell in the crowd herself. 'I'm sure she noticed everything, though.'

Trevelyan smiled at her. 'You don't like her, do you?'

Maddie was tongue-tied. 'I... It's not that I...'

'She's nice when you get to know her,' Trevelyan said, but what he might have thought were reassuring words hit Maddie like a blow to the gut. But why? She shook the thoughts and feelings away, she did not need this level of complication at the moment. And anyway, she was still cross at Trevelyan for arresting Nor and using her like that. Which reminded her...

'Any news on Jason Briggs by the way? Or Kieran Jones?'

Trevelyan shook his head. 'Briggs gave our guys the slip and is lying low somewhere, though we're keeping tabs on Hugo Pendergast.'

'Do you think Jason might have killed Clive?'

Trevelyan didn't answer. So Maddie conjectured further.

'If he didn't let him use Hill Top like he did Gran's barn? Or do you think Hugo might have killed his father? By all accounts, he must be a tricky customer if he was happy to dupe Gran. Urgh, I'd like to meet him and give him a piece of my mind.'

'I can't comment on any of that,' Trevelyan said and Maddie crossed her arms, missing the slight twitch at the corner of his mouth.

'It's hard to work out what you can and can't sometimes. On one hand, you tell me far too much about some of it, and on the other, you stay annoyingly quiet.' Maddie regretted her outburst almost as soon as she'd said it as she realised she was reminding

Trevelyan of his own shortcomings as a police officer. She blushed.

'Cheerio then,' Roger, carrying a tray of dirty glasses, said as he walked past Maddie, luckily changing the subject from the awkwardness that had fallen between them. 'Picked up some good pointers,' he winked at her and then Maddie, inspired by this, called after him.

'Roger, wait. Let me help.' Maddie gave Trevelyan a quick wave and followed Roger. When she'd caught up, she took the tray from him and kept him talking. 'Yes I did. Pointers, I mean. Interesting to see who spoke up about what. Just like you, it'll help us in the teashop when it comes to small talk. Anything you think I might have missed?'

Roger shrugged. 'You'll have seen what I did, and of course it all went a bit chaotic after your policeman friend there did his big announcement. Terrible about Clive. He was always very generous with straw bales for the town carnival. I hope his son will be as good when he takes over.'

'I wouldn't count on it. Hugo might not want to take over the farm.'

'Fair dos, fair dos,' Roger said, stroking his beard. 'There's a daughter too, of course. And with this planning up in the air. All very suspicious, don't you think?'

Maddie nodded, she couldn't help it, and she trusted Roger; he seemed nice and, as far as she knew, had no skin in the game, as it were. She'd noticed that he'd voted the same way as Marge and Julia to add houses to the east of the village. Unlike Archer.

'Any idea why Archer Lockwood would vote to build on Clive's land?' she asked.

Roger shook his head. 'Not something I'd really know.' He thought about it. 'He and his mum live up by the petrol station, so he might not want more traffic past the house. Whether you're in a mansion or a maisonette, no one wants more houses on their doorstep.'

Maddie nodded at Roger's wisdom. 'That's what I thought, too. Nimbyism. Is it nice up there?' Maddie couldn't picture the houses on the way out of town past the petrol station.

'Not bad, nice little new-builds, if that's your thing. Though, of course, the Lockwoods used to own quite a bit of land round here, I think. Young Archer's father's family, that is. But he's long gone and Archer and his mum ended up in Dolphin Drive.'

'Dolphin Drive?' Maddie queried.

'One of the roads up there. You know what developers are like. At least they're not Porpoise Place or Cuttlefish Close.' Maddie smiled at him. They'd left the Fisherman's Hall now and Roger had his old Volvo hatchback estate parked on the double-yellow lines with his hazard lights on. 'Better get these loaded before that policeman of yours sees me,' Roger said and took the tray of glasses from her.

'He's not my... Oh never mind,' Maddie said as she realised she'd rather rudely left Trevelyan in the hall, no doubt meeting up with his 'she's nice when you get to know her' colleague, Karen. She had meant to pass him the USB stick, but she'd lost sight of him now, and anyway, Roger had given her an idea. She reached a hand into her pocket and fingered the plastic stick drive that was still in there. She had a plan...

37

After a brief 'discussion' over who should drive, with Nor pulling rank and reminding Maddie that it was her car after all, and she was possibly more used to the clutch, Maddie and Nor had climbed into the old Morris Minor and driven the short drive back to Folly Farm. Maddie had filled Nor in on her conversations with Trevelyan and Roger and, similarly, Nor told her what Julia and Marge had to say.

'Both very keen for the new houses to be to the east of the village, where the not-so-new-builds already are. No one wants them near us, which is good. I can see the need for houses, but building them at Hill Top Farm would be ridiculous. There's no bus route there, and water would have to be pumped up from the town as the reservoir is inland. They don't think about these sorts of things when they lick their finger and stick it on a map.'

'I think you're mixing your metaphors there,' murmured Maddie, but basically agreed.

'And Marge says that she heard from Karen Mitchell's mother that they've had a decent lead on Kevin—'

'Kieran?'

'Oh yes, Kieran. Closing in on finding him.'

'That's good. I don't know what motive he'd have for killing Chloe, but if he thought Clive had killed *her*, he – assuming he'd heard about her murder wherever he was hiding out – could well have gone there and got his revenge. His train ticket was found by the farm gate after all. But if that's the case, why did Trevelyan make that announcement?' Maddie looked at her gran. 'Apparently he had—'

'Plain-clothed officers in the crowd,' Nor completed her sentence.

'Yes!' Maddie said and remembered at that point wishing that her grandmother would keep her eyes on the road, not look at her in triumph. 'How did you know?'

'Guess really. Karen Mitchell was there, but not sitting with her mum and dad, which was odd, because if she wasn't working, she'd have been with them.'

'Out of interest, how did they vote?' Maddie asked, as they'd pulled into the farmyard.

Nor waited until Maddie had let herself out of the car and opened the gate, then closed it after Nor had driven through, and popped back in again for the last few yards to the house.

'Hill Top all the way,' Nor said, raising an eyebrow and then getting out of the car.

Maddie put the kettle on and looked in the pantry to see what she could rustle up for a quick supper. There were eggs, of course, and luckily some mushrooms and an end of ham in the fridge. She went about knocking up a couple of perfectly cooked omelettes – set on the outside, carefully rolled out of the frying pan and deliciously oozing in the middle. Along with a mug of tea each, the omelettes formed a decent supper so late in the evening. They ate and chatted, and only once Nor had fed the cats and said goodnight did Maddie get the USB stick out of her pocket. She pulled her laptop over to her, and plugged it in, then waited for both the machine and the file icons to come to life. In a moment, she clicked once again on the USB's icon and saw the password demand come up. She typed in DOLPHIN and pressed return.

Nothing.

Then she typed in D0LPH1N, exchanging the O and I for a zero and a one.

Still nothing.

A blue light outside caught her attention and she got up from the table. The familiar rumble of a diesel engine greeted her as she opened the farmhouse's door. She watched as Trevelyan stepped out. He was alone, so she assumed that neither she nor Nor was about to be arrested again. What could he possibly want now, though?

'Tom?' Maddie asked. 'What's up?'

'Sorry to catch you so late, but I thought you'd like to know that we've found Kieran Jones.'

'Oh.' A million thoughts ran through Maddie's mind. Why had Trevelyan come all this way out of town to tell her in person? Why wasn't he there in the interview room interrogating Kieran? Couldn't he have texted? And also... gosh, he looked quite handsome with his tie loosened and his top button undone. She remembered the smell of soap she'd caught that first day and blushed. Trying to distract from that, she continued, 'I mean, that's great news. Is he talking? Where was he?'

'He was at St Ives train station. Apparently he was dodging the CCTV cameras and only came into view just before the evening train to Penzance pulled out. He jumped on, but an alert was sent down the line and he was picked up at Carbis Bay. I'm heading back to the station now to meet him.' He glanced at his watch. 'I just thought you'd like to know.'

'Thank you,' Maddie said and resisted the urge to reach out and touch his arm. 'I'd be interested to hear what you find out.

You know, if you can. I don't want you to get into trouble though.'

'Look, I...' Tom Trevelyan looked stuck for the right words. 'I really shouldn't tell you anything about the case, but I feel bad about what we did to your grandmother the other night.'

Maddie looked more sharply at him. The wrongful arrest, which by rights she should still be really cross with him about. And she was. Well, not *really* cross.

'She's fine – Nor, I mean. I think it was a bit of a wake-up call for her not to trust every Tom, Dick and Harry—'

'Toms aside,' said Trevelyan hopefully.

'Toms *especially*, if they go around arresting you for no reason,' Maddie said, though she couldn't keep the smile off her lips.

'Well,' Trevelyan said, looking suitably abashed. 'I feel like I owe you and your grandmother something. We did think she might be involved. She owns the barn, she acted quite shadily when we first asked about them and her relationship to Jason—'

'She was scared. And more than that, her pride was dented. I think she just wanted it all – you all – to go away.'

Trevelyan nodded. 'We realised that as soon as we got her in the car. She told Karen that she'd have a sharp word with her mother and then basically told us everything before we even got her into the interview room where you joined us.'

'Hence the not exactly protocol interview.'

'Yeah. And quick release. I am sorry, though. We should have examined the evidence better before pulling her in. So, I owe you.'

'Thank you, Tom.' Maddie used his first name and it felt nice. 'I'd be really interested to know what Kieran says and I might have some more info for you too. Shall we have a coffee tomorrow? Here at the teashop, if you like. I think it'll be a busy one, thanks to tonight's meeting, with no doubt townsfolk having a gander at the fields of Hill Top and, well, you know, seeing what they can see of the farm.'

'I'd like that,' said Trevelyan. He looked at her and Maddie could see that, despite the dark circles under them, his eyes twinkled. And she noticed, too, just a little colouring of his cheeks as he got into the Land Rover and leant out of the window before saying, 'It's a date.'

38

Maddie closed the front door of the house and leant back against it. Tom Trevelyan... She played with the name in her mind for a moment, then felt bad as she remembered Pascal in the kitchen at Chez Lucie and the multiple unanswered messages he'd sent her. She took a deep breath. She would reply to him; she couldn't not. But not right now. Right now, she needed a calming cup of something herbal to help get her heart rate back to normal.

Maddie made sure the front door was locked and bolted and then headed back to the kitchen. She put the kettle on the Aga hotplate and waited for it to boil, allowing her brain to pinball around a few ideas – mostly on what she might wear tomorrow in the teashop and what she'd say to Tom when he asked what info she had, and why on earth she hadn't handed over the USB to him there and then before he spent hours interviewing Kieran without what might be vital information. As she poured the boiling water into one of the stoneware mugs with a few leaves of mint in it, she hit on a plan. The police in St Ives wouldn't necessarily have the tech to crack the USB's encryption, but she could keep trying. That way, tomorrow morning, she could present Tom with some proper information.

Maddie sat herself down at the table, reached over and pulled the old recipe book towards her. The USB stick was still sticking out of her laptop and she opened the machine and waited while the screen lit up and the spinning wheel of doom had sorted itself out. Clicking on the USB's icon, she let the password box come up, then looked at the flapjack recipe – or at least the words written alongside it.

Clive Pendergast – Hill Top Farm – 'of all people' – related
Old cow shed – fallen stones
Last words – aren't you rock would tree help
Bloodied stone = murder
1965 – missing woman SAME PLACE Esther Pendergast
Clotted cream?
Litter
Planning – houses at Hill Top
HER backpack – OUR barn. Jason?!
C&K – lovers' tiff? Him more than her
Entitled
Archer – family tree
Sheila at Seaside B&B – accident – new sash?
Brick – warning!
USB stick – AL – Bella or Archer?
Bad review – dirty floor

Would any of these have anything to do with Archer? If her hunch was correct, one of these jottings here might help her crack the hacker's code. The thought of it made her laugh, though the sound that came out was a hollow sort of one. How could she? But still, she ran her finger down the 'recipe' and found something she thought could work.

ROCKWOULDTREEHELP.

Nothing.

CHLOEPENDERGAST.

Nothing.

She thought back to her original train of thought.

DOLPHIN1965.

The box closed and the folder opened from the icon. Maddie's heart almost jumped out of her chest. She'd done it! It was an old password-creator's trick – combining two different inspirations so it was harder to crack. Not for her and her secret recipe, though...

Excitedly she double-clicked on the folder and let it open up. There were a few documents inside and Maddie clicked on the first one her cursor hovered over. It was a PDF of a family tree, with a time stamp of its download time and the logo of the Truro Register Office. She scanned her eyes along the bottom. Chloe's name was there, descended from her parents; and her father was the son of Martha Hardy, whose sister was Esther Pendergast.

This proved that Chloe was descended from Esther Pendergast, Gerald's first wife, via her grandmother. And Gerald must have inherited Hill Top Farm when Esther died. In fact, it was there in black and white, Esther Pendergast née Martin, d.1965. And a second line from Gerald with his new wife Debbie Pendergast, née Burns-Lacey and their son Clive Pendergast, born 1966, and in turn, his son Hugo born 1992 and daughter Beatrice born 1994. If her gran was right and Hill Top was Esther's before it became Gerald's, then Chloe would have possibly had a better claim to it than Clive. This must have been what Archer had found and told Chloe the night before she'd been killed.

Maddie minimised the spreadsheet family tree and clicked

on the next document. It was a PDF of a newspaper article. *LOCAL WOMAN DISAPPEARS – HUSBAND SUSPECTED OF MURDER.* A picture accompanied it, and Maddie looked at Esther Pendergast, ethereal in a flowing kaftan. Maddie read the article and it stated that Gerald had been arrested but then released on bail. A second PDF showed a similar article, but a week or so later: *LOCAL MAN CLEARED OF ALL CHARGES.* This one recounted how Gerald had had all charges against him dropped due to there being no evidence of foul play, no body and no sign of any type of violence, especially in the location of the ruined cow shed. One name caught her eye, though, and Maddie read to the end of the piece:

> ... the eyewitness who had seen Mrs Pendergast at the cow shelter was Mary Nuttall, who was with her daughter Daphne. Mrs Nuttall, of Pendragon Creek, reported to the police that she had met Mrs Pendergast at the shelter in order to help plan a VE Day celebration barn dance and picnic. She had been in good spirits, Ms Nuttall said, and did not mention plans to leave the county. The investigation continues.

Maddie clicked the PDF shut, and closed down her laptop, pulling out the USB stick. All of this information pointed towards one person having the ultimate motive to murder Chloe Hardy. Clive Pendergast.

But Clive Pendergast was currently in a morgue in St Ives with two shotgun blasts to his chest. Maddie winced at the thought and placed a hand on her own chest. Could Kieran have shot Clive to avenge Chloe's death?

Maddie brought her hand up to her neck – meaning to massage a crick in her shoulder, but it put her in mind of poor Sheila from the B&B and her own accidental – or not – death. Could Kieran have had anything to do with that too? He had been staying at the Seaside View and Sheila had been the last person to see him alive after all? But had Sheila been murdered, or was it just a horrible accident with an unbalanced sash window? That theory didn't sit right with Maddie though – not so soon after those windows had been renovated.

But there was something in the news reports and family tree, or maybe not in them, but behind them, clues that she couldn't quite grasp but knew were there.

Clues that she was sure could solve not one, not two, but possibly three murders. If only she could work it out.

39

Thursday morning started early, and Maddie was relieved that she had managed more than just a few hours' sleep. Her brain had taken a while to switch off – busy brain, she called it – but in the end, the exhaustion of the day had won out and she'd drifted off between thinking about Hugo Pendergast and if he could have anything to do with Chloe and his father's deaths, Kieran Jones and if he could be responsible, and indeed Jason and if he could still be hanging around and behind it all. Oh, and whether Crumpet and Toast would wear tea-cosy-style jackets to promote the teashop in the quieter winter months. Her summary this morning was yes to the first three queries and a resounding no to the last.

Toast had made himself exceptionally comfortable in the warm place Maddie had left as she'd got up, and for once she didn't feel jealous of his plan for sleeping all day. She was keen to get up and get cooking, with the lure, of course, that Tom Trevelyan would be stopping by the teashop at some point this morning for their 'date'. She took a little longer in the bathroom that morning and even pushed some make-up around her face and tried kohl around her eyes, but the look gave her more of the appearance of a tired goth than a sultry sex goddess, so she wiped it off again. She settled for a bit of blush and some mascara, as well as a proper blow-dry to her hair, so instead of the wayward curls, it fell over her shoulders in soft conker-brown waves.

'That'll last until the urn starts steaming and the oven belches out heat again,' she said to a passing Crumpet, who chirruped in reply, which Maddie took to be a sign of agreement.

Flinging her battered old denim jacket on over her T-shirt, she felt ready for the day – whatever this one might throw at her...

As predicted, the teashop was heaving. Luckily, with both Nor and Maddie on baking duty earlier that morning and manning the till and counter now, they could just about keep up with demand for Nor's famous coffee and walnut cake and the scones. Maddie had adapted a recipe she'd used in Chez Lucie's kitchens and, despite the oven's best attempts at both sabotage and arson, she'd been able to dish up warm, double-chocolate brownies alongside Nor's infamously delicious cake and both cheese and fruit scones. She was just whipping up another batch of brownies and was selflessly testing the batter from the end of the wooden spoon before it went in the sink, when a now familiar voice said her name from the other side of the counter.

'Maddie?'

She turned and saw Tom Trevelyan standing there. He looked exhausted. She didn't know if it was same shirt as last night, but it was crumpled, and he'd given up on a tie, though he was still wearing his suit.

'Tom,' Maddie said, gesturing for him to sit down at a recently vacated table. 'You look like you need a coffee.'

Tom grinned at her and she wondered why until he said, 'And you look like you need a napkin.'

'Oh blast,' Maddie said, swiping the corners of her mouth with the tea towel that was tucked into her apron. A dark smear of chocolate brownie mix came off on the towel and Maddie cursed herself for being so greedy.

Once she'd checked her reflection in the glass of the cake dome (which wasn't advised on a normal occasion unless you wanted the impression that your head was the size of a beach ball stuck in your mind for the rest of the day), and made Tom and herself a coffee, she joined him at the table.

'Sorry about that,' she said, putting the coffees down.

'Got to test the goods, I get it.' Tom grinned again and Maddie saw how it crinkled the corners of his eyes. His exceptionally tired eyes.

'And they get five stars from me,' Maddie smiled at him. 'Thanks for pointing it out, though. The only thing worse than having something on your face is no one telling you you've got something on your face.'

Tom laughed. 'True, true.'

'So, any news?' Maddie sat down and leant her elbows on the table.

'Kieran's in custody. He insists he's innocent—'

'Is he charged with murder?'

'No, not yet. We can't bring a charge until the Crown Prosecution Service decides there's enough evidence and so far all we have is his train ticket near the Pendergast farm, which his solicitor rightly pointed out is highly circumstantial.'

'Circumstantial sounds a bit like coincidental to me, and we all know how there's no such thing as coincidence.'

'Except in a court of law, where there is, unless it can be proven otherwise.'

They both deflated a little. Then Maddie asked. 'Do you think it's him? Do you get a feeling? What else did he say?'

Tom sighed. 'Nothing. He's clammed up. Solicitor told him not to say anything else.'

Maddie made a face. 'How frustrating.'

'You're telling me,' Tom said, rubbing one of his eyes with the heel of his hand.

'So he didn't say anything about Sheila? She said she saw him leave – in fact, until he was picked up by that CCTV camera, she was the last person to see him. And now she's—'

'Dead,' Tom completed her sentence. 'You're right, there's something off about Mrs Laverstoke's death.' Maddie nodded – and tried not to think about how good it felt that Tom agreed with her. He carried on. 'We've looked into it, and the post-mortem is still to come back, but initial reports are that it's consistent with a crushing injury from a heavy window right across the windpipe.'

Maddie grimaced and subconsciously touched her neck again. Then she said, 'If Kieran was hiding out near Hill Top, and then St Ives, assuming he was heading there for the station, could he really have got back to Seaside View in Pendragon Creek without being seen? And be able to sneak back into the B&B and kill Sheila, all for what? Why? Because she'd seen him leaving in a huff, taking his bags with him, hours before his girlfriend was killed?'

'You're certain Mrs Laverstoke was murdered?' Trevelyan asked. 'There's still a chance it was an accident. The forensics team haven't called it yet.'

Maddie shrugged. Then she remembered that she owed it to Tom to tell him about the USB stick. She slipped it out of her apron pocket and handed it over, summing up what she'd found out by cracking the password.

'So, you see, Chloe did have an excellent claim to Hill Top Farm. Or at least her dad does, via his mum, who was Esther Pendergast's sister, who had moved away to marry a farmer in Lincolnshire.'

Tom had taken this all in in moderate silence. Then he shook his head. 'Why didn't you give me this last night? I mean, this is a murder investigation. I could have you arrested for withholding evidence.'

'Pish.' The voice that replied to him wasn't Maddie's, who had gone beetroot red at the gentle telling-off… and the interruption by her gran. 'Maddie was just checking it wasn't Bella's homework. She's an Arabella, you see – Arabella Leach, AL. If Maddie'd handed that in last night, with a big hoo-ha and called you out of a tense interview just at a vital moment, and it was just some French verbs or an essay on the Tudors, you and DS Mitchell would have had her over the coals for wasting police time.' Nor stood her ground, her arms folded in defence of her granddaughter.

'What she said,' said Maddie, pointing to Nor.

Tom just shook his head. 'OK, OK…' He looked at Maddie. 'And well found, by the way, and even better cracked. What was it again? Dolphin 1965?'

'Yes. Caps. And the 1965 I think relates to when Esther went missing. And the Dolphin is Archer's address. Those articles on the USB that Archer had found for Chloe say Gerald was arrested and then let off as there was no case to answer. No body, no sign of a struggle, she just disappeared.'

Nor rolled her eyes. 'I know I said we'd all called her a bolter, but there was plenty of folk who thought Gerald had done it. Debbie's parents included. Worried the hell out of them that their daughter was marrying a man with such a cloud over his history. It's not just fishermen and sailors the salty sea takes to its depths, you mark my words.'

'But you liked Gerald? You said he and Debbie threw amazing parties? Barn dances and the like?' Maddie had turned in her seat and was quizzing her grandmother. 'And now you think he was a murderer?'

Nor shrugged. 'Just because a man throws a nice party

doesn't make him a saint. And don't forget, the Pendergasts only have Hill Top due to Gerald marrying Esther, and then her disappearing, else he couldn't have married Debbie and had Clive.'

Maddie and Tom exchanged a look. Then Tom continued, 'And speaking of Pendergasts and disappearing, guess who's done a runner?'

'Who?' Maddie asked, a sense of urgency in her voice.

'Hugo Pendergast. Timing couldn't have been worse for him. Yes, we've hauled in Kieran, and yes, he's definitely not off the hook, but for a man to disappear just after his father's shot dead, with him the only other definite person in the house – well, that's suspicious.'

'Him and Jason alike,' said Maddie, looking up to her grandmother. 'Suspicious indeed.'

40

Maddie watched Tom Trevelyan's police Land Rover disappear through the farm gates. She still hated the fact that Nor had been through a wrongful arrest, but it was helpful that Tom now felt so bad about it that he was sharing so much of the case's info with her. And what she'd just learned was interesting indeed. And she appreciated Nor sticking up for her about the USB stick – and smiled at the fact that her gran had exactly the same excuse lined up for her as she had, even though they'd both known by last night that USB stick contained nothing in the way of French verbs or history essays. The grin disappeared from her face when she walked back into the teashop and saw Nor arguing with a woman wearing grey trousers, a blue blouse and holding a clipboard.

Uh-oh, Maddie thought, recognising a bureaucrat when she saw one. Without needing to be told, she knew that this was the lady from the council who had threatened to close the teashop. The lady who had said something about Nor's use of the farm's own eggs and probably very much not enjoyed Nor's own style of revenge. The laxative style.

Maddie smiled at a few customers, hoping they couldn't see the worry behind her rictus grin. As she got within earshot of Nor and the lady from the council, she heard the conversation...

'Mrs Penrose, it says here that you were arrested the other night.'

'Slander, libel! Who told you that?' Nor was standing with her arms crossed.

'It's not slander if it's true, and my friend Karen told me—'

'Karen Mitchell can mind her own beeswax,' huffed Nor. 'And so what if I was? It was a wrongful arrest and I'm an innocent and free woman. Plus, you just said yourself that you've tested some of my eggs and they're as wholesome as they come. So what's the problem?'

'The problem, Mrs Penrose, is the small matter of you poisoning a member of the council—'

'Hello...' Maddie interrupted. She introduced herself, shooting a look at her gran which she hoped was interpreted as 'zip it, for now', and gave the lady from the council a quick rundown of her qualifications and experience. '... And with the NCASS level three certificate it means I'm qualified to run a kitchen, plus I'm trained in first aid and...' Maddie carried on, hoping this would all knock the lady from the council's socks off, or at least make her forget about the laxative-laced coffee.

'Miss Penrose, I don't need your CV,' the lady from the council said, cutting Maddie off before she could get into her results from her culinary college. 'What I need is proof from you that no other customers will be harmed by your lax... attitude to health and safety.'

Out of the corner of her eye, Maddie was sure she could see her gran stifling a laugh that turned into a cough. She covered it well though, and Maddie continued. 'Well, I've just made a fresh batch of award-winning double-chocolate brownies, can I tempt you? Perhaps box some up for you to take home?'

The lady from the council looked doubtful, which wasn't surprising given her last encounter with freebies from this teashop. It didn't help that Nor was grinning and Maddie had a sneaking suspicion that the rest of her supply of Dulcolax might have just made it into the brownies. What must this woman think of them?

'I won't, thank you. Tempting as they sound.' The lady from the council put the lid back on her pen. 'I can see you're busy, so I won't stay any longer, but be warned, if this venue is connected in any way to the recent' – she lowered her tone – 'goings-on, then I will have to look closely at your permissions. The Pendragon Creek area is a very special one, and we don't need dubious establishments tarring our reputation.' With that, she clutched her clipboard under her arm and left.

As they watched her get into her car, Maddie turned to Nor and raised an eyebrow. 'Dubious establishment, eh? Shall we put that on the sign?'

Nor rolled her eyes, then gestured with her hand as if reading a grand sign in front of her. 'Folly Farm Teashop – Keeping the Council on Their Toes since 1983.'

'Toes? On the run more like.'

Nor grinned. 'Or runs...'

With the lady from the council finally gone, and Nor looking furtive behind the counter, Maddie could get her brain back onto the murders at hand. She took a payment for three teas, two brownies and a slice of cake while smiling to the customer and thinking about the coincidence that Kieran Jones had just been caught, and Hugo Pendergast had disappeared. She didn't doubt the police's intel, but she did wonder if perhaps she might find out a bit more if she headed up to Hill Top Farm herself after closing.

As four o'clock came around, the teashop emptied and for the last hour, Maddie and Nor pottered around, clearing away crockery and generally having a tidy. Nor chattered away about her friends Marge and Julia and filled Maddie in on some more local news. And for news, read 'gossip'.

'Marge says Daphne Lockwood was in buying something nice the other day,' Nor said, folding a tea towel over the Aga rail.

'Archer's mum?'

'That's right. A piece from the cruise collection, which is shorthand for the "we saw you coming" collection, though don't you dare tell Marge I said that. But, honestly, a kaftan for seventy quid! Who buys that sort of thing?'

'Rich people, Gran,' Maddie said, rather automatically as she was concentrating on fixing the rotor handle of an old hand whisk.

'Well, Daphne's never been rich. Not since her husband walked out on her anyway. It was a real struggle to send Archer to university, Marge said. Anyway, Julia said her husband has banned her from going to Marge's shop until the sales are on, and then she's not allowed in for more than twenty minutes at a time,' Nor nattered on and Maddie half listened as she tried to wangle a screwdriver into the tiny cavity. 'And apparently we'll hear next week about where the council want to put those houses, but there's been a last-minute, very confidential, approach from someone about Hill Top.'

'Really?' Maddie dropped the screwdriver on the table and gave her gran her full attention. 'What does that mean? Clive's probate can't have come through yet, he's not even had a funeral.'

Nor tapped her temple as she tried to remember. 'Ah me, it's slipped my mind. Julia said Bob on the council had spoken to someone local who had information about the ownership of

Hill Top Farm and that it could probably be released to the developer by the summer.'

'Wow, that's news indeed. It can't be a coincidence. I wonder if it's got anything to do with Hugo disappearing?'

Nor shrugged and went back to wiping down the tables. Maddie let the screwdriver and hand whisk rest between bouts and instead got the recipe book out. She looked at the list of words she had written:

Clive Pendergast – Hill Top Farm – 'of all people' – related
Old cow shed – fallen stones
Last words – aren't you rock would tree help
Bloodied stone = murder
1965 – missing woman SAME PLACE Esther Pendergast
Clotted cream?
Litter
Planning – houses at Hill Top
HER backpack – OUR barn. Jason?!
C&K – lovers' tiff? Him more than her
Entitled
Archer – family tree
Sheila at Seaside B&B – accident – new sash?
Brick – warning!
USB stick – AL – Bella or Archer?
Bad review – dirty floor

She wrote *developer?* after the line about planning at Hill Top Farm.

Did any of those words help her come up with a motive that tied both Chloe and Clive's death together? Not to mention poor Sheila from the B&B. With three murders – for she was convinced that Sheila's death had been one – within the last few days here at Pendragon Creek, things were looking decidedly dicey. And with the lady from the council's very real threat of closing Folly Farm teashop down if anything else were to happen, Maddie knew she had to think hard. Before it was too late.

41

'Still graffitiing my old recipe book, eh?' Nor called over from the far side of the teashop. 'Careful, the original recipe for the coffee and walnut cake is in there, I think.'

'Ooh, with the secret recipe for the nuts too?' Maddie's train of thought was diverted from murder – but then Maddie reckoned her grandmother's sweet and crunchy caramelised walnuts could probably have made Sherlock Holmes drop his pipe and raise his deerstalker.

'Oh no, that's firmly up here.' Nor tapped her temple again and Maddie laughed.

'What you can do with a walnut is nobody's business—'

'I'm not putting it on Only Buns though,' Nor interrupted, a twinkle in her eye.

'I'm still not entirely sure, that you're entirely sure, that you know what that means, Gran.'

Nor raised an eyebrow. 'Don't I just?'

'Gran!' Maddie whipped out her tea towel from her apron's waistband and flicked it at her grandmother, who laughed as she easily dodged it. Then she flicked through the recipe book, as if for the first time realising that it held treasures far greater than just her list of suspicions. 'Gosh Gran, there's some corkers in here. Maybe we could add some to the menu? Create a fuller offering to the walkers. My brownies went down well today and they keep well too, so I could batch bake and freeze some so we don't have such a panic in the kitchen in the morning. And you know what, on one of my walks, I was thinking about the scones... well, due to the cream and everything.'

'You've sorted that though, haven't you? Bella and the cats?'

'Sounds like a sixties folk pop group,' Maddie said, going off topic, then pulling herself back to it. 'But yes, the cream got me thinking. How about instead of cream, we serve cream cheese, but' – she carried on despite Nor's shocked face – 'we serve it with the cheese scones and some chutney? A savoury cream tea. For those who want something around lunchtime and don't want a sweet cream tea. Also, I'm sure almost every teashop in Cornwall serves a cream tea, they all probably claim to serve the best—'

'Well, I've never done that. Not with Crumpet as part of the package, ready to get your cream before you've even spooned it onto your scone.'

'Well,' Maddie continued, 'we could claim to serve the best *alternative*. It rather suits us; Folly Farm, well it might be madness, but we could try it. Might even get into the CornwallNow website or the local radio.'

'That's not a bad idea, my girl, not bad at all. There's my mother's old cheese scone recipe in that book of ours – just be careful not to write your Christmas list all over it.'

Maddie reached over and gave her grandmother a spontaneous hug. She didn't know how to put into words, as she hadn't really put into thoughts, how grateful she was for being here, and being encouraged – or at least not actively discouraged – for having ideas and being creative. The savoury cream tea was an idea she'd been noodling since she'd wondered about Crumpet and Toast and why they weren't called Coffee and Walnut (though she thought to herself that she should keep those names on standby in case Nor wanted to get puppies). Anyway, she squeezed her gran and released her, then let her help her finish the tidying and cleaning up, ready for the busy day tomorrow would no doubt be.

As they both walked across the yard, Maddie, who'd been pondering Nor's information about the ownership and a possible developer at Hill Top Farm, told her gran she wanted to walk back up there again.

'There'll still be police all over it, won't there?' Nor asked. 'And if there isn't, you be careful.'

'I will, I promise. I just can't help but think there might be something I can glean from taking a peek around the farmyard. Not that I want to see where Clive was murdered,' she gave an involuntary shiver, 'but I just feel like it's an itch I need to scratch.'

'And if it gives you fodder to talk to your nice policeman about, the more, the better, eh?'

Maddie smiled at her grandmother and for once didn't correct her.

After a bolstering cup of tea made on the Aga from the ever-warm kettle, not from the urn, and half a left-over chocolate brownie (waste not want not, though Maddie wondered if her waist wanted it at all), Maddie was up and out, following the path along the hedge line towards the old cow shed, the tumble and the sycamore tree. She turned at the right spot to take the path across the fields to Hill Top Farm and before too long she could see the corrugated roofs of the barns and the farmhouse. Maddie could also see the yellow and black of police tape, and as she approached the large metal five-bar gate, she could see the tape fluttering in the breeze. This must have been where Hugo broke it and drove off, never to be seen again – for now.

'He'll be inheriting the farm, along with his sister,' Maddie muttered to herself. 'He'll have to come back at some point.' Saying it out loud made her realise what a strange thing it was for the police to have assumed he'd done a runner. Surely he'd just gone to stay with Beatrice in London, or drown his sorrows at a pub in St Ives. The fact that Tom had said he'd *disappeared*... well, that was odd.

Maddie stepped over the flapping police tape and closed the farm gate behind her, out of habit more than anything else. She didn't think the cows would escape. *Who's looking after them?* She suddenly worried, realising that a herd of cows would need feeding and mucking out on an industrial scale. It was then that she realised the farm was totally silent. She peeked into the barn that had held the gently lowing cattle during the shoot day and there was no sign of them. *At least they're out in the fields*, Maddie surmised as she gave the steel-framed barn a double pat, as if to punctuate her thought on their whereabouts. She regretted it, though, as the clang from even her gentle pat echoed around the empty yard.

A scuffling from the other side of the farm made her turn around, but she could see nothing, no movement, nothing out of place. More cautiously, and with a shiver thanks to both the breeze and the odd atmosphere around her, she edged her way along the barn, keeping its metal wall close to her back. One of the doors was slightly ajar and Maddie poked her head in. The barn still smelt of fresh hay and recently departed cows, but otherwise there wasn't much in there.

Something bright orange sticking out from one of the haphazard piles of straw in the corner caught her eye and with a quick check over her shoulder, she slipped fully into the barn and tiptoed over to the brightly coloured thing. A few careful brushes with her hand revealed an item Maddie wasn't expecting. As far as she knew, Hill Top was a beef and dairy farm. Clive, according to Nor, had bought in feed and hay for the cows, only making a bit of it himself from the pastures when the cows weren't out in them most of the year anyway.

So why would he need a brand-new Chisel Plough 3000?

42

Maddie stared at the Chisel Plough 3000. She flicked a few more strands of straw off it and then noticed the big green tarpaulin that was stretched over something only a few yards away. Gingerly, she lifted a corner and saw another piece of equipment. She couldn't identify it, but it looked brand new and was painted the same lurid orange as the Chisel Plough 3000. And it was definitely agricultural.

Maddie furrowed her brow as she released the tarpaulin. This was a cow barn. There was still, in the nicest possible terms, 'evidence' of cows being in here. This wasn't an arable or mixed farm. So again, she thought to herself, why was there this brand-new machinery here?

That it was similar – and, indeed, in the case of the Chisel Plough 3000, identical – to the pieces that Jason had stored at her gran's hadn't escaped her. Hugo had recommended him to Nor after all, having had his own father say no. But now Clive was dead...

'Oh, gosh,' Maddie exclaimed to herself, then continued thinking out loud. 'What if Clive had said no to Hugo, that he wouldn't store this stuff, so Hugo, the rat, targeted Gran. But now Clive's dead, Hugo can use the farm for what he likes. Maybe Jason only came this far up the hill when he left us? What if—'

'Jason's still here?' The gruff voice caught her by surprise and she turned in an instant to see the angry face, on the burly body, of Jason Briggs. 'Question is, sunshine, what are you doing here?'

'I... I...' Maddie was stumped.

'Notcha Gran's farm this time, so you can't use that excuse. Aren't cha a bit out of your lane coming up here, nosing around?' Jason's tone and his large, looming presence scared the hell out of Maddie, but a few of his words rang a bell in her mind. If only she could press pause on this horrible situation and whip out the recipe book and run through her list. She was sure he'd just said something important... but the pause button didn't exist, and Jason, and his angry words did. 'Probably time you was taught a lesson about nosing your way in other people's business, yeah?'

Maddie gulped as she watched him reach into his back pocket and then, in one swift movement, pull out a baton and flick his wrist to extend it. It was the type of thing police carried if they needed to defend themselves against rioters. Maddie stumbled back and felt the sharp prongs of the Chisel Plough 3000 press, once again, into her back.

'I'm so sorry, I... I was looking for Hugo P-Pendergast. I knew his f-father,' Maddie stammered, hoping that some sort of legitimate connection to the farm she was effectively trespassing on would help her cause.

'Hugo, eh? What's he told you?' Jason edged closer to her, and with nowhere for Maddie to retreat to except closer to the sharp prongs of the Chisel Plough 3000, all she could do was cower backwards, hoping she didn't lose her balance and end up speared by one of the sharp points.

'I h-haven't spoken to him. I haven't even m-met him yet.'

Maddie hoped this wasn't the wrong thing to say. Since Jason and Hugo were obviously in cahoots, it would probably have helped her cause if she could say she was Hugo's friend.

Jason slapped the baton down on his open palm and the sound of it made Maddie wince. 'What are we goin' to do with you, eh? Aren't cha our little problem?' Jason growled, but Maddie was distracted again by something he'd said.

'We?' Maddie all but whispered.

Jason looked, for the first time, as if he was now on the back foot. Maddie could see the thought process cross his brow. His eyes twitched as he worked out what to say. If she needed proof that Hugo Pendergast had been a part of this dodgy farming equipment business all along, she had it, without Jason even needing to say a word. Sadly for Maddie, though, it was the only positive in this whole terrifying experience and Jason soon made up his mind what he was going to say.

'I'm gonna have to sort you out.' He emphasised the first word and then slapped the baton against his palm again, and then again slowly, menacingly, until...

'Oh no you won't.' The voice came from the other side of the barn. 'Step back from her and let her pass.'

Jason didn't even bother turning around and smirked as the voice, familiar to them both, didn't necessarily instil much fear into him.

'Oh yeah.' He raised his voice, still glaring at Maddie, but now talking to the voice behind him. 'And how are you going to make me, Granny?'

Finally, with another smirk and a raised eyebrow to Maddie, Jason turned around to face Nor Penrose. It was but a moment before Maddie saw his shoulders fall and the baton drop out of his hand, and as she peered around his bulky frame she could see why.

Nor was standing there, empty-handed and unthreatening... but not alone.

43

'Move slowly towards me, with your hands where I can see them,' DI Trevelyan said, the authority in his voice strengthened by the presence of two police constables who flanked him on either side.

Maddie felt herself start to shake and she carefully sidestepped her way along the Chisel Plough 3000 as Jason complied with Trevelyan's orders. As the bulky man was put into handcuffs and read his rights, Maddie felt the comforting arms of her grandmother wrap around her.

'Oh, Gran.' Maddie collapsed into the hug, squeezing her grandmother tight. 'Thank you, thank you. How did you know?'

'There, there, ducky,' Nor comforted her. 'It's all fine now. And I knew you were here, you told me so yourself.'

'Yes, but...' Maddie pulled away and wiped a tear of relief from her eye with the end of her sleeve. 'But how did you know I'd be in danger? How did you get Tom and the police here so soon?'

'As soon as you said you were coming up here, I phoned that nice policeman of yours—'

'He's not... Oh never mind.' Maddie wiped a tear from her other eye.

'I thought to myself, if Maddie's going sniffing around up there, it'll be for a good reason. Or a no good reason perhaps, depending on which way you look at it. No smoke without fire. You had a hunch and I believe in you, ducky. You've got a chef's sense when things aren't right.'

Maddie furrowed her brow, but there was a truth in what Nor was saying. She had always been able to tell when a dish she was cooking wasn't working. A sixth sense for a sunken soufflé. Though, in some cases, like when smoke billowed out of an old, broken oven, it was hardly a psychic power, more of a looking at the bleeding obvious.

Maddie smiled at Nor. 'Thanks, Gran, I know what you mean. And yup, I just knew there was something fishy about Hugo, or at least goings on here at Hill Top that didn't make sense. Who would kill Clive? Is it Hugo? Or Jason? Kieran? Or someone else altogether?'

Tom Trevelyan appeared next to them and gently placed a hand on Maddie's back.

'Are you OK?' he asked and Maddie's knees almost gave way.

I was... she thought, but smiled back up at him and nodded.

With that reassurance, he carried on, answering her rhetorical questions that he must have heard as he'd walked up to them both. 'And you're right. We still have no clear idea about who killed Clive Pendergast, or if his death was linked to that of Chloe Hardy.'

'They have to be, surely?' Maddie replied.

'Even I can see they must be linked,' Nor said. 'Barely a week between them and her thinking she'd be the one to inherit his land, or even take it off him, thanks to Archer and his research.'

Maddie suddenly turned to her grandmother. 'Say that again, Gran.'

Nor looked at her. 'What again? A week between them? We all know that.'

'No, the bit after.' Maddie gestured for her to keep going, repeating the words she'd just said while she reached behind her and pulled the folded recipe book out of her back pocket. Opening it up on the flapjack recipe, she ran her finger down her list as Nor spoke again.

'I just said that Chloe thought she'd be inheriting Clive's land—'

'Thanks to Archer and his research,' Maddie finished Nor's sentence for her as she ran her finger down the page. A thought sparked and she closed the recipe book and looked at DI Trevelyan. 'I think I have an inkling, but it's just that. Just the germ of an idea.'

'What? Who?' Trevelyan asked.

'I don't want to waste your time on it, if it isn't right,' Maddie said, garbling her words a bit. 'But there's just something Jason said earlier and then Gran just said that thing... it could just be... I mean, it would make sense for why Chloe was killed... and maybe Clive too, although that could still be Hugo or Jason, unless... I'd need to check that at the council... hmm, and Sheila's murder too... oh my, I think the walls had ears...'

'Maddie...' Trevelyan looked quizzically at her. 'What are you thinking? What's on your mind?'

Maddie looked at him, and then her gran, and felt her face flush. She did have an inkling but nothing to back it up yet, and no motive she could see for it, and the last thing she wanted, in this fledgling friendship with DI Trevelyan, was to waste his and the force's time on some random thought of hers.

And let's face it, she thought to herself, *my thoughts can be as random as sausages in a salad.*

'I... I don't have anything. Not really. Not yet. But I'll let you know as soon as I do. I promise.'

Maddie and Nor covered the distance between Hill Top Farm and Folly Farm as quickly as they could, bearing in mind one of them was eighty-two and the other had recently had her knees turned to jelly by both an unsettling thug and then a very handsome policeman. On the way, Maddie went over a few things with her grandmother.

'I hope Tom didn't think me a bit weird then,' she said, helping Nor over one of the stiles. 'He could have given you a lift home, you know, if you wanted?'

'Got to keep myself fit, and there's nothing like a stile to help you keep getting your leg over,' Nor replied and Maddie, despite the stress of the day, suppressed a giggle.

'I just don't think that means what you think it means, Gran,' she said, but all Nor would do was wink at her. 'Anyway, the more I think about it now, the more I'm doubting myself, Gran.'

'What's that phrase? Doubt whom you will, but never yourself,' Nor said as they entered the gate to their farm, each of them greeting a cat as they pushed the gate open and then closed it again after them.

'That's easy for you to say.' Maddie sighed as she thought through her theory again. There was one missing ingredient from her list that would bind the whole investigation together. And rather than wasting Trevelyan's time, if she got it right it might put her straight to the top of his good books. Which was somewhere, she had to admit, she liked the sound of being.

Maddie and Nor ate supper together, with Maddie showing off her air-light batter with her own version of toad-in-the-hole –

adding fresh sage and rosemary from the bushes by the back door into the pan as the sausages sizzled before pouring in the well-beaten batter. After a day on their feet in the teashop, and the drama at Hill Top, they decided this old family favourite was needed.

'What will you tell your parents?' Nor asked, having finished her meal, and Maddie wondered how much she'd tried to put the air of nonchalance in her voice.

'Oh, I don't know. Just enough,' Maddie said, pushing a piece of batter around her plate in order to scoop up some of the onion gravy she'd made to go with the toad, aka sausages. 'Maybe a few of the more juicy details once this case is over and the murderer among us is caught.'

'Yes, possibly best to wait until then. We don't want your mum and dad driving down from Surrey in high dudgeon, thinking this is no fit place for their daughter to be staying.'

'Gran,' Maddie reached over and took her gran's hand. 'They'd never think that. I wouldn't let them.'

'I can't have you leaving me now, not with all those good ideas you're having for cream cheese teas and chutney biscuits and what have you,' Nor carried on and Maddie squeezed her hand, both reassuring her and so relieved at the fact that her grandmother obviously seemed to want her to stay. She wasn't sure what chutney biscuits were, but that didn't matter.

Maddie was going to ask more about what Julia had said on the subject of Hill Top being handed over to the developer when she and Nor both jumped at the sound of a crash in the farmyard. It was dark outside by now and with no curtains at the kitchen windows, all they could see as they glanced over was blackness.

'What was that?' Maddie asked as she got up from the table and Nor shook her head.

'Horses maybe? Cam can kick out a bit when he's bored.'

'I don't think it was...' Maddie edged her way along the table to one of the windows, as quietly as possible so as to keep tuning in to the sounds outside. There it was again, heavy footsteps and a crash as if a blind man or a drunk was stumbling around.

'I'll get the torch,' Nor said, but before she could push her chair back from the table, Maddie had screamed.

For there, at the window, suddenly illuminated by the light from the kitchen, was what looked like the ghostly pale and bodyless face of a man.

A man she recognised.

Clive Pendergast.

44

Maddie screamed and rocked back from the window.

'It can't be...' The face had retreated, but the image of it stuck in her mind. It had been Clive. The nose, the red hair... but younger.

Maddie assumed that ghosts weren't much afraid of the physical realm, but it didn't stop her from picking up a sturdy wooden rolling pin and brandishing it at the window.

The face appeared again.

'Get away! Shoo!' she yelled through the glass, but the face just grimaced – not a smirk or a sneer, but contorted into what looked like pain.

Could this apparition in the darkness really be the tortured soul of Clive Pendergast? Despite the abject terror she was experiencing, a thought did occur to her. If this *was* Clive, or his ghost, it would be pretty bloody handy if he could tell her who shot him.

Nor came up behind Maddie, a hefty torch in her hand, but she lowered it as she saw who was at the window.

'Well, I never. That's Hugo Pendergast, that is.'

The head outside the window either heard her, or hoped that he might have been recognised and started gesturing for them to open the back door for him.

'Hugo...' Maddie shook her head. 'For a moment, I thought it was Clive.'

'Looks like him, doesn't he? He really is the spitting image.'

'Scarily so,' admitted Maddie as Nor moved towards the door. 'Are we letting him in, Gran? He looks a bit, well, hacked off.'

'I think he's just accidentally stepped in the bucket of chicken shit, which I left out there 'til I could be bothered to swill it away tomorrow morning. Judging by the look on his face, and that clanking sound we heard, I reckon his foot's right in it.'

Maddie lowered her rolling pin.

The face outside the window frowned, but nodded, which meant he probably had heard what Nor was saying.

Maddie looked at him. In her mind, she'd painted Hugo as some shady, good-for-nothing character, ready to rip off old ladies and latterly shoot perhaps even his own father. Not this hapless-looking young man with his foot in the chicken bucket.

Maddie walked over to the back door and opened it.

'Hugo?' she called out and watched as a man, dressed in jeans, a Viyella checked shirt and a fleece gilet, but with a galvanised steel bucket on his foot, clanked his way towards them.

'Yes, that's me. Hugo Pendergast, how do you do?' The man stuck his hand out and Maddie, too shocked to do anything else, took it and accepted his rather limp-wristed shake.

'What are you doing here?' Maddie asked. 'The police are after you.'

'And we'll call them, too, if you come anywhere near my nice clean floor,' Nor added.

Maddie smiled at her grandmother, but again, something

touched the edge of her brain, tingled in a way a squirt of lime might do in a glass of soda water, and she put the thought aside as she stood in the calamitous runaway's path, not letting him in.

'Hello, Mrs Penrose,' Hugo said, looking past Maddie into the kitchen.

Nor moved closer, but was still standing behind Maddie as she spoke. 'You've got a nerve showing up here, boy. What are you doing skulking around my farm in the dark? Moving more stolen goods?'

'I'm sorry, Mrs Penrose.' Hugo Pendergast looked like he was about to start blubbing. 'I didn't mean to get you involved, but Jason said he'd play ball and pay well and be out of your hair in a matter of weeks. Didn't realise he'd need so long to find buyers. Or be such a Johnny Rotten.'

Maddie, who was still confused as to why a wanted man, who was on the run, was now standing by the back door on the verge of tears, held her hand up. 'Hang on, so tell me, from the start, what business you and that horrid Jason bloke are in.'

Hugo looked sheepishly up at her. 'You must be Maddie. Hello.'

'Hello,' Maddie said, hoping she wasn't about to get another feeble handshake.

'So, yah, right.' Hugo's posh, slightly foppish, accent instantly told her he'd attended a public school, albeit a minor one most likely, where he probably wasn't all that academically successful but learned how to say hello to a chap and shoot a clay and think he was awfully clever by getting into money-making wheezes with common chaps who really knew what they were doing. Her assumptions were mostly proved correct by what he said. 'So, yah, um, well, I'd met Jason in Truro, and I say met, he came up to me in the car park of the Coach and Horses and said he was in the same business as me, and muggins here hadn't really thought about it until later, but of course it seems obvs now to one that of course how did he know what business I was in, but he said he needed some farms in the locale of Pops' farm.' At that, he stuttered, and Maddie remembered that if he wasn't the murderer, he was just a young man who'd lost his father. 'And said if I could grease the old wheels of getting the farmers to rent out the barns to him, for good dollar he said, he could see to it that I didn't have any trouble.'

'What sort of trouble?' Maddie asked.

'Um, well, yah, he didn't say. But when Pops said categorically no to it, I thought I better suggest somewhere else pronto and I'm really sorry, Mrs Penrose, but your farm came to mind and I didn't think you'd mind the moolah, and to be honest I thought Jason might be one of those hard men who got all soft over grannies, so rather hoped for the best that you might be a bit win-win out of it, know what I mean?'

'No, not really.' Maddie shook her head. Of course she knew what Hugo meant, but she didn't want to let him off that easily. 'You're telling me that you thought it would be a good idea to send your dodgy new friend round to my grandmother to bully her into storing his, what... stolen goods?'

'Hmm, yah, well, when you say it like that. Yah. Bad form of me.' Hugo shuffled his one bucket-less foot like a schoolboy in the head teacher's office.

'Yeah, pretty bloody bad form, Hugo,' Maddie agreed. 'And? What are the tractors and ploughs? Stolen from local farms?'

'Um, no, well, yes. In a sort of way. They're expensive things, you know, that big one was a Fendt and it was over quarter of a mil.' Hugo sort of huffed out a laugh, the sort that stupid posh men do when they're genuinely impressed by something, like a batting average, or the top BHP of a convertible car. 'So yah, Jason had a guy down in the Lizard and he released these bad boys from their contracts, so to speak—'

'He stole them?'

'I mean, yah, I don't think that word was used, but now I think about it, umm, well, yah. Insurance, you know, victimless crime and all that.'

'You prat, Hugo Pendergast,' Nor said, standing next to Maddie in the doorway. 'Is that why you've run away from the police?'

'So, yah, I saw Jason and he said now Pops was gone that I had no excuse about not letting him store the equipment at Hill Top, especially as the harridan – oh God, sorry, I didn't mean to say that out loud...'

'I've been called worse,' Nor said.

'Me too,' added Maddie. 'Go on?'

Hugo was reddening as he did so and Maddie took the chance to look down and note how well and truly his foot was stuck in the steel bucket of chicken muck. She tried not to smile and concentrate instead on what Hugo was saying.

'I thought to myself, "Hugo, you've got to sort this out," but then Jason said he was prepared to take our business to the next level and I thought, cripes, I'm barely out of Ag Col—'

'What?' Maddie asked, pulling her eyes away from the bucket again.

'Agricultural college. Wasn't much prepped for uni, and Pops thought it might work best if I had a more practical higher education, you know, so I could run the farm one day. But last week he told me about Chloe and her claim to it all and then I didn't know what to do, except maybe offer to marry her, but Jason said he wanted to move in with me and I just, well, I just bolted. I thought, "Hugo, mate, you've got to get out of here before you become some patsy for this gangster dude."'

'You realise it made you look incredibly suspicious, Hugo? Running away just as your dad had been killed? And you said he definitely knew about Chloe's claim via your grandad's first wife?'

'Yah, Pops had just found out about it, but he didn't kill her. I can promise you that. He didn't know it was her under those rocks, when he, well, found her. And I came here as it sounds like you're in the know and I wanted to see if you knew anything about who killed Pops?'

'Do you promise me it wasn't you?' Maddie asked, as solemnly as she could to a man in a fleece gilet with a bucket stuck to one foot.

'Scouts' honour. Not me. But I did see someone. And now Jason's arrested—'

'How did you know that?' Maddie asked. 'You'd disappeared before then.'

'I might not set the world alight with the old noggin, but I know these fields like the back of my hand... well, not that hand, it's got a few new scratches on it from the hedge. That's where I was hiding.'

Maddie shook her head, but urged him on. 'So you saw Jason arrested...?'

'Um, right, yah, and that was a mahoosive relief, but I don't think he killed Pops. I think it was... Um, look this is going to sound really weird.'

'Who was it? Who did you see?' Maddie pressed him, wondering why Trevelyan hadn't said anything to her about this titbit of information. 'Did you tell the police this?'

Hugo looked down at his feet, and the bucket, then looked back up at Maddie and Nor. 'No, I didn't, as I sound like a bloody idiot saying this out loud, but I know what I saw. I know what I saw.' He nodded to himself in reassurance.

'Who? Who did you see?' Maddie asked again. 'Whoever it was is most likely your father's murderer. And maybe Chloe's too.'

Hugo looked up at Maddie. 'Promise you won't laugh?'

'We definitely won't,' Maddie answered for Nor too.

Hugo girded himself. 'OK then, well, the person I saw

running away from the barn just after the gun went off was...' He shook his head in disbelief at himself.

'Who?' Maddie said, a little sharply.

Hugo looked up at her, the colour drained from his face, and solemnly answered.

'Esther Pendergast.'

45

'What?' Maddie took a step back in shock and knocked into Nor, who was shaking her head in disbelief.

'I know you've not got much between the ears, Hugo,' Nor said. 'But this is mad. Esther would be in her nineties, or perhaps even over one hundred by now. And she's most likely dead at the bottom of the sea. It couldn't be her.'

'It's what I saw!' Hugo protested, clattering his bucket on the ground.

'I can see why you couldn't tell the police this,' Maddie said, exasperated with this clod-headed man.

'I told them what I could definitely put my hand on a Bible for, which was that I was having a shower and had just got out when I heard the shots...'

Maddie narrowed her eyes, remembering Trevelyan's account. She thought this 'recipe' matched and nodded for Hugo to carry on.

'But, you see, the window was all steamed up and it's not unusual to hear shots, so I didn't think much of it, except that we weren't scheduled to shoot clays so early and the shots sounded bloody close. I looked through the window, and as I said, it was steamy, but I saw her, I think, leaving the barn where Pops was...' He gulped and regained his composure in the way men like him had been trained to do since first being dropped off at boarding school at age seven or eight. '... Where Pops was later found. By me, I found him. It was grim.'

'I know, I'm sorry.' Maddie felt bad that this entire discussion was being conducted at the back door while this poor man's foot was stuck in a bucket of chicken poop, but then she remembered that he'd stitched Nor up like a kipper and her sympathies crumbled faster than a shortbread biscuit. And thinking of Nor, she noticed that her gran had sidled away and if the blue lights on the horizon were anything to go by, she'd made a quick and subtle call to Trevelyan, who would now be on his way to pick up Hugo, bucket and all.

With a few moments left, Maddie racked her brain for anything else she might want to know to help her with her inkling of an idea.

'OK, Hugo, so what made you think it was Esther Pendergast? What did this woman look like?'

'She was wearing a kaftan, you know like the one Esther was wearing in the picture the police put out all those years ago. You can't be a Pendergast around here and not know about that picture. And at school I was bullied for living in a house that must surely be haunted by Grandpa's first wife, like that Du Maurier story, *Rebecca*.'

Maddie was mildly impressed at his literary reference. But then it was Cornwall and Du Maurier was bigger than Shakespeare down here. 'So you thought you saw the ghost of Esther Pendergast fleeing the scene.'

'In a flapping kaftan, yes,' said Hugo, and then he hesitated. 'But it all happened so quick. And you know, steam.'

The blue lights flashed closer.

Maddie changed tack. 'And what was your dad planning on

doing about Chloe? I mean, he knew the farm might be claimed, if not by her, then her family. Did you have a plan?'

'He didn't say. He just told me that Grandpa's first wife's family were in touch. Like I said, I suggested maybe I could marry her and that would sort it all out—'

'Hugo this is 2026, not 1826.'

'Yah, yah, you're right. Just wanted to do the right thing by Pops, you know. I suppose he would have spoken to them, but he wanted to check something with the council first. Some chat about another heir? I don't know. It wasn't looking peachy for the Pendergasts though, I can tell you that.'

'Enough that *you* might have killed to stop it from being lost? If your dad was willing to do the right thing?' Maddie could see the blue lights get stronger over the fields and knew Hugo would notice them soon too.

'No, honestly, not me. Not to Pops. Oh...' Finally, Hugo saw the echoes of the blue flashes across the stone of the farmhouse. 'You've called the police.' He looked genuinely shocked.

Nor appeared behind Maddie. 'I did, Hugo. Because you've been a naughty boy, and by the sounds of it, and the fact you've come skulking around here looking for a safe place to hide, I reckon you're scared to go home in case any of Jason's pals show up. So perhaps a nice safe pair of bars and some firmly locked doors might be the best place for you.'

'Fair play, Mrs Penrose, good thinking.'

'Do you know what it was that he wanted to check with the council?' Maddie asked as the first police car pulled into the farmyard.

'Um, no, like some family tree he wasn't sure about or something. I don't know. He said some local bloke said he had a claim on the farm too, better even than Chloe's. But Pops was unsure about it. Said he'd never heard of the possibility of it and all that. Plus, the old two buses coming along at once thing, haha, you know there's been no scandalous claims on the land we've had for decades and then two come along at once. Dodgy or what? Ah, hello, officer...' Hugo broke off speaking to Maddie as one of the local constables placed his wrists into handcuffs and tried to escort him to the squad car, his steps one clank after another.

Maddie looked up. Tom Trevelyan was standing there, having jumped down from the Land Rover, DS Mitchell next to him. He gave the two Ms Penroses an informal sort of salute and then headed over to the apprehended suspect, reading him his rights and waiting for the constable to remove the bucket, before seeing him into the squad car and driving away.

Maddie slept badly and awoke the next morning about as fresh as a three-day-old dishrag. Hugo hadn't been their only nocturnal visitor, with Toast bringing in one of the four-legged and long-tailed variety too. Once Maddie had been up at five in the morning trying to catch the little thing with an empty Tupperware and a stiff envelope, she couldn't get back to sleep so had lain awake and thought about the things she'd learned in the last twenty-four hours, and if any of it swayed her in her current thinking.

That Hugo hadn't been the criminal mastermind she'd pegged him for didn't get him off the hook altogether. He did know about the threat to his family farm and could be putting on an act while being much more devious underneath. And he'd incriminated Jason too, saying that Jason had been keen to move the stolen tractor operation to Hill Top as soon as Clive had died. Maybe he'd hastened Clive's death in order to get the use of the barn?

And Kieran, well he'd apparently kept his trap shut, but he was connected to Chloe, obviously, and to Clive by the fact that his train ticket was found at Hill Top at the time of Clive's death. But how did all of that relate to the inkling she'd had yesterday during Jason's arrest or her 'recipe'? Maddie had brought the old recipe book up to bed with her with a cup of tea after 'mouse-gate' and read down the list.

Clive Pendergast – Hill Top Farm – 'of all people' – related
Old cow shed – fallen stones
Last words – aren't you rock would tree help
Bloodied stone = murder
1965 – missing woman SAME PLACE Esther Pendergast
Clotted cream?
Litter
Planning – houses at Hill Top – developer?
HER backpack – OUR barn. Jason?!
C&K – lovers' tiff? Him more than her
Entitled
Archer – family tree
Sheila at Seaside B&B – accident – new sash?
Brick – warning!
USB stick – AL – Bella or Archer?
Bad review – dirty floor

Clive had been her first introduction to it all, and with him now dead, he was definitely central to the whole recipe. Those last words he'd heard Chloe say, 'aren't you rock would tree help'. Maddie tapped the page with her finger and saw the line above. The cow shed... now Maddie knew that Chloe had believed that land to be rightfully hers. Had she met Clive up there and been murdered by him? Yet Clive had already told his son about her claim to the land and was apparently about to go to the council to look into another, so it didn't feel like he was covering anything up. If he'd wanted her – the problem – to go away, surely he wouldn't have breathed a word to anyone?

Then she looked at the date of the disappearance of the missing woman, who she now knew to be Esther Pendergast, Clive's father's first wife. She closed her eyes and pictured her in her kaftan – could Hugo really have seen her leaving the scene of his father's death? She was related to Chloe too. And there was proof that the farm should rightfully be going to the Hardy family, not the Pendergasts. Was Hugo upset about that, having found out about it from his dad? So upset he'd kill her and then Clive, only to be too easily manipulated by his dodgy business partner that he ended up running away from the farm he now stood to inherit?

Maddie kept looking down the list, ignoring for now Chloe's backpack and its belongings; they had been explained by her personality and lifestyle. But her finger hovered over the entry about the USB stick, and Archer finding out about her family tree. And the fight, of course, between her and Kieran. She dwelled on the phrase 'him more than her', tapping her finger on it as she let it settle into her subconscious mind. Sheila, before she'd died, or been killed, had heard him arguing with Chloe – *him more than her* – that phrase again...

Maddie had to solve this case before it drove her mad, and as the dawn light strengthened and sunbeams flooded her bedroom through the open curtains, she decided just how she was going to do it.

46

'You're off to where, ducky?' Nor asked, while her hands were busy making breadcrumbs out of the flour and butter mix, the basics of scone making.

'The council offices,' Maddie replied, slipping the recipe book into her handbag.

'Not to see that woman?'

'Different department, Gran. There's some information in the archives there that might prove my theory.'

'Which is?' Nor asked, looking up from her mixing bowl.

Maddie hesitated. 'I don't want to say yet, Gran, in case it's laughable. You know me. It's probably as stupid an idea as Crumpet stealing the clotted cream.' At the sound of his name, the ginger cat looked up from his nap on the sofa and chirruped at Maddie. 'Don't worry, Crumps, you're off the hook.'

'Well, you be careful. I've got my hands full here this morning if you're not here to open up with me.'

'I won't be long.' Maddie leant over and kissed her grandmother on the cheek. 'And don't worry about me. I texted Tom and he's meeting me there.'

Nor raised an eyebrow at her granddaughter but suppressed

the smile that was twitching at the edge of her lips. 'Good plan, ducky, glad you've organised your own backup this time.'

'I doubt much could harm me in a council office beyond death by bureaucratic boredom, unless that lady from the Food Standards Agency chooses to enact her revenge... but fingers crossed I might just be on to something. Can I take the car? I'll see you in a bit.'

Maddie drove her gran's Morris Minor round the winding Cornish lanes that took her from Folly Farm, past the turning down to Pendragon Creek and up to the main road to St Ives. 'Main road' was a bit of a glossy term for the 'slightly wider than two cars' winding road that skirted fields and ancient hedgerows and followed the old holloways and drovers' tracks that first marked out this route centuries before she clattered down it, struggling with third gear on the sixty-year-old car. Maddie wound down the window, which got stuck halfway, for some fresh air, as the day was now proving to be a warm and sunny one. Coaxing the car into fourth gear, she cruised – if that was the word – into St Ives and followed the brown information signs to the council offices. She appreciated the cool air which flowed in through the half-open window, despite her lowered speed as she navigated the town's narrow streets, and she counted only stalling once at some traffic lights as a win. As she pulled into the council offices' car park, she felt herself blush as she remembered how quickly Tom had responded to her text message this morning.

Re that germ of an idea... would you meet me at the council offices in St Ives with the USB stick this morning, 9 o'clock?

It was hardly steamy stuff, but Tom's reply had been speedy and positive.

Of course. See you there Maddie. This could be useful. T.

Again, not exactly something out of a Richard Curtis film, but she was looking forward to seeing him. Even with the preoccupation in her mind of working out who killed Chloe Hardy, Clive Pendergast – and now, more than ever, she believed, Sheila Laverstoke – she had made sure she'd brushed her hair and put on a bit of make-up. It was nice to look nice after all.

The ancient handbrake proved it was still working, as Maddie pulled it up and felt the car tense underneath her. Climbing out, she was a little embarrassed to be offered a hand straight away by Tom Trevelyan, who must have seen – or indeed heard – her coming. The Morris Minor was not a stealthy car.

'Where to, then?' Tom asked, getting straight down to business. Maddie could see that he looked tired and she wondered if he'd come directly from the police station in town, having had a night raking Jason over the coals, not to mention Hugo.

Maddie took the hint and rather than asking about them, she answered succinctly.

'The record office. We need to check something.'

Tom nodded and, thanks to his warrant card, they were whisked through reception and to the office of the local registrar, who was able to access the archives and records.

'So what are we looking for?' Tom asked, leaning over Maddie's shoulder as she flicked the cursor around the screen, choosing various options from drop-down menus.

'Something that I have a hunch might be here. Which shouldn't be here.'

'Cryptic,' mumbled Tom, and Maddie had a sudden panic that she really might be wasting police time, not to mention that of the nice registrar who had taken herself off for a cup of tea while the two of them searched the system. At least she had been one council employee who hadn't shuddered at the sight of a Penrose. Maddie made a silent prayer and then clicked through to the page she wanted.

'Yes,' she whispered. 'That's what I thought. It should be Martin... Print.' She pressed the button and the laser-jet in the corner powered into life. 'Just a few more things.'

'What are you looking for, Maddie? And apart from being a useful warrant-card holder, what am I doing here?' Tom looked at his watch.

'I'll tell you everything, I just wanted to be sure. And now I am. I know who killed Chloe Hardy and why, and I know who killed Clive Pendergast and why. And before you even get the post-mortem results back, I know who killed Sheila Laverstoke, and why. And these records, especially when viewed side by side with those on the USB stick, prove it.'

'So, who is it?' Tom asked, and then followed Maddie's finger as she pointed to a name on the screen. He paused, stood back to rub his chin and then peered again at the computer monitor. 'Well, well, well. Looks like you've just caught yourself a killer.'

Identifying and finding proof that someone is a murderer is one thing; going ahead and actually finding that person is a different matter. Tom and Maddie printed out what they needed from the records office and headed back out to the car park.

'What now?' Maddie asked, fiddling with her car keys.

'We'll make the arrest.'

'Can I come?' Maddie asked and felt herself deflate as Tom shook his head.

'Sorry. Look, this is all really useful, the Crown Prosecution Service will be all over it, but I can't take you along for the ride. If there's anything untoward, it could jeopardise the whole thing. Bad people walk free all the time on legal technicalities.'

Maddie nodded. She understood, but had to admit to feeling a little put out as she drove back to Pendragon Creek from St Ives. She wound the window down again and tried to take her mind off murderers and motives – and most especially handsome policemen. She was pleased with herself for one thing, though. She hadn't stalled at those traffic lights. And she had cracked the case. And through her own slightly random way of doing it, too. Maybe she should write a book about it? The Recipe for Murder? Help other amateur food-obsessed sleuths crack cases as surely as they cracked eggs. She amused herself with puns and then more ideas for the teashop and tried to ignore the feeling of it all being a bit of an anticlimax when she pulled into the farmyard. Closing the gate behind her, she wondered why it was open in the first place. Toast was crouching in the hedge and gave Maddie a silent miaow in protest of her interrupting his hunting.

'Don't you shout at me,' she ticked him off, but accepted the rub around her ankles as he decided she might be a soft touch for a treat later. 'Why's this gate open? Honestly, if you two had opposable thumbs, I would lay so much at your cat flap...'

Maddie assumed Bella must be out on Cam, but the young girl, despite her age, was responsible enough to know about closing farm gates. Something prickled on the back of Maddie's neck as she realised the yard was far too quiet. Reaching for her bag in the car, she slung it over her shoulder and instinctively crept towards the farmhouse. Peering in through the kitchen window, she could see no one was in there. Maddie looked at her watch. It was almost eleven, and the teashop should be open, what with it being a Friday morning.

Almost a week since Chloe was killed...

The thought flashed through her mind.

Seven days for the killer to put that plan into action...

But what if...

Maddie pushed herself back from the kitchen windowsill

and ran towards the teashop. It was suspiciously quiet and the door was shut, not propped open by the novelty teapot-shaped doorstop. She pushed open the door and as soon as her eyes had adjusted to the dim light in the old barn, she saw a scene that made her blood run cold.

Nor Penrose was sitting very still at one of the tables. And pointing towards her was what Maddie could only guess was Clive Pendergast's shotgun in the hands of the person she'd just expected DI Trevelyan to have arrested. The murderer.

Archer Lockwood.

47

'Archer...' Maddie took a step forward with her hands raised up in front of her. He swiftly moved the gun through about ninety degrees so that both barrels were now pointing at her, and not Nor.

'Don't come any closer,' the young man said.

'You don't need to hurt us.' Maddie took her eyes off Archer for a second to check her gran was all right. Nor looked pale, but stalwart, and kept quiet. 'We can't do anything to you. You can just walk out of here. We won't call the police.'

'You already have. They're at my house now, pulling apart my rig.'

Maddie silently cursed, but was also genuinely confused. How had Archer known she was onto him? She kept her gaze on him, trying not to look at – and draw attention to – the gun. 'Why did you come here? How did you know I'd worked it out?'

'Your visit to the council this morning set off a virtual trip-wire. It alerted me to the log-on address and I activated the built-in webcam. Saw you and that policeman gormlessly staring back at me. Not enough people turn those cameras off, you know. Bit of sticky tape, all it takes.'

'I'm sorry, Archer.' Maddie kept her hands up, and silently berated herself. He'd mentioned those virtual alerts back when she'd first met him at the Two Pelicans. She hoped she hadn't missed anything else important as she carried on. 'But you killed Chloe, Clive and Sheila. You must have known people would have found out once your planning application to the council had been approved.'

Nor nodded, which distracted Archer enough for Maddie to move a little closer to her gran. She wanted to swap places with her – if Archer wanted a hostage, which she assumed this little stunt was all about, then he could have her. And if he wanted revenge for being found out, then, Maddie gulped, he could have her too. Her gran didn't need to be part of this. She hadn't told Nor about her theory as she'd been embarrassed in case she was wrong. That she'd been very, very right didn't feel as good as she thought it would right now.

'Don't come closer,' Archer snapped. He was still paying attention, it seemed. Perhaps if she could keep him talking, then it would give Tom Trevelyan time to realise where he'd fled to, and that Maddie and Nor were in danger. It was worth a shot.

Maddie blanched. Hopefully not *that* type of shot.

'Indulge me, Archer, how right was I about everything... I'm going to get something from my bag, slowly, so don't shoot. It's just a book.'

'Hey! Slow, slow.' Archer kept the shotgun trained on her, which Maddie preferred to it being pointed anywhere near her gran.

'I've been making notes, like a recipe. It's how my mind works. Can you tell me if I was right about a few things?'

Archer looked at her keenly as she showed him that it was just a book that she was holding up. She even riffled its pages to show that there was nothing concealed in it. Then she turned to the flapjack recipe, and more importantly, the words that were jotted next to it.

'Go on then,' Archer, said, lowering his gun slightly and taking a sip of the can of Coke that he had in front of him. Nor side-eyed it and Maddie loved how loyal she was to tea, even at this traumatic moment. And, of course, it reminded Maddie of when she'd first met Archer, even though she hadn't realised it then.

'OK, so you were here, almost exactly a week ago. It was my first Saturday on the job and Clive burst in covered in blood, not jam, as I first thought, and told us about Chloe's death. But you were here already. You were the bloke looking at your screen who'd come in, bought a Coke and then plugged your headphones in.' Maddie placed her finger near the bottom of the list. 'I remember noticing the floor of the teashop had stones and grit on it, as did someone else that day who bothered to write a bad review about our cleanliness, which I think was a little unfair—'

'Get on with it,' Archer demanded. 'My patience is wearing thin.'

'Of course, so yes, the muck on the floor was just the same as the type on the path up to the old cow shed. And it was on our teashop floor as someone had just come down that path with their big bovver boots on and sat themselves down at a table. You.'

Archer nodded. 'Not exactly proof, that. Go on.'

'Well, I remember wondering soon after Chloe's death if the killer could have been in the teashop and now I know it's you, that places you here close to her time of death.' Maddie knew this wasn't evidence enough, but she had more. She glanced at the list, then carried on. 'And I found a discarded Coke can up by the ruins. I didn't think anything of it at the time, but I made sure I brought it down here as Gran's been getting into trouble with the council about litter. I gave it to Trevelyan earlier,' she lied, though she knew she could probably find that can in the farmhouse's kitchen bin and send it to forensics. 'I think it'll have your DNA on it, and prove you were there at the scene when Chloe was killed.'

Archer's expression told her she had been correct in linking the soft drink can to him and she gave a silent prayer of thanks for the lady at the council who'd raised the issue about the littering.

She concentrated on Archer again and carried on. 'When Clive came in and I spoke to him, he told me that Chloe wasn't quite dead when he found her.' Maddie stopped and let that sink in, now she was here facing the killer. 'You left her there to die?'

'I thought I'd...' Archer looked uncomfortable, took a swig of his can, looked at it as if it had just betrayed him, then held the gun more firmly and demanded, 'Go on.'

'Right, so, Clive told me her last words. "Aren't you rock would tree help" is what I wrote down. They don't make much sense. Clive and I wondered if Chloe was talking about the tree and if it could be used to help get the rocks off her... but I knew that wasn't it. A few days later I realised that the "tree" part could refer to her family tree, but still, it made no sense, until last night. While I was being attacked by Jason, he said something which has nothing to do with all of this, except that it made me think. It was just the way he pronounced "what are you" and "aren't you". *Wotcha and arncha.* I think Clive assumed that's what Chloe was saying too. So when she said your name, Archer, he thought she was also saying "aren't you" and interpreted it as that. So, her dying, misheard words weren't "Aren't you rock would tree help", but "Archer Lockwood family tree help".'

Maddie could see Nor nodding her head encouragingly and carried on.

'And it makes sense, as she'd asked you to look into her family tree and a claim she had through her great-aunt to Hill Top Farm. She found you on a forum because you had the best skills when it came to searching archives. As you said yourself, you could get into places – hack systems – like no one else. Gran told me your mum was worried about you a few years ago as you'd left your computer science degree and got in with some real hackers, so you'd know all about this stuff. And you did help her, you put all the findings onto a USB stick.'

Archer rolled his eyes. Maddie could see that he was annoyed at himself.

'Which you lost the other day, but I'll come back to that. Anyway, on that USB there were time-stamped documents. You realised this, which was why in the end you didn't give it to her. Hence the fight at the B&B.'

'That was with Kieran,' Archer said, with rather too much authority, as he rubbed one eye with a fist.

Maddie looked down at her recipe again. *Him more than her*. She looked up at Archer again. 'Was it though? Sheila from the B&B told me she'd heard the argument and had heard Kieran speaking more than Chloe. "Him more than her", she told me, and that when she'd asked them to keep the noise down, Kieran had had the cheek to reply to her in a Cornish accent. She'd assumed it was a put-on one as she thought it was Kieran, but it was you. Oh poor Sheila, she died because you overheard her telling me all this? You were the noise at the door we heard. She thought it was a seagull, but I saw a shadow.' Maddie paused and shook her head. 'Archer, you killed her with one of her own sash windows? That's just horrid. She'd only just had them refurbished, she'd proudly told me that, so there was no way one falling on her was an accident...' Maddie paused again as another memory came back to her about the sash windows. 'And she said she had to close them once a room was aired out to stop the seagulls from flying in and stealing the marzipan fruits. Those definitely don't sound like windows that accidentally close themselves. Sadly, I don't think the post-mortem can prove either way, but now it's a working theory, I reckon the forensics team will find evidence that you pushed her head out of the window and brought the sash down on her.'

Archer rolled his eyes, but had started to drum his fingers on the gun grip. And Maddie was sure she'd just seen him stifle a yawn too. She couldn't see how this could possibly be boring him, but also didn't want to lose his attention. She carried on, using her list to jog her memory over Sheila's words.

'You were the one that Chloe threatened would "pay for this" and that you were "selfish" and "why were you doing this" to her. It's because, as you said to me, it hadn't been the plan that she would come to Cornwall so soon. So you had to let her down, said you wouldn't pass over the USB stick with the proof on it that would secure her claim to the farm.'

'Why wouldn't he do that, ducky?' Nor asked, risking having the gun turned back on her.

'Because her own good fortune, and his and his mum's lack of any. And the fact that one of the articles Archer found involved his gran, Mary Nuttall, with her young daughter Daphne, his mum. It gave him an idea. An idea that was cunning and evil and could only have been put in place by someone with his very special set of skills. Archer did what no one else could.'

Archer cocked an eyebrow at her, but Nor asked the question.

'Which was?'

'Tamper with history, change the records and put his own family well and truly in that tree.'

48

'You did what now, Archer?' Nor turned to him as he stifled a yawn. 'Hope we're not keeping you up, young man. All those shoot-'em-ups on your Nintendo or whatever is bad for you. Gives you naughty ideas, no doubt.'

'I think the idea came from the fact that Clive's father may well have got away with murder and claimed the farm for the Pendergasts,' Maddie said, and Nor nodded.

'Like I said, the sea is a deep, dark well full of secrets and not just the grave for sailors and fishermen.'

Archer rolled his eyes. 'So what if I did change the records? Surely that would mean I didn't have to kill her.'

'Of course you'd have to, she'd been studying the links you'd no doubt sent her already. The links that had got her so excited she decided to jump on a train and come and see her birthright for herself. You couldn't risk that she hadn't already printed them out. She'd have time-stamped proof. So you wouldn't have shut her up that easily, especially if she realised you'd changed the records in favour of yourself. She was an influencer, after all, with a huge social media following. There was no way she'd back down quietly, not after all the journalling and manifesting she'd been doing. Not to mention telling her followers in a video that she had exciting news. And Kieran didn't like you, or you him. Lucky for him that he didn't walk up to the old cow shed with Chloe after that big argument, else you would have killed him too. And it was clever making Chloe's death look like an accident, but then Crumpet found the stone with blood on it where you hit her. Honestly, if those cats had opposable thumbs, we'd all be in so much trouble.'

'What?' Archer looked confused, and with the hand not holding the gun, he pinched the top of his nose, as if he was trying to focus.

'Doesn't matter,' Maddie replied with a wave of the hand. 'Anyway, you'd been able to hack into the central government computer and change Esther Pendergast's maiden name. That's what DI Trevelyan and I were researching at the council this morning, when we set your tripwire off. On the USB stick, time-stamped from a couple of weeks ago, her maiden name is Martin, just like Chloe's grandmother's name, but this morning at the council archives it's, surprise surprise, Lockwood.'

'I was worried you'd been to see that woman who doesn't like my eggs, or, come to think of it, coffee,' Nor said, and Maddie noticed she'd regained her usual air of confidence.

Archer on the other hand, looked more cautious. And decidedly more knackered.

'Nope, avoided her like the plague – just in case she decided to shut me in a broom cupboard until you'd apologised. But the nice lady in the archives was much more helpful. Finding that the maiden name had been altered, along with a bit of local gossip that had your mum treating herself to really expensive clothes, which indicated she was about to come into some real money, clinched it for me. Oh, and Julia telling Gran that Clive had said there was another claimant to the farm, not to mention the rumours that after Clive's death someone had submitted

Hill Top Farm and its land for the town local plan. Hugo would never do that.'

'You're accusing me of killing Clive too then?' Archer said, his voice quieter and less cocky than it had been before. Maddie noticed the gun droop slightly in his hand, but frowned all the same. *What's wrong with him?*

'Yes. Despite you planting Kieran's train ticket at the gate.'

'That's his gun there, isn't it? Bad show that, killing him with his own weapon. Stealing it too. Tut tut,' Nor said, leaning back in her chair and crossing her arms. Maddie was pleased that Nor seemed so calm. She'd read enough books and watched enough TV to know that stand-offs like this were only made worse by nervous hostages, but still, she was a little surprised at Nor's insouciance.

'Each gun is licensed, so the police will easily identify it as Clive's. And if that's not evidence enough, then I can testify that I found the USB stick on the path on the way to Hill Top Farm. I remember thinking your bag was full of holes when I met you at the Two Pelicans. It must have dropped out as you made your way to kill Clive, which places you at the scene.'

Archer snorted and Maddie admitted to herself this was tenuous but she carried on.

'And Hugo saw you. He thought, and this is laughable really, that you, with your flowing overcoat, were the ghost of Esther Pendergast. I guess you used your long coat to conceal the gun as you left. You didn't dump it, like you had with Chloe's backpack – in our barn.' Maddie looked at Nor, who nodded. 'You took her ID out, but you left her phone in it. I remember in the pub you even called the murderer an idiot for doing that – was that the first time you realised you'd missed it? It was tucked into a narrow little side pocket, to be fair, but even me in Gran's Marigolds found it.'

'Told you they'd be fine for rootling through the bag, didn't I?' Nor said, looking completely at ease.

Maddie nodded, then looked back at Archer. 'So, you thought you'd take the gun properly away this time. No more mistakes.'

'And maybe use it again,' Archer slurred.

'I don't think he will,' said Nor, matter-of-factly, uncrossing her arms.

'What's wrong with him?' Maddie said as Archer's eyes slowly closed and opened again. The gun slipped from his hand and rested on the table, his finger loosened from the trigger. Maddie let herself breathe a little sigh of relief.

'There, there, Archer,' Nor said, finally getting up from the table next to him and carefully lifting the gun away from his sleeping figure. Finally, Maddie realised.

'You drugged him?' She almost laughed. 'How? When?'

Nor grinned back at her. 'When he came in. I could see that gun clear as day, though he thought he was hiding it in that long black coat of his. Nothing good ever comes of someone walking into your teashop with a shotgun, even if I was doubtful if it was loaded—'

'Because both shots had been used on Clive...' Maddie clocked.

'Exactly. Anyway, I thought on my feet. Luckily, he demanded a Coke, so I snuck in a couple of my sleeping pills when I pulled the tab. You know, the ones the doctor gave me so I could sleep through with my painful knee? Shame I'd run out of laxatives, really, though that might have been a messy mix. Anyway, I thought it might buy us some time before that nice policeman of yours turned up.'

'He's not my... Oh never mind.' Maddie shook her head, then gave her gran a massive hug. Pulling away, she said, 'Speaking of police, I better call him.'

. . .

DI Tom Trevelyan was at the teashop barely ten minutes after Maddie called. He and DS Mitchell picked up the slumbering Archer Lockwood and managed to get him on his feet and just about awake enough to read him his rights and get him safely in a police car. With the urn bubbling away, and the teashop still firmly closed for business – Archer had ensured he wouldn't be disturbed in his hostage-taking by putting out the A-board closed sign in front of the gate on his way in – Nor and Maddie made tea and cut generous slices of Nor's infamous coffee and walnut cake for Trevelyan and Mitchell.

'Did Kieran say anything about the argument? Has he confirmed Archer was there too?'

'He did, yes,' DS Mitchell replied. 'He told us Archer was in the B&B with them. He hadn't wanted to talk about it before as he thought Archer would make the case that Kieran and Chloe had been fighting, and be a false witness against him.'

'I'm not surprised,' Maddie said. 'I thought it was odd, you know, thinking about it, that Archer had told me so much about what he was doing for Chloe. It was him who told me all about the reason she was here in the first place. And in the same conversation pretty much accused Kieran of killing her.'

'Confident that you'd leave it there and not investigate further,' Trevelyan said.

'Overconfident, if you ask me. Never underestimate my Maddie.' Nor nodded approvingly.

DS Mitchell looked at her notebook and carried on, ignoring the grin that Trevelyan was giving Maddie. 'Well, you were right. Archer had paid them a visit, told them to leave and that he wouldn't help anymore and threatened to hack the records to do all sorts of things to them if they didn't go straight away – wipe national insurance numbers and all that. Kieran didn't think it was worth it, hence storming out, but Chloe had stood up to him and said she'd take it up with Clive personally.'

'She already had, by the sounds of it,' Maddie said. 'And

Clive, bless him, was quite accepting of it. I think, deep down, he knew his father might not have been a good man.'

'You started suspecting Archer when we arrested Jason Briggs, didn't you?' Tom asked, and between mouthfuls of cake said, 'But how did you put it all together?'

Maddie pushed the recipe book towards them. 'It's all in the ingredients.'

DS Mitchell frowned. 'Three million, one thousand, nine hundred and sixty-five grams of oats? Butter?'

'No,' Maddie laughed and looked up to see the corners of Tom's eyes crinkling with a smile too. 'The other ingredients. My ingredients. It's like writing down a recipe, but only finding the ingredients as I go along.'

'And as discussed,' Tom added, 'pen and paper can't be hacked.'

'Ha, yes.' Maddie smiled at him. 'So, like you, whenever I heard anything about the case that interested me, I jotted it down. Like when I saw that Archer had been the one doing all the research for Chloe, and that his grandmother had been around when Esther went missing. Plus he was at every scene: here at the teashop on the day of Chloe's murder, he dropped the USB stick the day that Clive was killed and, most importantly, he was with Kieran and Chloe when they argued – hence why Sheila was targeted. Archer was the one who cast a lot of doubt, to me at least, on Kieran, saying he was a jock and not very nice, not to mention leaving his pilfered train ticket, no doubt taken from Chloe's backpack when he removed her ID from it and planted it in Jason's rented shed. He then voted for Hill Top Farm to be included in the local plan so that when he'd taken ownership of it, he could sell it to developers. Plus, he's got the skills to hack the system. And that long coat of his could easily be mistaken for a kaftan, which through a steamed-up window made not-too-sharp Hugo think he saw a Esther back from the 1960s.'

'But why did he do it?' DS Mitchell asked.

'Greed, I suppose,' Maddie said, looking at the rather large slice of cake in front of her. 'But, more than that, entitlement. Roger at the pub had used the word to describe Chloe, but when Gran told me that Archer's family, the Lockwoods, had once owned a lot of land around here, it was one of the things I'd looked up in the council office this morning. You were right, Gran, generations ago the Lockwoods owned about five hundred acres. And now Archer and his mum live in less, well, posh circumstances. I think he saw a chance to change history, and give the Lockwood family some land back, if not their original land, then Hill Top would do. He felt entitled to it. More, in the end, than Clive did.'

'I can see how it all pieces together now,' Tom said, nodding approvingly.

Maddie popped one of her gran's secret-recipe walnuts into her mouth, crunched down on it, then winked.

'Just like the perfect recipe.'

49

'No, no, noooo...' Maddie whipped the tea towel out of her apron pocket and frantically waved it in front of the oven door as yet another cloud of smoke poured out of it. 'Why do I do this to myself?'

'We'll have to get one of those air-dryer things,' Nor chuckled, nudging Maddie out of the way and pulling the oven door down so she could rescue Maddie's tray bake of brownies.

'You mean air fryer, Gran,' Maddie laughed. 'And no, we don't need one. Just a new oven.'

The teashop had been busy since word had got out that the Pendragon Creek murders had been solved by the handsome policeman who often popped in for his morning coffee. Not that Maddie or Nor had advertised that fact, or that it had been Maddie who had actually been the one to work out it was local computer whizz kid Archer Lockwood. But Julia and Marge had broadcast the news as quickly as any CornwallNow website, proving the Pendragon Creek grapevine was more efficient than ever, even in this modern age.

Maddie had heard from Tom Trevelyan that Hugo Pendergast would most likely not get a custodial sentence as he could give so much evidence against Jason Briggs and help them catch the big fish at the heart of the stolen farm equipment ring. Whether he'd stay at the family farm now was still up in the air though. And in regards to Hill Top, Nor had heard from Marge that morning that the council had voted against building up there and instead the local plan would include the disused patch of land next to Dolphin Drive.

'It makes sense for the town,' Marge had said, sitting in her dryrobe, sipping her coffee. 'Those houses won't need cars as they can walk into the town for their groceries or to the pub. And we need affordable homes, not executive boxes, and those kids who need affordable homes don't want the expense of a car. Putting houses up on Hill Top Farm would have meant they'd be second homes for down-from-towners in a year or two, you mark my words.'

Nor and Maddie had nodded, and been relieved to know that the fields around them weren't about to become a building site. And with the cattle from Hill Top safely farmed out to neighbouring farms, it was now a waiting game as to what would become of the place.

Maddie had spent a couple of days recovering from the excitements of the case, and finally dealt with her admin, too. She'd plucked up the courage to call Pascal and officially end things with him. And she'd handed in formal notice to her landlord in London on the poky room she'd been renting. She and Nor had decided that she should at least spend the summer at Folly Farm, and agreed that the old tractor barn, which still housed the boneshaker, would make an excellent place for supper clubs and local events which would bring the teashop more customers and remind the town that they were just on the doorstep. As for appeasing the council, Maddie had made sure that both the nice lady from the archives and the not-so-nice lady from the food standards department had received boxes of freshly baked flapjacks – from Nor's own recipe, of course. And

Nor had instructed Derek from the builders' yard to make some smart wooden bins, which she attached to the gate and near the outside tables so no one could ever accuse the teashop of adding to the litter problem. Maddie had written this in the note she'd popped in with the flapjacks and hoped that no news, so far, was good news.

Maddie let the brownies cool down and turned the oven off. She wiped the back of her hand over her forehead, hoping some of that chocolate mixture that she might have swiped from the bowl with her finger wasn't now smeared across her face. She had to admit, though, that she didn't really mind if it was. Everyone seemed so down-to-earth here in Cornwall. With her fraying and battered old denim jacket, she felt like she fitted right in. She loved being here and she loved that Nor wanted her to stay on. She could really see a life for herself here among the green hills, sunken lanes, sandy beaches and old farmsteads.

Maddie looked at the clock. Not because she was pressured by time, or worried about doing anything. Just that elevenses was usually the time that...

The door to the teashop opened and Maddie grinned.

'Morning, Tom,' she said. 'The usual?'

A LETTER FROM FLISS

Dear reader,

I want to say a huge thank you for choosing to read *Murder in a Cornish Teashop*. If you did enjoy it, and want to keep up to date with all my latest releases, just sign up at the following link. Your email address will never be shared and you can unsubscribe at any time.

www.bookouture.com/fliss-chester

Thanks,

Fliss Chester

www.flisschester.co.uk

facebook.com/flisschester

instagram.com/flisschester

EXTRACT FROM NOR PENROSE'S OLD RECIPE BOOK

Coffee and Walnut Cake with Secret-Recipe Nuts!

FOR THE SPONGE

65g/⅔ cup walnut pieces, finely chopped
2 tablespoons instant coffee dissolved in 1 tablespoon boiling water, cooled
225g/2 sticks salted butter, softened, plus extra for the tin
225g/1 cup soft light brown sugar
225g/1 cup plain flour
3 teaspoons baking powder
pinch of salt
4 eggs
1–2 tablespoons milk, if necessary

FOR THE BUTTERCREAM

350g/3 cups icing/confectioners' sugar
165g/1½ sticks butter, softened
2 tablespoons instant coffee dissolved in 1 tablespoon boiling water, cooled
pinch of salt
4 tablespoons double (heavy) cream

FOR THE SECRET-RECIPE NUTS

8 walnut halves
1 tablespoon granulated sugar
5g/1 teaspoon butter

1. Line the bottom, and butter the edges, of two 20cm/8in cake tins.

2. Pop all the cake ingredients except the milk into a bowl (count them off as you do, you know you'll forget otherwise) and mix thoroughly, adding a dash of milk if needed to get dropping consistency. Divide between the two tins and smooth out. Lick the bowl (first taste test).

3. Bake at 160°C/350°F/under cool shelf in Aga until firm and springy. If baking in teashop, can start from cold oven – 28–30 minutes, or in pre-heated oven/Aga – 23–25 minutes. Leave to cool for 10 minutes, then run a knife round the edge to loosen and transfer to racks. Cool completely.

4. Make the buttercream – beat the butter till soft, sift in the sugar, add everything else and beat till smooth.

5. Put one sponge on serving plate and spread with half the buttercream, then top with the other half and remaining butter-cream. Lick the bowl (second taste test).

6. For the secret recipe walnuts, place a piece of baking paper on a board. Put the ingredients in a small pan, then stir constantly 'til the sugar is melted. Bring slowly to the boil and simmer over a medium heat until the walnuts and syrup darken (5 mins). Quickly transfer the sticky walnuts to the baking paper, separate them using a pair of forks and leave to cool. Arrange on the cake to mark servings. Serve with a nice cup of tea (third taste test).

The decorated cake will keep 2–3 days in a plastic box in a cool place, unless third taste testing has been completed...

ACKNOWLEDGEMENTS

It's been really exciting starting a new series – a blank page like no other! And a huge thank you must go to the team at Bookouture for encouraging me to start something new, and helping me form the germs of the idea that became *Murder in a Cornish Teashop*. As a sounding board *extraordinaire*, and a whizz with coming up with solutions to the many problems I sent her way, a thank you must go to my editor, Cerys Hadwin-Owen. It's been fantastic knowing I have such an excellent cheerleader on the team and someone who is as passionate about Maddie and Nor (and Toast and Crumpet!) as I am. I'd also like to thank my literary agent, Emily Sweet at Aevitas, for her constant support and advice throughout... and for having an Instagram account that's brimming with baked goods and an inspiration in itself!

As a keen – but amateur – baker myself, I was thrilled when my friend and fellow crime writer, Orlando Murrin, offered to come up with a recipe for me, to match the story in the book. You'll find it just before the acknowledgements in this book – with the secret trick for the walnuts too! I've made it, and can guarantee that it's utterly scrummy – do give it a go, and do look up his murder mystery books, starting with *Knife Skills for Beginners*; they're as brilliant as his recipes.

And Orlando isn't the only crime writer who has been a tremendous support – I have some wonderful friends who understand better than anyone what it's like to write crime books. Huge thanks to Lou, Heather, Jo, Rach, Niki, Kate and all the rest of the Criminal Minds WhatsApp group – whether our chats are silly or serious, they're a lifeline during the loneliest parts of the writing process.

Support comes in all forms, and sometimes from across the world too! I'm very lucky to have been included in some great fun 'Facebook Takeovers' – where I get to virtually chat to readers via Facebook posts on specialised Cosy Crime groups. Historical Mystery Mavens and Cozy Mystery Lovers/Meg's Cozy Corner have been particularly supportive and engaging, and congratulations to competition winner Debbie Burns Lacey for getting a mention in this book!

Finally, a huge thank you as always to my amazing husband, Rupert. He's always been a massive champion of my books, but I think this new series resonates in particular. His mother, my late mother-in-law, Viv, used to own and run her own teashop, down by the riverside in the small country town that Rupert and I both grew up in. She could crack an egg into a mixing bowl with one hand, while taking an order and working the cash register with the other, just like Nor can in this book. Her cakes were legendary. Viv sadly passed away before I ever became a published author, but I hope she would have been proud to see a teashop not unlike hers, bustling and busy, in these books.

PUBLISHING TEAM

Turning a manuscript into a book requires the efforts of many people. The publishing team at Bookouture would like to acknowledge everyone who contributed to this publication.

Audio
Alba Proko

Commercial
Lauren Morrissette
Hannah Richmond
Imogen Allport

Cover design
Ami Smithson

Data and analysis
Mark Alder
Mohamed Bussuri

Editorial
Cerys Hadwin-Owen
Charlotte Hegley

Copyeditor
Jade Craddock

Proofreader
Anne O'Brien

Marketing
Alex Crow
Melanie Price
Occy Carr
Cíara Rosney
Martyna Młynarska

Operations and distribution
Marina Valles
Joe Morris

Production
Hannah Snetsinger
Mandy Kullar
Nadia Michael
Charlotte Hegley

Publicity
Kim Nash
Noelle Holten
Jess Readett
Sarah Hardy

Rights and contracts
Peta Nightingale
Richard King
Saidah Graham

RAISING READERS

Books Build Bright Futures

Dear Reader,

We'd love your attention for one more page to tell you about the crisis in children's reading, and what we can all do.

Studies have shown that reading for fun is the **single biggest predictor of a child's future life chances** – more than family circumstance, parents' educational background or income. It improves academic results, mental health, wealth, communication skills, ambition and happiness.

The number of children reading for fun is in rapid decline. Young people have a lot of competition for their time, and a worryingly high number do not have a single book at home.

Hachette works extensively with schools, libraries and literacy charities, but here are some ways we can all raise more readers:

- Reading to children for just 10 minutes a day makes a difference
- Don't give up if children aren't regular readers – there will be books for them!

- Visit bookshops and libraries to get recommendations
- Encourage them to listen to audiobooks
- Support school libraries
- Give books as gifts

There's a lot more information about how to encourage children to read on our websites: **www.RaisingReaders.co.uk** and **www.JoinRaisingReaders.com**.

Thank you for reading.

hachette UK

www.ingramcontent.com/pod-product-compliance
Lightning Source LLC
Chambersburg PA
CBHW022240020426
42400CB00023B/140
* 9 7 8 1 8 0 5 5 0 4 4 3 6 *